THE LONELY MARGINS

Recent Titles by Ted Allbeury from Severn House

CODEWORD CROMWELL
THE GIRL FROM ADDIS

THE LONELY MARGINS

MARGINS

Ted Allbeury

This first hardcover edition published in Great Britain 1995 by
SEVERN HOUSE PUBLISHERS LTD of
9–15 High Street, Sutton, Surrey SM1 1DF.
Originally published under the pseudonym of
Patrick Kelly in Great Britain 1981.
This title first published in the U.S.A. 1996 by
SEVERN HOUSE PUBLISHERS INC of
595 Madison Avenue, New York, NY 10022.

British Library Cataloguing in Publication Data
Allbeury, Ted
  Lonely Margins
  I. Title
  823.914 [F]

  ISBN 0-7278-4881-X

Typeset by Hewer Text Composition Services, Edinburgh.
Printed and bound in Great Britain by
TJ Press (Padstow) Ltd, Padstow, Cornwall.

*To Lord and Lady Willis of Chislehurst with respect –
and to Ted and Audrey Willis with love.*

'Out here on the lonely margins of military life, heroes seem more heroic and blackguards more blackguardly than they do in the ordinary line of battle, where companionship keeps men steady and women are not expected to fight at all.'

M. R. D. Foot
SOE in France

Part I

One

The head-waiter showed him to the table that had been booked in the corner, and he half-smiled at being addressed as Mr Bishop. His field name was Archevêque, and SOE enjoyed these little touches of humour disguised as security. He sat quite still, his eyes looking around the restaurant. He supposed that even in peacetime the Savoy looked much the same as it did now. There was a sprinkling of uniforms but the men looked the kind of men who would have been there anyway. A few couples were dancing and he looked over towards the band. It was still Carrol Gibbons, and they were still playing 'A Nightingale Sang in Berkeley Square'. He had heard them sometimes on the radio before the war had started. Carrol Gibbons and the Savoy Orpheans.

Only twenty-four hours before he had been standing in the frosty moonlight in a meadow just south of Lyon, watching the dark shape of the Lysander come in low over the trees. He had been the only passenger to be picked up and they had been well inside the statutory change-over time of three minutes when they took off. Some idiot from his network had flashed '*Au revoir*' as they started the take-off run. It was one of those warning signs that indicated over-confidence, and over-confidence could wipe out a successful network in days.

Then he saw them walking over towards him. Carter and Pardoe. They were smiling as they sat down. They were wearing best battledress and infantry arm flashes.

'Did you get any sleep, James?' Carter said.

'A few hours.'

'You look fit enough.'

'I am.'

'It's nice to see you, anyway. Let's order a meal and then we can talk. There's not much choice but I can recommend the omelettes or there's generally liver on the menu.'

'Omelette for me. Cheese or mushrooms, I don't mind which.'

Carter pushed the menu to one side and looked across at Harmer and opened his mouth to speak. He closed it with irritation as the waiter arrived. He ordered for the three of them and when the waiter had gone he leaned forward.

'How are you managing for food over there?'

'It's very bad for the city people. Outside in the country it's not so bad. We've got good connections so we get by.'

'Is there anything they need urgently?'

'Detonators for *plastique* and spares for the transmitter. I've got a list I'll give you tomorrow.'

'Nothing else?'

'I'll need to take back more cash. We need tyres very badly. And I'd like to talk about providing an armourer for the Communists. But that can wait.'

'Are they playing ball with you?'

'Not really. They're already working out who's going to be mayor of Lyon when it's all over. But putting in the armourer for them would be a good move for us.'

They sat in silence as the waiter served the food and poured the wine. When they were alone Pardoe said, 'Have you got all you need at Sloane Street?'

Harmer smiled. 'It's luxury after my bloody attic.'

12

Carter raised his glass. 'To you and your chaps, Jimmie.'

Pardoe nodded and raised his glass. And despite the fact that he found such displays embarrassing Harmer raised his glass, too, and took a sip of the wine.

Looking over the top of his glass, Carter said, 'How are things in general with Curfew?'

'You've seen my signals traffic?'

'Of course.'

He smiled wryly. 'They'll survive for a week or two without me.'

'D'you feel rested enough for a meeting tomorrow morning?'

'Of course. What time?'

'Say ten. At Baker Street.'

'OK.'

They quizzed him for an hour or so about two networks working south of Lyon and his relationship with the Communists' network working in Lyon itself.

He walked back to Sloane Street alone, ill at ease with the lack of responsibility and tension, only half believing that he was entitled to be walking up the Mall. Still freezing inwardly at the sight of a uniform and, without thinking, keeping to the shadows from the trees. The blacked out windows of Buckingham Palace made the building look empty and neglected, and there was no Royal Standard on the flagpole.

He let himself into the flat at the bottom of Sloane Street and as he switched on the light he saw that since he had left somebody had put a pile of mail on the small hall-table. His accumulated mail from the past seven months. There were ten or more envelopes but he felt no inclination to open them. They belonged to a different world, and there was little or nothing from that world that much concerned him. Tomorrow would be soon enough.

He lit a cigarette as he sat on the edge of the single bed and looked casually round the room. It was sparsely furnished, and by reflex he had already checked the two doors and the windows as soon as he had been left alone that morning. Lieutenant James Harmer, Intelligence Corps seconded to SOE, believed that security should be second nature. Time spent in reconnaissance was seldom wasted.

The room had an air about it, almost an odour; it was a room for strangers, a transit camp that had absorbed nothing from its occupants; the men who came back to report their successes or excuse their failures. Men to whom English had almost become a foreign language. Whose glibness or reticence was weighed in the scales by their fellows, who debriefed them and then formed their own judgments. And who listened to their complaints. There were few heroes and fewer cowards; when you had had enough you could say so, and there were times when others decided it for you. When twenty or more people's lives could depend on one man the stakes were too high to take risks; and loyalty was a two-way traffic. Like most other agents Harmer felt less loyalty to the individuals who ran SOE, than to the concept, the organization. It was all-pervading, and as natural to Harmer as breathing. It was much more than an organization. It was a cause. A cause he totally believed in.

Switching off the light, he opened the curtains and undressed in the moonlight. He looked up at the night sky. The moon was two days into waning but that night, and maybe the next night, it would still be bright enough for the Hudsons to drop their loads of arms and stores and parachutists, and for Lysanders to bump down and pick up their clandestine passengers. He stubbed out the cigarette, fished around in the darkness for the packet and the matches and lit another. He knew why he was smoking the extra cigarette. It was the people at the Savoy. He had never been to a luxury hotel

14

before in his life but it wasn't just that. It wasn't envy either. But he knew that he felt a bitter resentment against the people he had seen in the Savoy, uniformed or not. There was a kind of indecency about the whole thing. There was a war on, Russians were dying in the snows of Kiev, all over Europe people were starving, French girls were selling their bodies to Germans for a bar of soap and in all the occupied countries people lived every day and every night in fear. But those bastards snapped their fingers to the waiters for a light for their cigars or another bottle of wine. And the servicemen weren't only men on leave, they were the knowing ones who always managed to stay in staff appointments where the bright lights still shone. Was there really any difference between them and the arrogant Germans dining with their mistresses at the Ritz in the Place Vendôme? War after war it was always the same, ordinary people bore the burdens and the others lived as if nothing was happening. He knew that he would be glad when he was back with his network. With real people, whose only thought was to defeat the Nazis.

Despite his thoughts, when he pulled up the army blankets over his shoulders it was only a few moments before he was asleep.

Seahouses is a small holiday and fishing port on the Northumberland coast. You can look to sea from the end of the jetty on a clear day and see the Farne Islands. It's not much more than a straggle of shops and houses up its only real street, and on a winter's day most of the shops will be closed. In the ten weeks of its northern summer, Seahouses is crowded with trippers from Newcastle and holiday-makers from further south and, despite the visitors, its miles of long golden beaches are almost empty. But local yachtsmen can navigate at night by the smell from the fish and chip shops.

At the end of the row of shops is a pair of large, solid,

stone-built semi-detached houses. Built to last several lifetimes, a southerner might find their appearance rather grim. But old houses built near the Scottish border had been built for defence as well as for living.

The left-hand house of the pair was now a boarding house of excellent reputation for both food and service. That reputation had been built up over the years by hard work and careful budgeting. Its proprietor, Anne-Marie Harmer, was the driving force of the enterprise.

She was a Frenchwoman from Honfleur who had married the British soldier she had met at the end of World War I. Hector Harmer was a quiet man; some said that he was dour rather than quiet. Whichever it was, he had been quite content to serve his time as an insurance agent for the Prudential, riding through the countryside on his bicycle to collect the monthly or weekly payments. In his thirty-five years he had twice been offered promotion and had twice refused. His wife, with the boarding house, earned them twice what he made from his agency, and when he was 55 he had opted for an early retirement so that he could help her run it. James Harmer was their only child and was a fair reflection of his parents. Single-minded, courageous, hard-working and reliable, he had done well at grammar school. Bilingual and Francophile because of his mother and the long summer holidays with relations in Bordeaux, he had found a job in Alnwick at its only bookshop. Called-up early in 1940 to the Royal Northumberland Fusiliers, the War Office's wheels had eventually turned so that his language qualification had been highlighted and he had been transferred to Field Security; and from there he was recruited into Special Operations Executive.

Throughout his training he had done well at almost everything but, despite this, there had been doubts on the part of the training staff as to his suitability as an operator in the

16

field. There was no flair; courage but not boldness; he seemed almost too reliable, and he stood out as a rather negative personality compared with the more piratical temperaments that were attracted into SOE. They had marked him down as a first-class potential instructor. But the operational heads of SOE saw him as excellent agent material, just the kind of man who would survive in the field. They had to spend too much time unravelling the crumbling networks that were run by leaders who saw it all as a sport – 'knocking the Boche for six' – not to be glad of a man like Harmer.

Lieutenant Harmer had been dropped near Angoulême as second-in-command of a shaky network. And when, four months later, the network had been smashed by the Sicherheitsdienst he had taken over the survivors and pulled them out of the area until they could be picked up by London. Six months later he had been parachuted in again to take over the Lyon network. For seven months they had harried the Germans, blowing bridges and power lines, wrecking trains and cutting communications. Nobody had fallen into German hands although one member of the network had died from natural causes. The harassed men in Baker Street had been justified in their choice. But they wanted him now for other things. Men who could hold crumbling networks together in enemy-occupied territory were few and far between. And such men who did what they were ordered to do, without question, were rarer still.

By 5.30 the next morning Harmer was dressed and shaved, and he sat in the ancient armchair opening his mail. There were two letters from his father with brief postscripts from his mother. Both letters were quite short. There were no complaints and there was no affection, they were limited to news of a few neighbours and a couple of his school-friends,

17

and the death of a distant uncle whom he had never met. They hoped that he was well. There was a long gossipy letter from the owner of the bookshop enclosing a paperback entitled *Fair Stood the Wind for France* by Flying-Officer X. A statement from the Bank of Scotland showed a credit balance of £450.12.0. A duplicated newsletter from his grammar school gave details of the activities of some of its Old Boys. He featured in a one-line mention as a rifleman in the Fusiliers. A leaflet from the Reprint Society offered him special introductory terms, and a typewritten note from Alnwick library threatened legal action unless he returned the overdue copy of J. P. Marquand's *The Late George Apley*. A postcard from a jeweller's in Newcastle informed him that the repair to his wristwatch would cost 12s.6d and they awaited his instructions. Finally, there was a stilted but friendly letter from one of the girls at the tennis club. He recognized the name but he couldn't remember the face. He burnt them all in the empty grate and mashed up the ashes with the poker.

It was still dark when he walked slowly down to Sloane Square and bought a paper before he turned into the King's Road. He read the *Daily Mail* and lingered over two coffees and a round of toast at the Kardomah.

There was a message for him at Baker Street. He was given an address in Bryanston Square. The number was on the west side of the square, and just inside the door a counter with a flap cut off the rest of the passage. A Field Security sergeant asked his name, checked his identity card and reached for the telephone. He watched Harmer's face as he spoke in what sounded to Harmer like Arabic. When he hung up he said in English, 'They're sending someone up for you, sir.' A tall girl in her early thirties came for him, and although she smiled at him as she lifted the flap for him to go through, she said nothing as they walked to the end of the corridor, down to a basement and along another passage that seemed to go on and on. Finally she knocked on a door and in response to a shout from the inside she opened the door and Harmer walked into the room.

It was quite a small, windowless room with white-painted walls and ceiling, and with a pine parquet floor. Carter waved him to a chair at the table alongside Pardoe. There was a Thermos and cups on a tray, and Pardoe poured him a coffee.

'Did you sleep well?' Carter said.

'Like a log.'

'D'you mind if we pile in right away?'

Harmer shrugged. 'Not at all.'

'We're going to pull you out of Curfew, James. We need you somewhere else.'

Carter waited for the protests but there were none, and he continued.

'We'd like your recommendations as to who should take over in Lyon.'

'Who did *you* have in mind?'

Carter smiled. 'You first, James.'

'I'd say de Salis then.'

Carter looked surprised. 'But you sent a report that he'd been approached by RF section. And he's not been trained by us.'

'You could pull him out for a course but he doesn't really need it. And as far as RF section is concerned he's not a de Gaulle man. Never was. Apart from that he's ambitious enough to prefer heading up his own network.'

'Will he follow instructions?'

'That would be the weak point, but if you give him good reasons he'll do what you want.'

Carter smiled. 'We can't always give reasons, James, good or bad.'

19

Harmer half-smiled. 'Then make them up. Give him reasons he's likely to go along with.'

He noticed the quick glance that Carter gave Pardoe.

'We'd thought that maybe it should be Cowan,' said Carter.

Harmer shook his head. 'He'd be the first to crack under pressure.'

'Why?'

'He's got a local girl he wants to marry. That's a pressure in itself. It also gives him a bolthole if the Germans got at the network. He would leave the rest of them to fend for themselves.'

'Any other reasons?'

'Yes. He's a bit of a bullshitter. He'd like to be a hero, and it's too early for that sort of stuff. There'll be time enough for that after the landings.'

'You think there *will* be an Allied invasion?' Carter smiled as he said it.

'If I thought there *wasn't* I wouldn't be over there. And you wouldn't be here now.'

'You'd be happier with de Salis?'

'Yes.'

Carter nodded. 'OK. Now let's talk about you. Do you know any of the people in Seagull?'

'No. That's one of the *réseaux* in Paris isn't it?'

'Yes. You never met Paul Gethin?'

'Not that I know of. What's his field name?'

Carter ignored the question. 'Have you any objection to being moved?'

'No. None.'

'We think that it's possible that the Germans have penetrated Seagull.'

'Gestapo or SD?'

'We're not sure, but the indications are that it's the SD.'

20

'What do you want me to do?'

'We'd like you to look them over and let us know what you think.'

'You want me to take over Seagull?'

'No. We don't want you to have any contact with them. Just carry out a surveillance.'

'How do I report back to you?'

'We'll give you your own radio-operator and courier.'

'Experienced?'

'The courier has been operational for nearly a year, and the radio-operator is just finishing training.'

'French or English?'

'Bilingual, a Scot.'

'How old?'

'Twenty-three.'

'Where is he now?'

'It's a girl. You can interview her later today. Or tomorrow if you prefer.'

'Is there an alternative?'

'Possibly. Why?'

'She's too young.'

'Wait till you've seen her, James. Then we can talk again.'

'What's her background?'

'Pardoe's brought along her ''P'' file for you to read.'

Pardoe slid two red files across the table and said, 'There's both files there, James. We'll leave you to read them. Just press the bell when you want us back.'

Jane Frazer was born in 1920, the daughter of an Edinburgh solicitor and his French wife. When Paris fell she had been in her second year at Les Oiseaux. She had pleaded on the telephone for her parents to let her stay in Paris, but for the first time in her life her father had not been open to argument. He was adamant, the Germans were only days from the capital, she was British not French, she was at risk every hour, there was nothing she could do if she stayed, and he would instruct the Embassy to send her back if she didn't promise to return immediately. It was a bad line, but not so bad that she could not hear the panic in her father's voice, and the tears in her mother's pleading.

It had taken her five days to get to Bordeaux, and three days before she could get on a boat bound for Harwich. She had had to trade her British passport for her passage, and for the first time in her life she had been scared. At Harwich she had been quizzed by an official about conditions and morale in Paris and Bordeaux. She had been surprised that the conversation had been in French and that it had wandered over her family background and what she had been doing in Paris.

She had joined the FANYs a couple of months later and had been posted to HQ Scottish Command in Edinburgh. A year later she had been interviewed in a small office in Queen Street. The interview had been in French and had lasted for four hours. The interviewer was a man in his fifties, bald and round-faced, with a quiet voice that somehow didn't match his Marseillaise accent. Two months later she had been posted to London, to SOE's headquarters in Baker Street. For nearly two years she had worked as a cypher clerk decoding the signals from networks in the field.

She had a small basement flat in Sussex Gardens and spent most evenings being escorted to night-clubs and the restaurants of Mayfair's better hotels. Even at her finishing school in Paris her evenings had been spent in expensive clubs. At first she had been given the standard lectures on ladylike behaviour, but the staff at Les Oiseaux, and eventually at SOE, had come to realize that the pretty girl was in fact quite capable of looking after herself.

There was a pattern about the men she spent her time with, they tended to be what the English call bounders and the French call *louche*. Unorthodox, arrogant men, who knew their way around. Men who knew how to get scarce things and fix things. But, on the other hand, men who laughed, who didn't take life too seriously, amusing, worthless men. She was under no illusion about them, she didn't take them seriously but she preferred their company to more serious young men. And even when the evening ended in bed it was just that. There was never a relationship; she wanted it that way, and if a man pressed for more she dropped him. She was too pretty not to be the target of more serious intentions but she laughed them off as if they were only a joke.

SOE had checked on her after the first six months and were satisfied that she had stuck to her cover story with her parents and the casual acquaintances at the night-clubs that she was a clerk at a War Office unit of the Pay Corps. She did her work well, and willingly worked long hours when it was necessary. At the end of the first year she had been sent on a signals course and had done well. From time to time she was given a week as stand-by operator to receive the signals traffic from two networks in France. She had never actually taken over but when there was a desperate shortage of operators her name had been put forward for a full training course. At SOE's various stately homes she had been trained on security, self-defence, map-reading, firearms and explosives, surveillance and sabotage. There had been a special field radio-operators' course, and she was now at Beaulieu waiting for the training staff to decide her fate.

It was their report that Harmer sat reading. She had done well on all aspects of the course but they did not recommend her for field work on two grounds. Firstly because she was too pretty, and secondly because of her liking for night-life. The comments were not male prejudice; a girl, or a man, who was noticeable in *any* way was always a problem in any network. It was average people who could best blend into the landscape. Abnormal height, an obvious birthmark, a physical handicap or a striking appearance could make that person noticed in a routine check and remembered too easily. And the liking for night-life all too often indicated irresponsibility, and a proneness to boredom when night-life was impossible. The operations staff needed her but shared the doubts. Both Carter and Pardoe felt that she could be used provided the network leader was the type who could control her. They reckoned that James Harmer might be such a man.

When Harmer had read the 'P' file twice he put it on one side. He wouldn't decide until after he had interviewed her. The courier's file was straightforward. Like many recruits to SOE's 'F' section he was British but with a French parent, in his case his mother. He had been brought up with French as his mother tongue. His father was British and had a small restaurant at Dieppe until the Germans invaded the Low Countries. The family had moved to England and the father now worked as a waiter at the Mayfair Hotel. Marcel Thomas had been a successful courier for a network in the south of France and later a network in Nancy. He had been arrested once by the Gestapo, and had escaped and come back along the usual route over the Pyrenees to Gibraltar.

Thomas looked a good choice but he would also wait until he had talked with him.

They sent Harmer down to the SOE training school at Beaulieu. He was to be briefed there about his new mission, interview the courier and the radio-operator and be debriefed from his responsibilities for Curfew. They were also taking the opportunity of using him to lecture those trainees who had not yet been operational.

24

They gave him one of the cottages on the estate and, on the Sunday when he arrived at mid-day, the grey November sky emphasized the gaunt woods and bare trees where the daylight was already beginning to fade. Carter drove him down and took him for an evening meal in Southampton. It was while they were drinking their coffee that Carter tossed the two green-edged felt stars on the table and told Harmer that he was now a captain.

Two

Harmer sat on the scarred, oak table, his legs swinging slowly as he leaned slightly forward to add emphasis to what he was saying.

'The easiest way to give yourself away is to behave as if you were trained here. *Don't* look around to see if you're being followed. And if you *are* stopped in a check don't hurry to get your documents out. Have the reason already in your mind as to why you are where you are. But don't give more information than you need. Don't be friendly or try to charm them. They're too used to resentment and obstruction to fall for that, and they'd be all the more suspicious. Right. Any questions?'

A hand went up and a tall, thin man said, 'Who normally carries out the checks?'

'The Gestapo, the SD, the Feldgendarmerie, the Milice and, on rare occasions, the Abwehr.'

'What authority do they have to arrest?'

'Mainly Lugers.'

There was a titter from the trainees, but Harmer hadn't smiled. He reached with his feet for the floor and stood up. He looked at his watch. 'You've got a ten-minute break now. Report back to the projection theatre and you'll be shown the current newsreels. Tonight you will have individual interrogations on your cover stories. Be well prepared, gentlemen. And there will be no evening passes tonight.'

Outside, the ground was iron-hard. The frost had solarized the grass and the bare silhouettes of the trees. Harmer released the padlock from his cycle and tested the brakes before he free-wheeled down the long path that eventually forked so that he could pedal towards the cottage they had allocated for his use. It was a pleasant stone-built structure with a thatched roof, set at the edge of the woods, comfortably furnished, and looked after by an ATS corporal.

Carter was already there, waiting for him, his plump body sitting awkwardly in the comfortable chair, his tunic unbuttoned and his tie unknotted. Carter at 36 was already balding, his fluffy, reddish hair merging with the freckles at the edge of his scalp. His pale, grey eyes looked out from deep-set sockets overhung by sprawling hairy eyebrows. His fleshy nose made his full mouth seem less sensual. He had the appearance of a placid country priest whose cure of souls gave him no great problems. But Harmer was well aware that behind the placid looking mask was an alert mind that held and grasped the countless details of a dozen networks, and assessed men's strengths and weakness with accuracy and a feminine perception. He wondered what Carter had done before he joined the army, but SOE didn't encourage curiosity about its members' backgrounds. And if you asked questions the answers would generally be devious or untrue. Even their names were often spurious, and cover-names and field-names added their bit to the confusion. The kind of men and women who could survive in enemy-held country and fight back against the Germans, came from a variety of backgrounds, from bankers to gun-runners, from accountants to shop assistants, and from diamond smugglers to rich men's mistresses. But they all had a few things in common. A passionate love for France, a hostility to authority, and a willingness to take a dangerous chance. Their temperaments lay at the two extremes. They tended to be either calm and collected, or highly neurotic with a love of the dramatic. And it was the job of men like Carter in the operations section to use, and sometimes abuse, this *galère*. Despite their deliberate aloofness the operations staff all achieved a loyalty from the men and women they sent into the field that was based on their dedication, their understanding, and their meticulous attention to the details that would give the agents protection and support.

Carter waited until Harmer had made himself comfortable.

'How did it go?'

'It's hard to tell. Sometimes they look like lambs being sent to the slaughterhouse, and then, by God, all of a sudden they behave like veterans.'

'Have you spoken to the girl yet?'

'No, but I'm worried about her.'

'Why?'

'Just the things you doubted yourselves. She just *is* too pretty, and she's wild. I cancelled their evening passes tonight and she looked like she could happily kill me. Every night she's off to the West End or Southampton, to parties and night-clubs.'

'So are some of the men.'

'I know, but how do I control her in Paris? It won't be only Frenchmen. She'll be attractive to the Germans, and she won't know how to handle them.'

'She never breathes a word about what she's doing. We've checked on her again and again.'

'OK. I'll let you know what I think when I've talked to her.'

Carter stood up, stretching his long legs. 'I'll need your decision on her within a week if we're to have any chance of getting you a good replacement. How about a meal in Southampton?'

'I'm doing mock interrogations tonight.'

'Their field cover-stories, or just tests?'

'Their real ones. The tests are a waste of time.'

'Why?'

'There's no real incentive. You can't dig deep in an artificial cover. They make things up just to give an answer.'

Carter nodded, and stood buttoning his jacket and straightening his tie.

'Do you want leave to see your parents, James?'

'No. It's not necessary. It will disturb them.'

'As you wish. Is there a show in town you'd like to see?'

Harmer shook his head. 'I've got enough to occupy me down here and then there's my new briefing.'

'OK. I'll be down again in a couple of days.'

It was a small office, the walls a grimy white, one small, barred window high up behind the desk. The desk itself was the usual army issue, solid oak and ugly; and the only light was from a table-lamp that was facing the chair. The floor was covered with well-worn linoleum, and there was a gripping cold that emphasized the grimness of the room itself.

Harmer opened the service notepad, reached over and pressed the bell. A few moments later the girl came into the room. Seeing the chair she sat down.

'Stand up.' His voice was sharp and hard-edged.

She stood up slowly and he turned the lamp so that it shone directly on her face. He had looked her over before, in the classes he had instructed, but he looked more carefully at her now. Her hair was almost black, long, and tied at the back with a red ribbon. Ignoring her eyes she was extraordinarily pretty. A neat, pert nose, a soft, full mouth that showed her strong, white teeth, and a slender neck that emphasized the determined chin. But because of her eyes she was more than merely pretty, she was undoubtedly beautiful. The lids were heavy, and the large, grey eyes seemed luminous in the harsh light from the lamp. He looked down at the documents on his desk, and picked up the *carte d'identitée*.

'Your name?'

'Feuillet, Paulette.'

He made a note on his pad.

'Date of birth?'

'Twenty-fourth October 1920.'

'Place of birth?'

'Saint Omer.'

'Occupation?'

'Clerk.'

'Place of employment?'

'I'm looking for a job. I'm unemployed.'

'What were you doing in the place where you were arrested?'

'Just walking.'

'Where to?'

'To a café.'

'Which café?'

'No particular café. I hadn't decided. I was going to have a meal.'

'Where were you picked up?'

'The Champs Elysées.'

'Where do you live?'

'Rue Mouffetard 57 *bis*.'

He made another note on his pad.

'What time did you leave Rue Mouffetard?'

'I don't remember. Just after ten, I think.'

'Which bridge did you cross?'

'Pont de la Concorde.'

'It took you two hours to get to the Champs Elysées?' He sounded genuinely surprised. As if he was really interrogating her.

'Yes. I looked at the shops.'

'What shops?'

'Just shops, for God's sake. Any shops.'

He saw the flush of anger on her cheeks. He held out a bunch of keys.

'Tell me about the keys. Where are they for?'

'The street door. My apartment door. My car key. The key to a friend's apartment.'

'Where are your petrol coupons?'

'I haven't any. My car was sequestered. That key was a spare.'

'What is the name of your friend?'

'What friend?'

'The friend with the apartment.'

She hesitated. 'Madame Dupuis.'

'Where is her apartment?'

'Rue du Mont Thabor.'

'Ah, a wealthy friend?'

The dark eyebrows went up disdainfully.

'No, just civilized.'

'Sit down, mam'selle.'

'I prefer to stand.'

'Sit down.'

For a moment she hesitated but the harshness of his voice seemed real. When she was sitting he stood up and carried his chair round the desk and placed it in front of her. As he sat facing her he moved the lamp so that it still shone on her face, over his shoulder.

'You're very beautiful, mam'selle.'

31

She raised her eyebrows but said nothing.

'Have you a boy-friend?'

'Several.'

'German or French?'

'French.'

'Maybe you should also have a German protector.'

'I don't need protecting.'

'But look at you now. About to go to jail.'

'For what?'

'For using a forged document.'

'It was accepted at the Kommadatura when they issued my *Permis de Conduire*.'

'The Gestapo are different, my dear, from the simple soldiers.'

He put his hand on her thigh. It was warm and firm.

'I thought you would prefer to co-operate, mam'selle.'

'If you don't take your hand off my leg I'll scream the place down.'

The room echoed as his hand struck her face. The big, grey eyes looked at him, swimming with tears.

'You bastard,' she said softly.

He stared grimly at her face and saw the marks of his fingers on her cheek.

'Tell me the story of the poor young man.'

She looked at him big-eyed and amazed.

'You must be out of your mind,' she whispered.

'Tell me about *Monsieur de Camors*.'

He stood up, walked across to the door, and switched on the ceiling light. When he sat down in front of her again he nodded towards her.

'You did very well, Jane.' He reached round for his pad. 'A couple of points.'

He looked at his pad and then at her face.

'When I asked you your name you said Feuillet, Paulette.

That's far too official. A girl would usually say Paulette Feuillet. The Gestapo and SD would notice that straight away. And then "the story of the poor young man".'

She frowned. 'What the hell was that all about?'

'Your name's Frazer, yes?'

'Yes.'

'A Scottish name?'

'Yes.'

'Who's the most famous Scottish Frazer?'

'Sir James Frazer, I suppose. He wrote the *Golden Bough*.' Then he saw the comprehension in her eyes. 'Christ, you mean there's a famous Feuillet?'

'Yes. He was a novelist. He wrote sentimental novels, one of which was *Roman d'un jeune homme pauvre* and another was *Monsieur de Camors*.'

'D'you think the Germans would know that?'

'Maybe the Gestapo wouldn't, but the SD might. They're not all gorillas, and if they speak French well enough to interrogate a suspect agent, they may know. How did you feel yourself?'

'It was all right at first, but as you went on I was beginning to fumble. There were moments when it seemed real.'

'I'm sorry I had to hit you but I wanted to see your reaction.'

'I was bloody angry.'

'So I gathered. Most people are. It's not a good move for interrogators to make, it often makes people more resistant. At least until the interrogation gets really tough.'

'Would they really try and sleep with a girl?'

'Not if you were suspected of being an agent. Otherwise I guess they might. They're normal men. Have you eaten already?'

'No. The instructors advised me not to.'

33

'Well, come and eat with me. Corporal Bates will fix us something and I want to talk to you.'

She shrugged and smiled. 'OK.'

She walked with him down to the cottage, and after they had eaten they sat in the oak-beamed room on each side of the log fire.

'Tell me about your family.'

'My father is a solicitor, and my mother is French. I'm their only child.'

'Is your father successful?'

'Yes. He's well known in Edinburgh. He gets more work than he can handle.'

'Is he rich?'

'Well-off. He doesn't discuss money with me.' He noticed the disapproving curl of her lip.

'Why did you join SOE?'

She shrugged. 'They asked me, and it sounded fun.'

'Fun?'

'Yes, fun.'

He looked at her defiant face. They had been talking in French and he knew that her affected 16th *arrondissement* accent had already prejudiced him against her. She would grate on his nerves, and she had the arrogance that went with the affectation. She wasn't serious, and that could cost other people's lives as well as her own.

'May I ask you about *your* background?' she said.

'Of course. My father is a retired insurance agent and he helps my mother run a boarding house at Seahouses in Northumberland.'

'What did you do before the war?'

'I was a shop assistant.'

'What kind of shop?'

'A bookshop.'

34

She smiled. A broad, knowing smile and it was several seconds before she spoke. 'They told me that I was being considered by an agent as his WT operator. It's you isn't it?'

'What makes you think that?'

'You wouldn't be talking to me if it wasn't for that. You wouldn't waste five minutes of your precious time on me, because you only like humble people, and people who take life seriously.'

'I should certainly be scared of working with someone who thought fighting Germans was fun.'

Her eyes were big with anger as she leaned forward.

'Well, you look at my record, mister. I've beaten most of the men on this damn training course and that's what counts.'

'Why do you spend so much time in night-clubs?'

'Because I like night-clubs,' she almost shouted. 'And I like night-club people. They're happy, they have a good time, they enjoy themselves. So put that in my "P" file.'

He was tempted, and he fell. 'It's already in your "P" file.'

She saw his half-smile and burst out laughing.

'Jesus. You can't win against you bastards can you?'

'You know what they say . . .'

'Time spent in reconnaissance is seldom wasted.' She repeated the army adage mockingly.

'It's true.'

She shrugged. 'I'd better go.'

'You don't want to be my WT operator then?'

'But you just said . . . ' she raised her eyebrows and spread her arms in a Gallic shrug.

'I was just discussing the problems with you.'

She frowned. 'But you're prejudiced against me already.'

'I'm prejudiced both ways.'

'What's that mean?'

'You've got a first-class training record so I want to grab

you while I've got the chance. But on the other hand there are a couple of snags.'

'What are they?'

'First of all you're very beautiful. Too beautiful. You'll be noticed wherever you go. By Germans as well as Frenchmen. And secondly I'm afraid of the night-club business. The only people in Paris night-clubs are Germans and black-market barons. And that's dangerous for you, and therefore for the rest of us.'

The big, grey eyes looked at him.

'Will you answer me one question truthfully?'

'Sure.'

'You don't like me because maybe my father's wealthy, and you don't like me because I don't take life seriously. Am I right?'

It was a long time before he answered and then he said, 'Yes.' He said slowly, 'You're right. I'm sorry.'

'OK. I'll make a bargain with you. You take me, and I'll never go near a night-club unless you order me to.'

'Why are you so anxious to go?'

She shrugged. 'I guess it's my mother's genes. I loved my time in Paris. I belonged there. It's terrible to think of the Germans there. It's like men in hob-nailed boots treading on roses. I want to help throw 'em out.'

'You know we'll be dropping blind. No reception committee, no safe-house, no contacts.'

'I didn't know. But if that's what we're expected to do, I'll do it. I won't be a liability.'

'Think about it overnight. Tell me in the morning.'

'Are *you* going to think about it?'

'No.'

'Why not?'

And he saw the disappointment on her face.

'I've already decided. If you still want to go after you've

36

thought about it, I'll take you.'

She beamed at him, and then relaxed in her chair.

'Can I tell you something?'

'Yes.'

'You know, in your own sweet way you're just as much of a snob as you think I am.'

'How do you make that out?'

'You said you worked as a shop assistant.'

'Well that's true.'

'Yes, but a bookshop's different. Much posher than just a shop. Yours is a sort of inverted snobbery.'

He smiled. 'Maybe you're right. Anyway, I'll walk you back to the big house.'

She sat up suddenly. 'By the way. How the hell did you know about Feuillet the writer?'

'I checked on the phone at the British Museum library.'

'You didn't know already?'

'No.'

'I'll have to watch you, you know.' She tried to look serious but she couldn't hide her pleasure.

Walking back alone from the big house in the cold hard moonlight he thought about the girl. She would end up being either a fantastic success or a complete disaster, and for once in his life he was uncertain as to which it was more likely to be. There were plenty of pluses but the minuses could turn out to be big ones.

He undressed slowly, arranging his clothes neatly on the chair. It was almost three o'clock. As he pulled the rough army blanket over his shoulders he closed his eyes. And in the seconds before he slept he saw again those big, grey eyes filled with tears. He sighed as he turned over.

Three

Harmer spent the morning with the courier. Marcel Thomas had worked with two networks in the south of France until the Gestapo had eventually rounded up network Lucas in two days of mass arrests in Nice. Thomas had escaped the net and made his way to a safe-house at Perpignan until he was fed into the escape line that took him to Gibraltar and, finally, the deep-interrogation centre at Wandsworth. There was no need to go over his experience, they just gossiped about conditions in France, the problems of the Resistance networks, and the political manoeuvrings that were already going on. Thomas had finished his refresher course. He hadn't done well, which was perhaps more a reflection on the course than the man, and he was now waiting to join Harmer officially. He had been promised a month's leave, and Harmer walked to the admin. office to arrange his passes, his travel warrants, and his pay.

It was lunch-time before he saw the girl, she was checking over the guts of a new-looking B2 transmitter that was laid out on a green baize card-table. She glanced up as he walked towards her and then looked back at the wiring diagram on the table.

'You're lucky to have been given one of those,' he said.

She looked up, smiling. 'They didn't give me one. I twisted their arms. I've got to lug this thing around France until we find a safe-house. I think they had visions of palming me off with a Mark XV in three separate cases.'

'Did you think about what I said?'

'Yeah. I thought it was a lot of old baloney. You haven't seen me when I've just washed my hair. I look a real old hag.'

'You still want to go?'

'You bet I do.'

'Are you going to celebrate this evening?'

She laughed. 'I celebrated last night.'

'How?'

'Got smashed on champers with the two other girls in my billet.'

She gave him a teasing smile, and for a fleeting moment he thought that maybe smiling could sometimes be a good thing.

He phoned Carter and told him that he would accept the girl, but asked for a couple of days' practice jumps at Ringway. Her parachute training report indicated that she was an untidy jumper, which normally didn't matter too much, but they were jumping blind, with no reception team, and no safe-house. An injured WT operator would be too much to cope with.

Carter phoned back mid-afternoon. They were to travel up to Manchester that night and could use the next two days for training. The girl had to be fetched back from Southampton where she was part of a team practising how to get rid of a tail.

A staff car took them both up to Euston station, and two first-class seats had been reserved for them. The girl read a magazine and Harmer slept. They were alone in the carriage as it jolted and clattered through the night. When she put down her magazine she looked across at his face as he slept. It was an innocent sort of face, but it had no feature that could be described as beautiful or handsome. His hair was thick and wavy, but wiry and coarse, and with his almost swarthy complexion he could have been an Italian or even a Corsican. Most sleeping faces retain some aspect of their childish origin, but not Harmer's, even his eyelashes were merely practical. If he had an attractive feature it was his mouth. His lips were firm and curved, and at the corners of his mouth were two ridged muscles of determination that matched the stubbornness of his chin. The aspect of innocence came from a kind of vulnerability, a pulse that beat at his temple like some indicator of mortality, and, as with a child, his sleep looked untouched by fear or doubt. She wondered what gave such security to a man who seemed so alone and guarded. And she wondered what kind of woman he loved or slept with. He had no charm, but she knew that when he first looked at her he was aware that she was attractive. But his brown eyes hadn't lingered. They had looked and noted, but that was all. He lay back in the corner, his hands hanging loosely between his legs. They were broad and strong with spatulate fingers, and there were wiry black hairs at his wrists. But when his hand had touched her thigh during the mock interrogation it had been a gentle touch. His battledress blouse was unbuckled at the waist and his forage-cap with its Intelligence Corps badge lay across his thigh.

She tried to make herself comfortable in the corner seat and as she leaned back she wondered if the Flight-Lieutenant would still be on the permanent staff of the Parachute Training School. He was old for a Flight-Lieutenant, a wine-merchant in a small way before the war. Sophisticated and amusing, he had monopolized her evenings during the original training course and she had let him have her on the last night before going back to Beaulieu. She had meant it to mark the end of the relationship and had assumed that he would see it as such. She hoped that he wouldn't assume that this time he could take up where he had left off. He wasn't the kind of man who would appeal to James Harmer.

Harmer was standing, lifting down her kitbag from the rack, as she woke up. They were already at Manchester.

An army pick-up was waiting for them alongside the station platform, and Harmer left her to carry her own bag as they threaded their way through piles of mail-bags to the van.

It was too early on a grey winter's morning for conversation, and they sat in silence, thankful for the van's crude heating system. They were checked at the guard-room and then driven across to the commandant's office. It was four a.m. and the mess was empty. They were given breakfast and told that they should rest until mid-day.

During the afternoon they were taken quickly through the preliminaries of the static harness in the big hangar, the jumps from the back of a truck, and the routine visit to the girls who packed the parachutes. They were spared the usual hackneyed jokes about parachutes that failed to open, as they both already had their parachute wings. Their first jumps were to be from the static balloon the next morning.

The wickerwork of the basket creaked as it swung, and the mild wind whistled against the thick cable that led down to the capstan on the truck on the ground. It was already 8.30 but it was barely light. Harmer looked across towards the city where a pall of smoke from factory chimneys hung like menacing clouds where the sun's weak rays gave a pale glow on the horizon. Harmer and the girl stood in one corner watching the RAF sergeant coiling ropes and clearing the hole in the centre of the basket. Then the sergeant made his way over to them, balancing awkwardly against the random lurching of the basket. He checked their parachute harnesses carefully, and then shouted against the wind.

'Who's going first, sir?'

Harmer nodded towards the girl and the sergeant looked at her smiling and said, 'Just remember what your mother told you.'

She frowned. 'What's that?'

'Always keep your legs closed.'

The girl laughed and the sergeant looked amiably at Harmer to include him in the joke. Harmer's brown eyes looked back at him with utter contempt, and the sergeant turned away and took the girl's arm to steady her as she sat down and swung her legs through the jump-hole. The sergeant bent down, his mouth close to her ear. 'Don't worry about your face hitting the other side, love, it's further away than you think. Over six foot. When I tap your shoulder, straighten your back. When I tap you a second time you go. Make it a good jump. OK?'

She nodded, and almost at once he tapped her shoulder. She straightened her back and the sergeant saw her eyes about to look down and he tapped her shoulder again. For a couple of seconds she was spread-eagled as she fell, and then there was the sharp crack as the training parachute snapped open. From their different vantage points they watched the girl's descent. She went over on her back as she landed and the canopy filled with the ground wind, dragging her for several yards before she turned and spilled the air from the 'chute. She stood up, taking off her helmet and shaking out her hair. Then, as two figures on the ground led her out of the dropping zone she turned, looked up, and waved to Harmer. He didn't wave back.

The RAF sergeant raised his eyebrows. Harmer nodded

and walked carefully across the tilting basket and sat at the edge of the hole.

'You know the drill, sir. Warning tap, then second tap you go.'

Harmer nodded.

'Good jump, sir.'

At the second tap Harmer jumped. A regulation jump, feet together all the way, and when he landed the neat forward roll brought him to his feet with his back to the wind, and seconds later the silk canopy collapsed.

The Halifax jump in the afternoon was cancelled because of poor visibility but by mid-day the Met report indicated a clear sky after dark and it was decided to do a night jump from the Halifax.

There were two despatchers on the night jump, and Harmer sat alongside the girl on the hard metal bench. She was trembling violently, taking deep breaths to fight off the nausea. Harmer put his mouth to her ear.

'I'll go first, and I'll wait there for you. Come down straight after me and I'll be there.'

She looked at him and shouted, 'Are you scared?'

He shook his head. 'No. And I've booked us a table at the Midland for this evening.'

Then the RAF officer pointed to the red light.

Harmer got up and walked over and they hooked him up. The green light came on and he went, conscious of the girl behind him.

The wind had dropped, but the air was iron cold on his face and the cords were already slippery with frost. Far away, towards Manchester, a group of searchlights criss-crossed in the night sky and then the ground was coming up to meet him, fast. He bent his knees slightly and then he was rolling over, wrenching off the harness with one hand and looking up for the girl. She was swinging in a 60° arc but

43

bringing the parachute under control. She was going to land about sixty yards away. She landed perfectly and spilled the air from the canopy as he walked over to her.

'A good jump, Jane. A very good jump.'

She was grinning. 'Jesus, it seemed a long journey down.' She looked at his hand holding his left wrist.

'What have you done?'

'I think I've fractured a bone.'

'I can see the car coming. Don't move it about until they've checked it.'

It had taken a couple of injections to set his broken wrist and it was ten before the taxi got them to the hotel.

The best the restaurant could do was a soufflé followed by plaice, but the girl was obviously enjoying herself and slowly he relaxed. He was very conscious of the envious glances cast in his direction. The wine waiter had found them a bottle of Chablis and as he poured her the last remnants she said, 'They're playing our tune.'

He looked up and listened. They were playing 'The Last Time I Saw Paris'.

'Dance with me, Jimmy. Just this once.'

'I can't dance well. In fact I can't dance at all.'

'It doesn't matter. I'll guide you round.'

He pushed back his chair and stood up, and they walked onto the small dance floor. She looked up at him smiling as he took her in his arms.

'The plaster on my wrist will ruin your jacket.'

She grinned. 'You're scared, my boy.'

He smiled. 'You're right.'

He wasn't too bad, and the music and the wine both helped, and she stopped at the dais and asked the band to play it again.

It was nearly two o'clock when the taxi dropped them at the guard-room. She wondered if he would kiss her goodnight. He didn't. But he walked with her to her hut and reminded her that their final jump was at ten that morning.

There was a signal from London for him that came through as they were eating breakfast. When they had finished the refresher course he was to report back to Baker Street and the girl was to go straight back to Beaulieu.

They travelled down to London together and he saw her on to her train at Waterloo, and then walked up to Trafalgar Square. He took a taxi to Selfridges and walked the rest of the way.

Carter gave him eight 'P' files covering the Seagull network, and two box-files of their radio traffic.

'Read it all, James, and let me know what you think.'

'About what?'

Carter shrugged. 'Have they been penetrated? Just your general feelings.'

'When do you expect us to go?'

'About the end of January. Depends on the weather conditions. It may have to be the first moon in February. You'll have Christmas here anyway.'

'Can I show this stuff to Thomas and the girl?'

Carter looked down at his hands on the desk, one finger rolling a pencil on the green blotter as he thought. He looked up at Harmer.

'What good would it do?'

'The girl would get a good picture of actual messages and Thomas could give a second opinion about the network. He's got experience of two already.'

Carter looked across at the window to where a brown unwatered plant drooped from a clay pot. He looked back at Harmer.

'I think not, James. A "P" file is top secret. The girl has seen plenty of actual signals stuff in her previous duties.

Discuss it with them in general terms if you like, but keep the files to yourself.'

'Do you want me to stay in London?'

'Not unless you particularly want to, we're hard pressed for accommodation and you've got the cottage at Beaulieu.' Carter stood up. 'Let me have the files back in due course. They're signed out to me.'

'How long can I keep them?'

'A week, ten days, not too long.'

The flat at Sloane Street was free, and Harmer decided to use it for the night. For an hour he sat reading through the Seagull 'P' files. They all seemed typical SOE types, either old-school-tie chaps or brigands.

He walked up to Knightsbridge and ate at the Hyde Park Hotel. Old-fashioned and solid, it gave him a vague feeling of security. After drinking his coffee he walked to the bar and had a whisky as he listened to the nine o'clock news. Winston Churchill had presented the Sword of Stalingrad to Stalin at the Teheran conference, General de Gaulle was taking a few days rest outside Algiers, and a new drug had been discovered called penicillin. The bar was crowded and Harmer drank up quickly and left.

It was the 7th of December 1943 and it was beginning to drizzle. Harmer turned up the collar of his greatcoat and walked slowly down the hotel steps. At the bottom he hesitated and finally turned left, walking up Knightsbridge towards Hyde Park Corner and then along Piccadilly. He knew what he was going to do, but not for a moment did he acknowledge it, even at the back of his mind.

He saw the two girls at the corner of Sackville Street. The younger one was laughing, stamping her feet against the cold. As he glanced at them they both looked at him and, as he walked slowly past, the younger one joined him and walked alongside him. 'You want a nice time, soldier?' He

46

stopped and looked at her, and she shone her shaded torch on her face. She was very pretty.

When she switched it off he said, 'How much is it?'

'A quid.'

'What can I do for that?'

She laughed. 'You can do me.'

'Where's your place?'

'Sackville Street over the piano shop.'

She slid her arm in his, and they retraced their steps in the darkness.

He stood waiting as she unlocked the door and then followed her up the stairs in the dim light from a bare bulb in the ceiling. The doors that they passed carried the tatty name-plates of small import/export companies and insurance agencies, until finally they were at the top of the building.

Her room was small and gaunt. An unmade bed and a single chair. She sat on the bed taking off her shoes. She was about twenty and, even in the harsh light from the single bulb, she was pretty, despite her pale face and her garish make-up. She looked up at him.

'Have you got my present?'

He gave her the pound, and her hands reached for his buttons. She pushed up her skirt and lay back on the bed looking up at the bare bulb as he got on top of her. Three minutes later she said, 'You feel better now, soldier?'

She had walked back with Harmer to the corner of Piccadilly, and he had walked off alone into the black-out, heading for Sloane Street.

Harmer phoned the guardroom at Beaulieu from Southampton station and then sat in the steamy tea-room, waiting for the car to pick him up. When it arrived he was surprised to see the girl sitting in the back seat. He put his case in the boot and sat in front with the driver.

She was full of her final tests. She had done well on the obstacle course and unarmed combat, but not too well on the final small-arms shoot.

She went into the cottage with him, and the car went back to the pool. There was a small fire burning with a black wire guard in front of it. A note on the table said that there were sandwiches and a Thermos in the kitchen. And the ATS corporal was at a party in the corporals' mess if she were needed.

'Why aren't you wearing your uniform?' he said.

'Because I'm not on duty. Have you got any news?'

'About what?'

'About when we go.'

He turned to look at her. 'It'll be at least eight or nine weeks before we go.'

'That means we'll be here for Christmas and New Year.'

'Yes. I'll fix leave for you if you want. You're entitled to three weeks when you finish the course.'

'What will *you* do for Christmas?'

'I shall stay here.'

'But everybody will be away.'

'So?'

She looked up at his face. 'Why don't you go to your home?'

'There's only my parents.'

'But there'll be parties to go to. The conquering hero on leave and all that.'

He half-smiled. 'They think I'm a rifleman in the infantry.'

'They'll want to see you all the same.'

'It's not that kind of family. They've got their own worries.'

'Jesus. You're their son, for God's sake.'

'You wouldn't understand.'

'But don't *you* want to see them?'

48

He sighed. 'Not really. I've got my routine, and they've got theirs.'

She stood up. 'Let's see what there is to eat.'

They sat each side of the fireplace, the plate of sandwiches and the Thermos and cups on the low table between them.

'How about you come up to my folks for a few days at Christmas?'

'I'd be in the way.' But she had seen the surprise and momentary pleasure in his eyes.

'Don't talk rot. You're a friend of mine, that's enough.'

'It's very kind of you.'

She licked her fingers. 'You know, when this bloody war is over we'll have to send *you* on a training course to get you house-trained and civilized. You're a bloody zombie, Captain Harmer, sir.'

She was sorry the moment she said it, because it was true and his eyes had gone down to his plate and the remnants of the bully-beef sandwich. He leaned forward, put the plate on the table and looked up at her.

'I'd be very grateful, and perhaps you'd come for a day to my parents.'

'Great. I'll phone mine tomorrow. I'd better get back to my billet now.'

'I'll walk you back.'

There was a thick, yellow fog coming down as they walked slowly up to the huts alongside the big house. As her hand reached to move aside the black-out curtain from the door he said, 'Who gave you permission to meet me at the station?'

She laughed softly. 'Nobody. I didn't ask.'

'Why did you come?'

'You're being dumb again, sweetie. We're a team, and I came to welcome you back.'

'See you tomorrow.'

'OK.'

49

Four

Harmer read the Seagull 'P' files several times and the box-file of signals traffic he read again and again. He found no grounds on which to suspect or confirm the network's security. They were thin on the ground, and seemed to have far too many conflicting responsibilities, and that always meant the possibility of careless enciphering and slapdash procedures. But they seemed no worse than the average network. It was easy for armchair operators to criticize agents in the field. There was criticism enough the other way round. He sent the files back to Norgeby House by despatch rider.

There were patches of pale sunlight from the mullioned windows across the wooden lectern, and the reflected light emphasized the line of Harmer's jaw as he turned, pointing at the words on the blackboard.

'You're confusing the Sicherheitspolizei with the Sicherheitsdienst, my friend. They are both SS organizations, but their functions are different. The SIPO control section 4 – the Gestapo. They also control the German civil police, the KRIPO. And section 3 of the SIPO is the SD which is what concerns you.'

He turned to look back at the trainees. An arm was up. 'Yes,' he nodded.

'What about the Abwehr?'

'They are controlled by the army, the Wehrmacht. And they themselves control the GFP – The Field Secret Police. You can check the illustrations of their uniforms in your handbooks. That's the easiest way to remember them. But you're not likely to have any great trouble from the Abwehr.'

'Which is the most efficient – the Gestapo or the SD?'

'They're both efficient. Fortunately for us they are bitter rivals. Not only in France but in Germany, too.'

'How does that help us?'

'They don't compare notes. They don't share their records or the results of their interrogations. There's no cross-referencing, and they spend a lot of time and energy disparaging one another's information.'

'Which of them is best at interrogations?'

'They both get results. The SD men are generally more intelligent and better trained. The Gestapo are low-grade. They recruit on a different basis to the SD. They're not too fussy about background. They rely more on brute force than brains. But they're effective. They go for violence in interrogations but the SD tend to get more information. That's probably the main difference between them. The SD want to know and the Gestapo want to chalk up an arrest.'

Harmer walked over to the wall and switched on the light. When he was back in front of them the girl put her hand up and he nodded to her.

'What's the best attitude to adopt for interrogations?'

'Well, it's tougher for us than it is for a normal prisoner-of-war. A serviceman gives his name, rank and number, quotes the Geneva Convention and refuses to answer any other questions. Those are his orders and they know it. For us, we are being interrogated as suspect civilians. You've got to stick to your cover story through thick and thin. You've had plenty of experience from the mock interrogations here. You probably feel that the instructors were pretty rough. Believe me they were gentle as lambs compared with the real thing. And you know that they're instructors. They may have yanked you out of bed in the middle of the night. They may have used some violence on you, but they're men you know. You've seen them in the mess. You don't need me to tell you that it all feels a lot different when it's for real.

'If you stick to the basic rules you've been given that's all we ask. You stick to your cover story as long as you can. And no matter what, you don't talk for forty-eight hours so that your network has had time to disperse. And one last thing. It's not a rule and nobody demands it of you, but even when they've broken your story you don't have to tell them more than you need to. Make them work for it. It takes more than average guts so it's just a thought, not a rule and certainly not an order.'

Harmer looked at his watch, and then looked up.

'Travel warrants and pay are waiting for you at the office. Your leave passes are made out to the third of January. I look forward to seeing you all then.'

They turned off the road at Alnwick and took the narrow roads that led to the coast. At the T-junction Harmer turned right into the single main street of Seahouses. He parked the car alongside the row of small shops and turned to look at the girl.

'You'll take them as you find them won't you?'

'Of course I will.'

'And we don't stop the night, even if they ask us. We say we've got to press on.'

'OK.'

They crossed the narrow street together, and he opened the wrought-iron gate. There were long net curtains at the windows, and in the downstairs room there was an aspidistra in a big green china bowl, filling the space where the curtains parted. He reached out his hand and pressed the white bell-button, and she saw that he was trembling.

A grey-haired man opened the door, dressed in a seaman's jersey and grey flannel trousers. He looked from one to the other.

'Yes?' he said.

'It's me, dad, Jamie.'

The pale blue eyes looked at his son's face and then at the girl. Then back at his son.

'Well then. What're *you* doing up in these parts?'

'I've got a few days leave, dad. This is Miss Frazer, a friend of mine.'

The old man looked back at the girl.

'D'you come from these parts, miss?'

'My parents live in Edinburgh, Mr Harmer.'

'I see,' he said.

'Shall we come in, dad? We can't stay long.'

'Your mother's not in. She's buying offal at the butcher's.'

He stood to one side almost reluctantly, and the two of them followed him as he shuffled down the narrow hall to the back room.

Harmer pulled out a chair from the table for the girl to sit on.

The doorbell rang and the old man went off down the hall. The girl sat silently, looking at Harmer's grim face as they heard the distant voices.

'. . . with a girl.'

'Who is she?'

'I didn't catch her name. Comes from Edinburgh.'

And then the door opened. The woman had the same

swarthy complexion, the same brown eyes and the sensual mouth, that she had passed on to her son.

'Well, Jamie,' she said, as she put her basket on the table. 'You're just passing through, I hear.'

'Yes, *maman*. Let me introduce Miss Frazer, a friend of mine.'

The woman turned as if she had not realized the girl was there.

'Well, that's nice. And you're from Edinburgh, I hear.'

'My home is in Edinburgh.'

'And very nice too. Can the two of you stop for a meal?'

'We'd love to,' the girl said.

'And you, Jamie?'

'If it's not too much trouble, *maman*.'

The meal was superb, but the atmosphere was strained. It was as if they were intruders, and that the young man beside her was an acquaintance rather than a son. The talk was of the locals and their problems, and they asked no questions of their son. There was no leg-pulling or affection, just a distant politeness that was almost formal. When his parents had seen them to the door an hour later there were no kisses or good wishes, and the door had closed behind them before they reached the wrought-iron gate.

In the car Harmer sat in silence for a moment or two, and then, turning to look at her face, he said, 'I'm sorry about that. But I warned you.'

'They were fine, Jamie. We ought to have warned them we were calling in.'

'It wouldn't have made any difference.'

He turned the ignition key, started the engine, and drove down to the sea front turning left onto the Bamburgh road.

Two hours later they turned out of Princes Street, crossed Queen Street, and drew up outside the big house in Drummond Place. The girl had been very conscious of the contrast. The decorations, the warmth and the lights, the hugs and kisses, the excitement, and the ease with which her parents took the stiff young man under their wing. Relatives and friends were phoned, and people came in for drinks and sandwiches.

The girl's mother had shown him to his room and ten minutes later Jane had knocked on his door and had taken him downstairs to meet the visitors. And despite his aloofness he was James, Jimmy and Jamie to a dozen people inside half an hour. Nobody asked him about why he was there. He was a friend of the family and that was enough. And what surprised him most was that despite the laughter they weren't frivolous people. For the first time in his life he felt accepted, even valued, without having to prove his worth. People touched one another. Arms went round shoulders and waists, casually and naturally, and people listened when he spoke. They seemed interested in what he had to say. There were people who had been to Seahouses and Bamburgh and knew the wild countryside of the Cheviots and the long miles of sandy beaches.

As he lay that night in the comfortable bed he was tired but he couldn't sleep. It was a grand house, expensively furnished but the family treated it all as if it were just a background. They seemed unaware of the luxury; unaffected by it, and in two or three hours he had met more amiable, intelligent people than he had met in all his years at Seahouses. And her parents had accepted him so easily. There had been no cautious questions about his background or his relationship with their daughter. He was a friend of hers and that seemed to make him part of the family. He had read novels of families like this but he had seen them as idealized figments of some writer's imagination. Although they were nothing like his parents they were quite ordinary people, but they had a kind of dignity that allowed them to

55

be relaxed and friendly with all those people. And with him.

He had gone shopping with her in Princes Street the next day and while she was trying on dresses he had slipped out to a bookshop and bought her a copy of the *Oxford Book of French Verse*. It was the first time he had ever bought anybody a present, apart from the routine gloves or handkerchiefs for his mother.

There had been parties every evening, mainly young people and he had gone cold with anger when young men kissed the girl with obvious enjoyment under the mistletoe. But pretty girls had kissed him too, the girl had seen to that. His lips had not responded, but it made no difference, slim arms had gone round his neck and smiling girls had kissed him with apparent pleasure.

In the afternoons they had gone for drives into the countryside to Cramond and Duddingston, walking across soggy meadows, along muddy lanes and then back to Edinburgh for tea in one of the hotel lounges.

There was an hour or so in the early evening when she was helping her mother and he sat alone with her father. They generally had a whisky or two and the older man's questions about him were obviously prompted by interest rather than curiosity. He had asked about his life before the war, and about his parents. Not what they did but what they were like. What he hoped to do when the war was over. He passed no comment and offered no suggestions. He just listened, and Harmer was conscious that he was talking too much and too freely. Mr Frazer was a good and attentive listener and Harmer always felt somehow as if he had been praised or approved of after they had talked.

On the afternoon of New Year's Eve he had been shown how to do one of the Scottish dances. They had taken it all so seriously that he had more or less mastered 'The Dashing White Sergeant'. Enough to start the dance with a Jane he

56

hadn't seen before. Smiling but serious in full Highland dress. Pleased that he tried so hard, she made sure that he was on her right hand and her father on her left as they stood in a circle with their guests to sing 'Auld Lang Syne'.

Two days later they had headed south in the crisp winter sunshine and he was wearing the watch she had given him on Christmas morning. He had felt pleased and yet disturbed when he saw it in its blue velvet box and had been faintly jealous when later that day there had been gifts from her to other young men.

Because of the icy roads it took them two days to drive back to Beaulieu, and for Harmer it was as if someone had switched off all the lights.

He went with Carter and Pardoe to meet de Salis when the Lysander brought him to the airfield at Tangmere. They spent ten days in London discussing the new plans for his old network, and then he took de Salis down to Beaulieu to start his crash course.

It was the last week in January when he received his official orders. He sat reading them, alone in the cottage.

For Captain James Harmer; organizer of CYCLOPS
Operation Instruction No F65 29.1.44
Operation: CYCLOPS
Field-name: ARCHEVÊQUE
Name on papers: Jacques Hubert
1. Information
   You have been briefed on the personnel and the objectives of existing network SEAGULL and you have been informed of our concern that this network may be insecure.
   You have agreed to carry out a surveillance of this network and report your findings to London.
2. Intention
   (a) You will return to the Field accompanied by your

W/T operator and courier during the February moon.

(b) Your party will, for security reasons, drop blind in the area YMONVILLE

(c) You have been given details of RV and safe-houses currently held by SEAGULL personnel. These will not be used by your team.

(d) You have been given the address of a safe-house in CHARTRES to be used only in an emergency. The password there is AUDUBON.

(e) You will not make contact with any member of SEAGULL nor attempt any active operation.

(f) Decisions regarding transmissions are entirely at the discretion of your W/T operator.

Administration and finance.

You will take with you to the Field 300,000 francs and it is expected that this will be sufficient for a period of six months.

There was no signature.

He took out his large-scale maps and checked for Ymonville. It was a town he had never heard of. He found it on the map and read through his operational orders again.

He was relieved that at last they were on their way, but it seemed a strange operation, to be virtually spying on another network; not to help them, but to report to the staff who were controlling them. But there would be a reason, and it was not for him to ask what it was. If they had wanted him to know they would have told him.

In the following week he carefully briefed the girl and Marcel Thomas. He had her radio checked again, and confirmed the codes that she would use. And he gave them the address and the password for the safe-house in Chartres.

He arranged for the other two to be transferred to the cottage. But now that the time was approaching for them to leave, there was a tension between them all that he found impossible to ease. At 24 he felt like an old man. The other two were looking at him with calculating eyes. Their lives were going to depend on him, and he could sense them speculating on his capabilities. Neither the girl nor Thomas argued or queried what he said. He was the expert, and they would rely on his judgment. But they still wondered. Thomas had worked only in the ZNO, the unoccupied zone, and his experience of German harassment was limited. Harmer spent hours interrogating them both on their cover stories, and insisted that they all no longer spoke any English or used anything but their cover names.

Both Carter and Pardoe came down to visit them from time to time, but their brief visits were stilted and uncomfortable. The three of them were in a kind of limbo, and Harmer sensed that the girl's confidence was slowly ebbing away.

He took her to the cinema one evening in Southampton. It was a re-run of *Mrs Miniver* and it seemed to be about another world, and another, fairy-tale war. They left half-way through the film and went for a drink at a hotel. Sitting in the deserted bar there seemed nothing encouraging to say.

'Are you worried, Paulette?'

She looked up at him and sighed. 'I'm something. I don't know what it is.'

'Try and tell me.'

There were tears in the big, grey eyes, and her lips quivered as she spoke. 'I don't seem to belong anywhere any more. My parents in Edinburgh seem like the other side of the world. I feel like I've already left Beaulieu. We don't belong there any more. And we don't belong where we're going either. I can't believe I'll ever belong anywhere ever again. And I'm scared.'

'What are you scared of?'

'Everything. I'm scared of the drop. I feel that just being dropped is enough. And to go on doing things after that, to cause trouble, seems crazy.'

Harmer smiled. 'Everybody feels like that.'

'Do you?'

'I did the first time. I just wanted to go back and have my bacon and eggs with the aircrew. They looked so much belonging together. They were going back to proper beds and a routine they knew. And I had no idea what I was going to face. And when I was brought back here from my network in Lyon I felt the same. I wanted to stay where I knew the rules. I still feel an imposter in this battledress.'

'What sort of place did you live in, in Lyon?'

'I was never very long in the same place. My main place was in an attic.'

She looked at his face. 'D'you like me?'

He nodded. 'Oh yes. I wish I'd had a sister like you.'

She burst out laughing. 'You're a funny man, you really are.'

'In what way?'

She fiddled with a beer mat as she collected her thoughts, then she looked up at him.

'I know so much about you. I know things about you that I suspect you don't know yourself. But *really* I know nothing about you. Absolutely nothing.'

'Can I suggest something?'

'Of course.'

'How about you go up to town tomorrow and have a fling?'

'Would you come with me?'

'No. And I'd be a bore. You go yourself.'

She sighed. 'No. It's a nice thought, but it would be as phoney as *Mrs Miniver*. I'll stay put. How much longer do you think we have to wait?'

'About two days. The moon will be full then.'

'What a waste of a moon.'

'Come on. Let's go and find the car.'

Thomas was waiting for them. Carter had telephoned and Harmer was to ring him back no matter what time he came in.

The conversation with Carter was brief. Weather permitting they were to drop the next night, and a staff car had been laid on to take them up to the airfield at Tempsford.

Five

The dark green Humber staff-car picked up Carter at Baker Street on its way from Beaulieu to Tempsford and then they headed north up the A1. An armoured brigade, its tanks on transporters, ground past them going south from Stevenage, and it was followed by the long convoy of an American infantry unit.

At Biggleswade they stopped for lunch, and after they had eaten, Harmer and the girl walked down to the bank of the river. There was thin ice around the brown dead stalks of mace at the edge of the bank, and a pair of moorhens were busy in the reeds. Across the river a stand of oaks and elms stood bare-branched against the grey sky. It was barely two o'clock but the light was already going. In a thicket a bird sang a thin, cold, hesitant, winter song. The girl shivered despite her khaki greatcoat, and Harmer took her arm and led her back to the inn.

At Tempsford the gates in the overgrown hedge were closed, and two Field Security sergeants stood on the far side watching them.

Carter got out of the car and walked to the gate, fishing in his inside pocket as he went. He handed over some papers and stood waiting while they were checked. Then the gates were opened and the car was stopped at a makeshift guardroom while one of the sergeants spoke on the telephone. When he hung up he nodded to Carter, who got back in the car.

The headlamps carried the standard black-out covers, but even in that dim light they could see the long low wooden huts strung along the cinder pathway, and over to their right they saw the shadowy outline of what looked like a Halifax bomber. The car stopped at a brick building, and Pardoe was waiting for them.

They were taken to separate rooms and Carter went in with Harmer.

On a long narrow table were his documents. Carter handed them over one by one and took back Harmer's operational orders.

In the corner of the room was a glass panelled shower and it was a bar of French soap that Harmer used as he washed his body carefully. An RAMC orderly manicured his fingers and his toes, and then he carefully put on the clothes he had worn when he came back from France. They had been steam-cleaned, and as he put them on they seemed incredibly thin and light after his battledress. His Baretta lay on a piece of paper that said that it had been stripped down, cleaned and oiled, and re-calibrated. A brief note informed him that he was loading the cartridges incorrectly. They should be lip over lip. The note added that the magazine was fully loaded with one up the spout. The safety catch was on. A further note in a different hand said that despite the re-calibration the pistol had a tendency to pull up and right when there were fewer than four cartridges in the magazine.

There was a copy of the Part II orders notifying his promotion to captain and his attachment to the Inter-Service Research Unit, the cover name on the plate outside 64 Baker Street.

Harmer laid out all his personal belongings from his battledress and Carter put them into two small piles. Those that he could take, and those that would be returned to him when he came back.

'Are you satisfied with the girl and Thomas?'

'They'll be fine.'

'The training staff at Beaulieu are very impressed with what you've done with them so far.'

Harmer nodded. 'Are they looking after her?'

'Yes. Audrey Bowen's taken her over.'

'Is there any more new information on Seagull?'

'No. Nothing significant.'

'But you're still suspicious?'

'I think it's just a question of time before they're penetrated.'

'Maybe you've overloaded them.'

'Pardoe's in charge of them. I wouldn't think so.'

'What's our ETA tonight?'

'23.00 hours. We want to give you an hour before curfew.'

'Have you seen the Met report?'

'Not the latest, but this morning's forecast was clear skies until dawn tomorrow. We're putting on a little diversion to help you.'

'What sort of diversion?'

'A couple of fighter-bombers are raiding the SS barracks just north of Chartres to keep them occupied.'

Harmer looked at his watch. There were three hours to go.

'I'd like to take the others to see the plane and check our stores.'

'OK. I'll be coming with you myself as despatcher.'

Inside the aircraft, an RAF sergeant sat at a small metal

64

desk, using a celluloid protractor with a swinging ruler, on a folded chart. He looked up for a moment and nodded as they stood at the doorway. Two aircraftsmen were checking the maze of pipes that ran along the inner body of the aircraft.

Harmer showed the other two the exit hatch and the static line hooks, and the red and green signal bulbs. They talked almost in whispers as if they were in a museum or a cathedral, but Harmer sensed that the depression of the waiting period had gone. There was tension now, a concentration on what they were about to do that gave no time for introspection. He felt the same tension himself.

They walked back to the operations block and Carter took them into the canteen. Like aircrew back from a mission they could have the privilege of real eggs and bacon. They sat around afterwards reading old copies of *Picture Post* and *Blighty*.

Half an hour later they were joined by an RAF flight-lieutenant with the Met report.

'There's a bit of cloud over the French coast but that won't be any problem. The weather over the other side is much the same as here . . . damp but mild.' He smiled up at Harmer. 'Are you all ready to go?'

'Any time.'

'Come on, then, let's go.'

There was flak as well as cloud as they passed over the coast between Cherbourg and Le Havre, and they felt the big bomber struggling to gain height. Half an hour later the navigator came over to Harmer and bent to speak close to his ear.

'Another ten minutes, skipper. There's not much wind now so we can drop you pretty accurately. What's the jumping order?'

'Me first, then the girl, and then the other fellow.'

'OK. You've got your own despatcher, haven't you?'

'Yes.'

'I'll put the red light on three minutes before ETA.'

'OK.'

It was the girl who touched his hand as the light went on.

Carter unscrewed the two big wing-nuts and slid the hatch on its axis across the floor, and Harmer swung his legs down into the darkness and pointed at the girl and then Thomas. They both nodded to him. He gave Carter the thumbs-up sign and then the green light flickered and came on.

The undertow from the bomber turned him sideways then upside down, and for a split second he was at the edge of panic until he heard the canopy burst open above him. His body swung down, away from the shrouds. Far away in the darkness he caught a brief glimpse of fires and searchlights, and then the earth was rushing up to meet him. He landed sprawling, as his feet met tussocky grass, and then he was free of his harness. The canopy spilled its air and as he looked up he saw the other 'chutes falling slowly. The girl and Thomas were coming down in almost the same spot about a hundred yards away. He stood watching as they both landed, and in the bright moonlight he could see them struggling with their canopies. He flashed the amber light of his torch towards them and waited.

The girl got to him first, rosy cheeked and panting.

'The supplies 'chutes have gone in the next field. One of them's hanging from a tree or something.'

'OK. We'll get it in a moment. Are you OK?'

'I'm fine.'

'Good girl.'

Then Thomas came stumbling across in the thick grass, cursing softly as he ran. His red face was redder than usual and beads of sweat lined his forehead.

'You OK, Marcel?'

'Sure.'

'Right. We'll collect the 'chutes and get into the next field. There's a . . .'

For a moment they all froze as the all-clear wailed from a nearby village. Then he realized it was probably the aftermath of the raid by the fighter-bombers, and slowly they relaxed.

He bent down for his neatly folded canopy and harness, and they stumbled across the field together.

It took them an hour to find the second supplies 'chute but it was the one with the squat little spade strapped to its side. They dug out two rabbit holes at the edge of the small wood, and stuffed in the canopies and harnesses, tamping in the soil, and covering the entrances with dead leaves.

Harmer stood up, looked around, and then pointed. 'There should be a road over there. We follow that for about three kilometres and then there's a main road that by-passes the village. If there's traffic it will be Germans, and you go straight in the ditch. I want to make twenty kilometres before it gets light. We'll stop ten minutes in every hour. Don't talk, and don't make a noise. If a dog barks or somebody shouts just keep going unless I stop. OK?'

They went through three villages, walking silently in the shadows. And just like Harmer had warned, dogs had barked, and once somebody had flung open a bedroom window as they froze in a shop entrance. Only once had a car gone by, but its headlights had given them good warning. As the girl looked cautiously from the ditch it seemed incredible that there actually was a swastika pennant fluttering from the nose of its radiator.

They had done just short of twenty kilometres when Harmer called a halt at the edge of a wood on the crest of a hill. Harmer took over the radio as well as his own kit, and Thomas carried the other case. He took them back about fifty yards into the woods.

Irrationally, Harmer, despite his physical tiredness, felt a lifting of his spirit just from being back in France, and he sensed that the others felt the same. They could barely see one another in the darkness, but they had suddenly become a real team. Harmer's self-assurance on the journey through the night had worked its own magic and he was a leader again.

He made them each take a sip or two from his brandy flask before he gave them their orders. It was 4.30 a.m. and still dark, but Harmer knew that people would already be stirring on the small farms dotted along the valley. He was almost certain that he knew where they were but he would need good light before he could plan any further. He told the girl and Thomas to sleep until he woke one of them to take over after he had actually confirmed where they were.

The false dawn came an hour later and Harmer moved back to the edge of the wood but it was another hour before the first light showed in the sky. By nine o'clock the sky was clear but the temperature had dropped. He could hear the lowing of cows from the other side of the hill and two or three farm vehicles moved on the main road to Chartres. By ten there was sunshine and in the far distance it touched the roofs and spire of the cathedral. It stood out from the thin mist that shrouded the city, like a ship on an ocean. He had never been to Chartres, but in that moment it represented all that he felt about France. Gothic, magnificent, civilized and maternal, indifferent to the Nazi occupiers, the epitome of all that France stood for.

He scrambled to his feet and went back to Thomas and the girl to wake them. They were both awake, stretching arms and legs, red-eyed, despite their sleep, but smiling. He took them back to his vantage point at the edge of the wood to show them the cathedral. Marcel Thomas had slowly cros-

68

sed himself but seemed otherwise unimpressed. But there were tears on the girl's face and she turned to look at him, shaking her head as if in disbelief. 'I can't believe it,' she said.

They ate one of the ration packs and some of the glucose tablets but they had nothing to drink. Harmer gave them a look-out rota and told them to wake him at two o'clock.

The girl had to shake him several times to wake him and half an hour later he set off with her for the valley road. Two or three cars passed them before they got to the outskirts of the city. There were Wehrmacht everywhere and a few SS, their papers were checked twice but only cursorily and there had been no problem. The girl's unwashed face and ungroomed hair had been a useful protection.

Harmer walked her to the main square and then past the safe-house, an apartment over a bakery. Next door to the bakery was a café and they ate a bowl of soup and paid for the thermos flask to be filled with hot milk. The elderly patron was able to give Harmer the address of a widow in one of the neighbouring streets who had a furnished room to let.

It was small and backed on to a small tannery whose stench pervaded the whole house, but they paid a month's rent in advance and took it in Thomas's name. Harmer wanted him out of Paris until he had had a week or two to look around.

The girl glanced from time to time at his face as they headed back down the road to the hill and the woods. He was unshaven and his eyes red-rimmed, his thick jacket was stained and patched but she knew now why they had picked him. From the moment they had landed they had followed him like sheepdogs at a shepherd's heels because he knew exactly what they should do. He owed his leadership, not to SOE's edict, but because it came naturally. In an area that was as strange to him as it was to them he acted as if he had a right to be there. When the SS had checked their documents he had ignored them and had gone on talking to her as if there was no fear in his mind, and no problem. And there *was* no fear in his mind. There were things to be done and he was on his way to do them. He didn't give orders, he just explained, and took their agreement for granted.

There was a row of four small cottages about seven kilometres down the road. Harmer stopped outside the garden gate of the last cottage and told her to wait. He walked up the narrow garden path and knocked on the door. An elderly woman in black opened the door. He talked for five or six minutes but the old lady kept slowly shaking her head, until finally she closed the door in his face and he walked back to the road, his face impassive. When she asked him what had happened he ignored her question.

The light had almost gone as they turned off the road to climb the hill. The fine day was already turning into a bitter cold night and he knew that there would be no sleep for any of them that night, even in the shelter of the woods. There could be no question of lighting a fire.

Marcel Thomas's face looked raw red from the cold and Harmer gave him the key to the room in Chartres and told him to take just the smaller of his two cases and stay there until he received a coded telegram. It would give a telephone number in Paris which he should contact immediately. The order of the digits would be reversed.

After Thomas had left Harmer hid the radio and the two large kitbags under a pile of brown bracken and with only their toilet kit he led her back down the hill towards the road. Despite the rising moon they made slow progress as their side of the hill was still in shadow from the wood. Frost was already forming on the tussocky grass and they were panting and bruised by the time they got to the ditch at the side of the road.

Harmer turned left at the road, turning south, away from Chartres. He was sure that there had been a signpost marked on the large-scale map he had memorized at Beaulieu. At a crossroads, and the right fork should point to Loché. Half a kilometre further on he saw it. One arm had been broken off but as he looked up at the other the almost indecipherable legend said Loché – 2 kms.

In fact it was not much more than a kilometre down the winding lane and the small inn that had been marked on the map was there at the edge of the village. The village itself was no more than a huddle of twenty dwellings each side of a set of crossroads.

Harmer took her hand and they walked carefully along the edge of the narrow grass verge. There were no lights at the front of the inn but Harmer led her under the stone archway to the small courtyard enclosed by a group of stone outbuildings. Almost at the back door of the inn Harmer suddenly stopped. He turned to the girl and silently put his hand to his mouth and indicated that she shouldn't move. He walked carefully and silently towards where a headlight reflected the moonlight and put his hand on the engine of the motor-cycle. It was still hot and on the petrol tank were two painted shields. The leading one was white with the two lightning flashes of the SS in black. The second was also white but with the outline of a winged helmet in its centre. The divisional sign of the 38th SS Panzer Grenadier Division 'Nibelungen'. A five-figure official number was stencilled along the lower edge of the petrol tank. It was a 500-cc BMW.

He walked back, took her hand, and led her back silently to the shadow of the archway. There were no lights in any of the houses and nothing moved although it was barely seven o'clock. He squeezed her hand and pulled her forward so that he could look both ways up the village street. Then with his arm around her waist he hurried her across the road. They stood for a few moments in the shadow of church yard gates and then crunched up the gravel drive in the shadow of the yews and cupressus that flanked the pathway.

His hand reached for the rusted wrought-iron handle on the church door and turned it slowly and tentatively. The snap as the latch came up seemed to echo over the whole village. He opened the heavy door, pushed the girl inside, followed her, and closed the door behind them. The church was quite small, four or five gas jets in glass globes cast long shadows on the roughly plastered walls. The timbers of the low, arched roof were black with age and neglect, and at the far end a small vestry door stood ajar, and a light came from the vestry itself.

They walked cautiously up the aisle and as they turned towards the vestry door it opened, and a man with a tired, lined face stood there in the doorway. His black suit hung on him loosely and it shone with age and wear. His clerical collar hung loose from its stud as if he had been undressing when he was disturbed. For a few moments the priest looked at them both and then Harmer said softly, 'Good-evening, Father.'

The sad brown eyes looked back at him and the priest was silent for long moments before he spoke.

'Who are you?'

'We need shelter, Father. Just for tonight. The inn seems to be closed. Do you know someone who could help us?'

'Why did you come to me?'

'Because you are a priest.'

'Are you a Catholic?'

'No, Father.'

'Are you?' He looked at the girl.

She shook her head. 'No, Father.'

The priest hesitated and then turned and beckoned them

72

into the vestry, then down a short, dark corridor to a small living room. It was almost bare except for a small, worn table and four wooden chairs. There was half a dark loaf and a small piece of cheese on a plate and a glass of red wine. On the far wall was a crucifix and a photograph of the Pope. On the narrow shelf over the fireplace was a painted Madonna and Child.

The priest waved them to the chairs and sat down slowly, facing them.

'Do you pray, my son?'

'Not very often, Father.'

'When do you pray?'

'When I'm scared.'

'Are you scared now?'

'No.'

'Why not?'

'I think you'll help us.'

'Where do you come from?'

'I'm a stranger.'

The priest half-smiled. It was a Jesuit's answer, because *étranger* could mean either stranger or foreigner.

'Why did you choose this village?'

'For no special reason.'

'You chose very badly, my son.'

'I don't understand.'

'I can see that.' The priest paused, still watching Harmer's face. 'Ten days ago the German army ordered the evacuation of this village and our neighbouring village of Vers-les-Chartres. Many people refused. A German soldier was killed. Twenty villagers were taken as hostages and then shot. The government in Vichy made an official complaint. If you came from Paris you would know this. There are only four French people still living in the village. I am one. The others work for the Germans.'

Harmer stood up. 'I'm sorry, Father. We must leave.'

The priest sighed. 'Where will you go?'

'To Chartres.'

'There is a special early curfew imposed for a month in Chartres, because of an RAF raid on the SS barracks. You would never get through at this time of night, or find a place to stay.'

Harmer opened his mouth to speak, hesitated, then closed it and said nothing. The priest pushed aside the plate and leaned forward. He said softly, looking at Harmer, 'Why have you no accent?'

There was a long pause and then Harmer said, 'My mother is French.'

The priest turned to look at the girl. 'And you, mam'selle?'

Her lips trembled but she smiled. 'Mine is, too.'

'You must stay with me tonight. Maybe until tomorrow night would be safe. But no longer. There are at least thirty Germans, all SS, quartered in this village. You were very lucky to have got here without being seen.'

When he saw Harmer hesitate he said, 'Don't be afraid, my friend, you'll both be safe here for tonight. We can talk tomorrow about how you get away.' He stood up half-smiling. 'Somebody must have been praying for us. I was given six fresh eggs this morning. I think we should celebrate together tonight.'

After they had eaten they talked, the three of them. Never formally acknowledging what Harmer and the girl might be doing, but nevertheless talking as if it was only a question of time before the fight against the Germans would start.

'What do you think that the German attitude to an invasion will be?' Harmer asked.

'The German attitude to France has always been peculiar. They saw us as a decadent nation because they only talked pre-war to our traitors, then they defeated us and found

74

themselves in Paris. It was like a working man who suddenly found that the film star he worshipped was actually available. His to do with as he wished. They were here, but they only half believed it. They still only half believe it, but they'll fight like wild animals to keep what they've got. If France goes it's the beginning of the end for them. Subconsciously they have never expected it to last but when somebody tries to take their prize away they will fight like animals. Make no mistake about that. They are already hardening against our population; until a few months ago they wanted to put over an impression of correctness, but when the landings start they will be ruthless against us. What they did in this small village they will do anywhere where they find resistance.'

'What has been the reaction of the survivors? Are they frightened by now?'

'Not at all. They are angry, bitterly angry. They are waiting for the day when they will be revenged.'

'Father, there is a cottage on the main road to Chartres with blue shutters and a willow tree in the garden. There is a lean-to shed at the side of the cottage with two cycles in it. I offered the woman money for the cycles today but she refused. Could you possibly persuade her to sell them to me?'

The priest nodded. 'She's a widow. She was probably scared. I'll see her early tomorrow morning after matins. I am still allowed to use my car. I will have the blacksmith check them over, and I'll take you there later. Now you must sleep. Tomorrow morning there will be a little hot water for you to bath.'

They slept soundly, the girl on a hard wooden bed with a thin mattress, and Harmer on a pile of blankets on the floor. It was nearly ten o'clock the next morning when the priest shook them awake. The widow at the cottage was ready to sell both cycles for five thousand francs, which was a

75

bargain, and the blacksmith was already at her cottage checking them over.

They had some local cheese and bread for their lunch. Harmer had decided to move on, and the priest took them back up the road towards Chartres in his car, waiting patiently while Harmer went up to the woods for the radio and the cases. They paid the widow for the cycles and some rope to tie the loads to the cycles. At the garden gate the priest took Harmer's hand. 'If ever you need help in Paris go to the *Institut Catholique* and ask for Father Anselm. He is my brother. I shall telephone him when I get back. Just say you come from Father Francis at Loché.' He turned and looked at the girl. 'Somebody once said that it is better to have courage than beauty. You are twice blessed, mam'selle, and we shall not forget when it is all over. There will always be a refuge for you at my church. Good luck.' And he smiled, because he had said 'good luck' in English.

It took them almost two hours to cycle to the station. They had skirted the town and come in from the west on the road from Courville. But there was no problem at the station in buying tickets for Paris.

It was early evening when the train pulled in at the Gare Montparnasse. They separated as they got off the train and walked to the guard's van for the cycles. There were Germans in uniform and plain-clothes checking passengers at the end of the platform, and there were Wehrmacht soldiers with rifles checking that the carriages were empty.

Harmer watched the girl go through the two check-points and then walked away from the barriers to the far end of the platform. Under the road-bridge he saw what he wanted, one of the metal containers that held the fine grit that was used on icy rails to prevent the big drive wheels on locomotives from slipping. He lifted the lid. It was half empty and he hurriedly scooped the grit to one side and buried the radio in its leather case.

There was only a handful of people left at the checkpoints, and he could see that the Germans were checking all documents carefully. The uniformed man had passed his *Fiche de Demobilisation* to a plain-clothes man who looked at it carefully and then consulted a thick loose-leaf file. He ran his finger slowly down one of the pages then closed the file, nodding to the uniformed man as he handed back the document.

The girl was waiting for him as they had arranged, just past the theatre. They cycled down to one of the small streets opposite the cemetery and padlocked their cycles outside a small restaurant. Harmer had remembered its name from reading the Seagull reports. The patron was a sympathizer but not part of the network. They ate a good meal of liver and bacon and paid the blackmarket price. When Harmer was paying he asked the patron where he could rent a couple of rooms.

'How long for?'

'Six months, maybe longer.'

The shrewd eyes looked at Harmer's face.

'Just the two of you?'

'Yes.'

'There's two rooms upstairs, with their own kitchen but only a shared bathroom.'

'Can I see them?'

'Sure.' He pointed. 'Through the door, first left. Up the stairs to the top floor. There's no lift.'

The rooms were medium-sized, but comfortably furnished, and the sitting-room was on the corner of the building looking out on the Rue Roger and the small street that led through to the Rue Gassendi. The girl stood beside him looking out of the window and he turned to look at her.

'Are you happy now?'

'In a way. But not like I used to be. I'm glad to be here . . .' she shrugged, ' . . .but it's business this time. Last night was a lesson for me. It isn't just a beautiful cathedral. This isn't my Paris any more.'

Harmer nodded. 'We've both got to remember that.'

'Don't worry. I shan't forget.'

'I'll have to go back for the radio after curfew. I ought to have got out at Chaville. Or some other station before Montparnasse.'

'It might look better if I come with you.'

'No. But go downstairs and phone Marcel in Chartres. Give him the telephone number here but not the address.'

When he got to the Gare Montparnasse it was half an hour past curfew. He was carrying a half-empty bottle of beer in his hand. There were a few railway men on duty and a goods train was being unloaded. Steam hung in clouds under the old-fashioned roof and in the distance was the clanging of goods wagons being shunted on to the warehouse sidings.

Nobody stopped him as he walked through the double gates on to the platform. He passed two Wehrmacht corporals unloading mail from a van marked '*Feldpost*' but neither of them even glanced at him. As he approached the shadows of the bridge he glanced behind him, but there was nobody following him. He was alone now, and he could see the metal bin against the arch of the bridge. He stood in front of it and slowly lifted the metal lid. Carefully his hand scooped away the fine gravel, heaping it to one side. Then he thrust in his hand, deeper and deeper. He slid off his coat and his jacket and rolled up his sleeve, and reached again deep into the shifting grains of stone. Then again and again. He scooped again on the opposite side, panting from the effort, but when his arm went deep inside again, his finger-tips contacted the metal bottom of the bin. The case and the

78

radio had gone. He pulled his shirt-sleeve down and slid on his jacket, and then his coat, and turned to see if he was being watched. They were bound to have left someone to arrest whoever came to collect the case. It would be a routine. But there was very little light at that end of the platform and he could see virtually nothing in the shadows.

Slowly he walked on, further down the platform, until it eventually sloped down towards the railway lines and the signal gantry. Stumbling as he walked in the darkness, he crossed lines and points until he had counted three separate sets of rails. Then he walked back until he came to the furthest platform against the outer brick wall of the station. He kept to the shadows when he reached the lighted area, weaving carefully in and out of the empty trailers that were lined up on the deserted platform. On the centre track, in a shower of sparks, a man was welding some part of the valve gear on one of the big 4-8-2 locos. It was then, with his eyes slightly closed against the blue-white light of the welding torch that the hand gripped his arm. 'Keep walking,' a voice said.

He sensed that the man beside him was a big man and the grip on his arm was like a vice. Just before the ticket barrier the man stopped and turned him towards a door in the station wall. He caught a glimpse of the man as he leaned forward to open the door. He had red hair and bushy eyebrows and a heavy jaw. 'Go on in,' the man said.

There were two other men inside the small office and they looked from the big man to Harmer. The older one pointed to the chair.

'Sit down.'

When Harmer was sitting the red-haired man locked the door.

The older man was wearing an SNCF railway uniform.

'What's your name?'

Harmer didn't answer.

The man in the uniform sat down and pushed the papers on the table to one side before he leaned forward. His eyes were cold and hard.

'You've got the choice, friend. You talk to us or we hand you over to the Feldpolizei. You've got two minutes to decide.'

The two pairs of eyes watched his face as he sat in silence, then, without looking at his watch the uniformed man reached for the old-fashioned upright telephone and pulled it across the table towards him. As he lifted the ear-piece off the hook Harmer held up his hand.

'What do you want to know?'

The man put the ear-piece back on the hook and pushed the phone to one side.

'Who are you?'

'Jacques Hubert.'

'What were you looking for in the grit-bin?'

'Perhaps nothing. That would depend on who you are.'

'Give me your papers.'

Harmer reached into his jacket pocket and put his papers on the table in front of him. The man reached forward and took them. He read each one of them carefully and passed each of them to the second man. When they had both looked at every document the man looked back at Harmer's face.

'Who can vouch for you?'

'Nobody.'

'Where do you work?'

'I am looking for work. I am unemployed.'

'Where do you live?'

'In Montparnasse.'

'How long at your present address?'

'I moved there today.'

'Where were you last night?'

'Near Chartres.'

'Where?'

'I can't tell you.'

The man sighed and looked at his companion. The other man, a thin man with a pale face turned towards Harmer. He opened his mouth to speak then changed his mind and looked at his companion. 'Let me take him outside, just for two minutes.' The uniformed man looked surprised, but he nodded his acquiescence.

The pale man walked round the table, took Harmer's arm and led him through the door to the station platform. With the door closed behind them the man said, 'Let me tell you I have nothing to lose.' He tapped his chest. 'Both lungs. Maybe three months more. Maybe four. If you are working for the Boche it makes no difference to me. Are you working for them?'

'No.'

'Can you operate that radio?'

'Yes.'

'Are you with others?'

'Yes.'

'Can we meet one of them?'

'No.'

'Why not?'

'You know why not, my friend.'

'How do we resolve this?'

'You give me my case and let me go.'

'And what if you are a plant by the Gestapo?'

'They would have been watching all of you from the moment you took away the case. They would have seen you take me. They would have come into the office to arrest all three of you by now. You know that.'

'Tell me something. Why is there no crystal in the set?'

'It hasn't been used operationally yet.'

'When did you come over?'

'A few days ago.'

'How?'

'By parachute.'

'Where?'

'South of Chartres.'

'Let's go back inside.'

As Harmer sat down, the uniformed man went outside to talk with the pale man. A few minutes later they came back in. The uniformed man beckoned to the red-haired man to join him outside and Harmer was left with the pale man, who opened a cupboard door, and pulling out some ancient box-files reached in the back of the cupboard and took out the radio case. He lifted it up and put it on the table.

'It is just you and me. No others,' the pale man said. 'If the Germans catch you with that after curfew you'll be in the Avenue Foch in minutes.' The pale grey eyes looked at Harmer's face. 'I hope to God I'm not being a fool.'

Harmer smiled. 'I'll come back and see you one day. We'll celebrate.'

Then he realized what he had said. 'I'm sorry. I forgot. Are there any drugs I could get you that would help?'

The pale man shook his head. 'It's too late I'm afraid. A year too late.' He held out his hand and, as Harmer took it, the pale man said quietly, 'Vive de Gaulle.'

It was almost five o'clock when Harmer let himself in at the side-door of the café. The girl was sitting on the bed, shivering, despite the blankets wrapped round her.

'I'm sorry. I got held up.'

'My God, I was so worried. I nearly came out to look for you.'

'Don't ever do anything like that unless I've told you to. I have to rely on you being where I expect you to be.'

'The patron came up. I think he wants to talk to you.'

'He can wait. Have you slept at all?'

'No.'

'When will they be listening for you?'

'Five past every hour until we've made our first transmission.'

He pointed to the case. 'Can you set it up to transmit for the next timing?'

'Of course.'

He scribbled out a brief message to say that they had arrived safely in Paris. And then he watched the girl checking over the radio. He stood on the bed and fixed the aerial along the edges of the picture rail with plasticine pellets. She checked the encoding of his message again and again as she waited for the last few minutes to pass, her fingers resting lightly on the ebony knob of the Morse key. Then, glancing at her watch, she put on the headphones and a few seconds later she was watching the needle flickering on the meter as she started to transmit. A few minutes later she turned the switch to 'receive' and waited, her eyes closed. Then her eyes opened and she was scribbling on the pad on the bedside table. It was only a short message, and he watched her switch to 'transmit' to acknowledge receipt, and then, just as they had taught her, she went quickly and smoothly through the routine of closing down and storing the radio in its battered case. It took her ten minutes to decode London's signal. It acknowledged their message and congratulated them on their safe arrival, with instructions to keep to the pre-arranged transmission times from that day onwards. As she handed him the decoded message her hand went to her mouth and she whispered, 'My God, my God. What a fool.'

'What is it?'

'I forgot to use my security checks.'

He shrugged. 'They'll understand, for a first transmission. Maybe they didn't notice.'

'The duty officer will have noticed even if the WT operator didn't.'

'You can give them a rocket when we get back.'

He wore his overcoat when he eventually slid into bed alongside her, and was vaguely aware that she was shivering as he closed his eyes and slid into sleep.

Six

It was the knocking on the door that woke Harmer and when he opened it slightly the café patron stood there.

'There's someone downstairs wants to speak to you. He can't wait long.'

'Who is it?'

'He'll tell you that.'

'How does he know I'm here?'

'I told him.'

'Why?'

'I'd like to make sure who you are.'

'You tell him, whoever he is, to go to hell and mind his own business.'

The patron shrugged. 'You won't be able to move a step out of this place until you've spoken to him. Or one of them.'

'One of who?'

'Ask them.'

Harmer hesitated and then looked back at the girl in bed. He turned back to look at the patron.

'Tell him I'll be down in ten minutes.'

The man smiled. 'They're watching the back as well as the front. You'd better co-operate.'

Harmer shaved carefully and put on a clean pullover.

As he walked into the café he recognized the face of the man sitting at the table opposite the door. His code name was Pauli and he was one of the Seagull men.

Harmer went over to the bar counter and the patron nodded towards the man at the table. Harmer walked slowly across the room to the table and sat down. Pauli was fair-haired with blue eyes and a narrow face. He had looked shifty in the photograph in the SOE files and he looked shifty in real life.

'You wanted to speak to me.'

'Who are you?'

'What's that got to do with you?'

The washed-out blue eyes looked at Harmer with anger, and the man said, 'You'll tell me or you'll be in the morgue tomorrow, and your friends in the Rue des Saussaies won't be able to help you.'

'Maybe they're *your* friends in the Rue des Saussaies.'

The blue eyes stared at his face and he saw the pulse beating at the man's temple. Harmer could almost smell the man's fear and tension. He watched as the man's tongue touched his dry, scaly lips. The man spoke almost in a whisper.

'Do you like birds?'

'Some birds.'

'*Les mouettes par exemple?*'

And hearing the word 'seagulls' in French seemed strange. Harmer then knew that they must be terribly demoralized to risk using a word that the Germans could easily know of already. He slid his hand forward and touched the man's thin wrist where it rested on the table.

'Don't talk here any more.'

'The patron's safe. He's on our side.'

'It doesn't matter. He doesn't need to know.'

There were tears at the edge of the young man's eyes.

'We're in the shit. Really in the shit.'

'Don't say any more. I'll leave you now. Come up to the top floor and knock. The V sign.'

The blue eyes pleaded. 'Are you from London?'

The anger in Harmer's voice was unmistakable and the young man flinched. 'Do as I told you. Stop talking, you fool.'

Harmer stood up, pushed back his chair, walked over to the counter and paid for the man's drink. Then he walked upstairs to the top floor.

The girl was naked as he walked in the room, leaning forward to look in the small mirror on the dressing-table as she brushed her long hair. She turned as he closed the door, the brush in her hand.

'My God. I wish you wouldn't keep disappearing, Jimmy.'

For long seconds she was no longer a radio operator but a girl, a naked girl, with trembling, pink-tipped breasts and long legs, and a black triangle between her thighs. For a moment their eyes were locked and then he said gently, 'There's a man coming up in a moment.'

She reached for her skirt and her sweater, and as she slid her feet into her shoes there was the knock on the door.

Harmer waited for a few moments then opened the door, and, without introducing the girl, he pointed to the tapestry chair. When the man had sat down he closed his eyes for a moment. Harmer waited and, when the man opened his eyes, Harmer said, 'How long since you've slept?'

The man shook his head. 'God knows. Two days, it could be longer.'

'What's happened?'

'They've got René and the radio operator.'

'Who have?'

He sighed and looked up at Harmer's face. 'Our friends in

the Rue des Saussaies. The Gestapo.'

'When did they pick them up?'

'Two days ago.'

'Do London know?'

'We've no way to tell them, there's no other operator.'

'Did they get the radio?'

'Yes.'

'Were they transmitting at the time?'

'God knows.'

'Have the rest of you moved out?'

'There's nowhere for us to go.'

'Can you contact them quickly?'

'It depends on where they are.'

Harmer reached inside his jacket and gave the man ten thousand francs. 'Get all of them. Tell them to leave immediately. And I *mean* immediately. In seconds, not minutes. Tell them to meet me in the cemetery at the back of the School of Architecture an hour from now. You come there, too. The password is... *les lilas*... no – *Où sont les lilas?* Hurry up, don't waste time.'

When Pauli had gone Harmer turned to the girl. 'What's the earliest you can contact London?'

'This evening at four minutes past eight.'

'Why four minutes past?'

'It depends on the date.'

'Tell me.'

'I can't. I'm not allowed to.'

He smiled. 'Good girl.'

He pulled up his sweater and she saw the wide belt round his waist. He unbuttoned one of the small pouches and drew out a wad of thousand franc notes. He looked back as he opened the door.

'I'm going down to see the patron.'

The patron had phoned around, and in half an hour had

located five different places that they could rent. Three in Montparnasse, one near the Sorbonne, and one in a side street off the Rue de Vaugirard. It was a risk using him, but you took risks when five men's lives were at stake. But he was angry that he had been forced within hours to break the basic security rules that networks operated by. He would collect the keys himself as part of the deal.

There was thin, watery sunshine as Harmer paced up and down at the cemetery, and the green tips of crocuses pushing up through the frozen soil; and a wind that struck cold even through two sweaters and a coat.

Only three men came, and when they gave the password he sent them off to the café to each pick up a key. Finally Pauli himself came, shivering in the cold wind.

'I can't find the other two. Maybe they've already been taken.'

'How long has the patron been helping the network?'

'Almost from the beginning.'

'Do you trust him.'

'René trusted him.'

'Did you?'

'Somebody betrayed us, but I don't think it was him.'

'Is there anywhere we could meet safely?'

'I don't know anywhere that's safe in Paris any more.'

'OK. Come back with me to the café.'

Harmer went up to the rooms to the girl, and wrote out his long message to London. He told them of the arrests and the disintegration of the Seagull network, and asked their permission to take over the remnants to attempt a reorganization. He had to leave the girl to cope with the transmission on her own.

There was a small room at the back of the café that had

been used pre-war for wedding receptions and private functions, and Harmer hired it for a month. Aware of its insecurity but ready to accept the risks until he could find something safer, he sent Pauli on the cycle to arrange for the three others to come to the café immediately. He paid blackmarket prices for two bottles of wine and food for all of them. He forgot to order them to come singly, but Pauli at least had the sense to bring them through the side entrance.

He took them into the back room to the corner where the table was laid and two small paraffin stoves gave off their heat and fumes. There was cheese and bread, and a cold meat pie. And the two bottles of wine. When they were all seated he looked round the table.

'I'm Jacques. Introduce yourselves.'

A thick-set man with close-cropped, grey hair said, 'Albert.'

A man with a dark drooping moustache and big brown eyes said, very softly, 'Martin.'

And the third man, with dark brown wavy hair and sensual lips said with a half-smile, 'Beaucaire.'

Harmer turned back to the thick-set man who had given his name as Albert.

'Tell me about the network. How long you have been operating. What you've been doing. And what has happened in the last few days.'

'We have been operating for twenty months. At first in Paris and then more recently to the west around Evreux. We have been carrying out sabotage. Railways, bridges, telephone exchanges and a petrol dump. The usual targets.' He shrugged. 'I've only just come back, Martin knows what has happened in the last few days.'

Martin had been eating slowly as he listened, and as the other man finished he looked up at Harmer.

90

'We had two safe-houses near the Porte de Vanves. I used one and René and the girl used the other. René and I had an appointment for Monday afternoon at his place. I was ten minutes late, and when I got to the corner there were two men watching the entrance to René's place from the other side of the street. I walked on round the block and waited. Then I bought cigarettes and a paper and walked back the same way. They were shoving René into one car and the girl into another. I saw them putting the radio and some files into the boot of the first car. The Germans were all carrying guns. They looked very pleased with themselves. About two hours later I phoned René's number from a kiosk and a man answered in French with a German accent. I hung up.'

'Was anything planned for the next few days?'

'No. That was to be the planning meeting. We'd been having problems with London.'

'What kind of problems?'

'They seemed to be cool about everything that we were doing, and they refused us a drop.'

'What had you asked for?'

'Plastique, detonators and pencil fuses. Nothing special. They kept delaying decisions on our targets.'

'What was the radio traffic in the previous two or three days?'

'René sent a message that if they didn't agree targets soon we should go ahead independently. London signalled that he was possibly going to be recalled to London, and to contact the air organizer; meanwhile all operations were to stop. Two days later René was picked up.'

'What targets had you suggested?'

'The locomotives at Evreux and the power station at Nanterre.'

Harmer was silent for a moment and then he leaned

forward, his elbows on the table as he looked at each one of them.

'Right, gentlemen, unless anyone else would like to do so I shall now take over this network.' He paused for a few moments but nobody spoke. He went on. 'We will carry out the sabotage operation at Evreux when I have looked at the target. After that we will talk. Maybe a rest for a few weeks would help us all. We will see how we all feel, and what London has to say. But I want to warn you. If any one of us is taken by the Germans the others will leave even the new safe-houses immediately. Our emergency meeting place after an arrest will be in the Luxembourg Gardens by the small fountain. I've forgotten its name.' He paused and looked around.

Pauli said, 'The Medici Fountain.'

'That's the one. Eleven in the morning and three in the afternoon. Maximum wait – ten minutes. Understood?'

They all nodded and Harmer looked at his watch.

'Your rents are paid for two months in advance.' He took out four wads of notes. 'There's five thousand francs each. I shall want an accounting. I shall contact you through Pauli.'

He stood up and lifted his glass. '*Aux mouettes.*'

There were faint smiles as they lifted their glasses. But they were very faint indeed.

He watched them leave from the bedroom window. They went as they had been trained to do when leaving a safe-house. One by one, without looking back.

He turned to look at the girl. She looked strangely subdued.

'Did you get through to London?'

'Yes.'

'Any response?'

'They told me to stand by for an hour. I've decoded the reply.'

She handed him a folded sheet of paper. He unfolded it and read it carefully.

> archevêque figures 1094 you will break off all contact with seagull network immediately stop confirm next transmission stop your orders were specific and your duties limited to observation without contacts stop details of arrests noted stop message ends figures 1094

He read it again, then looked at the girl. 'You read it?'

'Yes.'

'They obviously don't understand. These people are demoralized, they would be rounded up in days if they were left to their own devices. When is the next transmission?'

'Tomorrow evening at eight seven.'

'There's no emergency time we can use?'

'They didn't give us an emergency schedule after our first transmission.'

He walked over to the wash-basin, struck a match and burned the message. It floated down like a black leaf into the bowl and he turned on the tap and flushed it down the plughole.

She watched as he walked back to the bed and sat down. Then he lay back slowly against the pillows, his eyes closed. She remembered looking at his face as he slept on the train to Manchester. But she knew that this time he wasn't asleep. From the moment they had landed in the darkness he had known what to do. And everything he had done had worked. Then he opened his eyes and looked at her.

'Why don't they want me to take over?'

'I don't know, Jimmy. Why did they send us at all?'

'They wanted a check on their security. They were afraid they had been penetrated.'

'Plenty of networks have collapsed before. What's so

special about Seagull?'

'What makes you think it's special?'

'They pulled you back from leading a successful network. They didn't send just you, but me and Marcel. Did they give you any secret orders to do something, apart from the surveillance?'

'No.'

'You wouldn't tell me even if they had, would you?'

'I suppose not. But they didn't.'

'Do you want us to leave here tonight?'

'If I did that they would be finished. I told them I had taken over. I was sure that London would agree.'

'And now?'

'I must explain how it is. There is a planned operation to carry out. Perhaps that will convince them. And after that I can get them out of Paris to somewhere safer. They deserve at least that.'

'You're sure you're not holding something back?'

'Like what?'

She shrugged. 'That the surveillance is just a cover for something else.'

He shook his head without speaking. Not realizing that that dismissal would change the whole of his life.

Seven

When she woke she saw him standing at the window, the curtain parted slightly so that he could see out. The bright moon made his dark-complexioned face look like the bronze head of a statue. She watched him for a few moments and then said, 'Come back to bed, Jimmy. You need to rest.'

When he didn't answer or move she cheated and said, 'I'm frightened, Jimmy.'

His head turned to look at her, but she was in the darkness of the room. Slowly he walked back to the bed and lay down, wrapping his overcoat around him. She stretched out her hand and took his.

'Try and sleep.'

He sighed. 'I can't stop thinking. I'm too tired to sleep.'

Slowly she took his hand and slid it between her legs and her soft mouth found his. As she pulled aside his coat she pressed her lithe young body to his and whispered, 'Love me, Jimmy. Love me properly.'

Half an hour later he reached over her and switched on the bedside lamp. She smiled as he pushed away the sheets to look at her body. And when eventually he looked back at her face he said, 'I'm sorry. It was . . .' And he shrugged. The grey eyes looked back at him. 'Captain James Harmer, you're a bit of an idiot so far as girls are concerned. Most other men would have had me months ago. Or tried to, anyway.'

His eyes searched her face and he said, 'I liked you too much to do that.'

She shook her head slowly. 'Those people in Seahouses have got a lot to answer for.'

'Why?'

'Nobody's ever loved you, have they?'

'I suppose not.'

'Well, they should have.'

'But I'm not that kind of man.'

'What kind of man?'

He shrugged. 'Sophisticated. Self-confident. That sort of thing.'

Very softly she said, 'You're crazy. You're 24, in occupied France, pulling together a bunch of men much older than you are. You've got all the self-confidence in the world. Those dour parents of yours fitted you up with a pair of blinkers when you were about four years old and it's time you threw them away.' She leaned up one elbow. 'D'you remember when you interrogated me at Beaulieu?'

'Of course.'

'D'you remember putting your hand on my leg?'

'Yes.'

'What did you think of when you did that?'

'I wanted to see what your reactions would be.'

'What was *your* reaction?'

'None. It was a question of routine procedure.'

'You're lying, Jimmy Harmer. You wanted me.' She watched the confusion on his face and when he didn't answer she said softly, 'And I wanted you too.'

They looked at each other for long moments, and then she said, 'I care very much about you.'

'Why?'

'You're honest, you're brave, I hate it when you're away, you're like a nice sunny island in a stormy sea and I'll hate it when all this is over. And that's crazy.'

He wanted to say something in return. Something loving, something nice, but you can't throw off a lifetime's blinkers as easily as that. But bodies can sometimes do what words can not. His hand reached up to cup her right breast and this time he took her slowly, and kissed her eyes as her arms went round him.

Before the war there were locals who claimed that Evreux was an outer suburb of Paris. For promoters of tourism the argument had considerable appeal. But in 1944 the only tourists wore field-grey uniforms or jack-boots, and Evreux was undoubtedly Normandy, not Paris. Despite a long history of fire and destruction, the raids by the Luftwaffe in June 1940 had done more damage in two days than had been done in the previous six centuries. With the centre of the town laid waste, the buildings had burned, out of control, for a week. The cathedral of Nôtre Dame was only half destroyed, and you could still see the remains of one blackened tower as you left the railway station that lies to the south of the town.

But Harmer and the man named Albert gave it scarcely a glance as they turned left out of the station. They walked slowly along the road that flanked the engine sheds, and found the bistro where Albert had arranged to meet his contact.

It was twenty minutes before he came. It was the pale, sick young railwayman from the Gare Montparnasse. Although they recognized each other neither of them gave any indication that they had met before. Albert introduced them merely as Jacques and Felix. Harmer ordered them drinks and they sat in silence until the waitress had gone.

'How many locomotives are usually in the sheds?'

'For the next two nights there will be three, possibly four. One under repair, one for routine servicing and the others for change of crew and route.'

'How are they guarded?'

'The sheds don't have a separate guard. There's a patrol at night. Six Wehrmacht men and a sergeant. Unless there are troop trains or supply trains coming through it's all pretty casual. But there are two anti-aircraft guns in the park across the road from the station. They've got full crews, and they're on stand-to every night because of the RAF.'

'Are any SNCF men around at night?'

'The night repair crew. Two men.'

'Do they have a break?'

'Two. Fifteen minutes at midnight and an hour between three and four.'

'Where do they go?'

'They rest in the waiting-room on the platform.'

'Do the guards use dogs?'

'No.'

'Any other information you can give us?'

'There will be four trains through tonight. None of them stopping, but they distract the guards.'

'What times?'

'We don't know. They're phoned down from Montparnasse or Saint Lazare after they've left.'

'Do you know the engineers tonight?'

'Yes.'

'Can they stretch the first break to twenty minutes?'

'Sure.'

'Is there a Gestapo detachment in the town?'

'Two of them. Real bastards. They're way over the far side of the town.'

'Have another drink?'

'No thanks. Is that all?'

'Yes.'

Felix went off quickly. No handshake and no farewells. Harmer felt a surge of excitement at the thought of what they were going to do and he reached instinctively to touch the canvas bag between his feet under the table. He looked at the tough little man who sat opposite.

'Have you done locos before, Albert?'

'No. Just the tracks.'

'But you've used plastic before?'

'Yes. Many times.'

'Where were you trained?'

'Sabotage at Hertford. The rest at Beaulieu and Scotland.'

'We just do the cylinders. The right one only. That's all it needs. One hour fuses. When we leave we don't go towards Paris, we go west on the Conches road. Pauli is bringing down the cycles this evening. We've fixed an RV and he'll wait with the cycles until we come. We'll cycle back and he'll come on by train later and tell us what he sees.'

They walked into the town to the cinema. It had been roughly repaired, but it was half-empty. They slept through the German newsreels and an old version in German of 'The Merry Widow'. It was ten when they left the cinema and headed for the road to Conches. Two kilometres from the station they climbed over the low fence and scrambled down on to the track. Half an hour later they were sitting silently in the darkness at the foot of the buttress wall facing the loco sheds. A dim, orange light seeped from the open doors of the shed, and they could smell the faint sulphur fumes from a coke brazier. The great hulks of two tanker locos stood side by side just inside the shed, and the steady ringing of a hammer on solid metal echoed across the whole area.

Only twice did they see a patrolling soldier, and he came no further than the end of the loco shed, standing there for a few moments, his rifle on a loose sling over his shoulder. A long troop train came through before midnight and under cover of the noise they had moved up to within a few feet of the shed.

At five minutes past midnight the shed was silent. Harmer squeezed Albert's arm and they moved quickly inside the open doors and stood against the wall peering into the foggy, yellow light. The charges had already been prepared, wrapped in grease-proof paper, and Harmer touched Albert's chest and pointed to the two nearest locos. Then headed deeper into the shed himself.

With black insulating tape he fixed the plastic to the smooth painted cylinder, pressed in the primer, and then the pencil fuse into the primer. A turn and it was activated. He hurried back to the entrance of the shed and saw Albert bent over his canvas bag. He tapped him on the shoulder and as he stood up he pointed silently to the door. Ten minutes later they were well clear of the loco sheds, and Harmer led the way up the side of a steep cutting and across the road. Lambs bleated in the darkness as the two men crossed a field until they came to the bank of a river.

With their sleeves rolled up they carefully washed their hands and arms in the freezing water to get rid of the tell-tale almond smell of the explosive.

It was the false dawn by the time they got to the edge of the wood where he had arranged to meet Pauli. There was no sign of him, or the cycles, and Harmer walked a few yards inside the wood. With a felled tree trunk at their backs they sat quietly as the birds in the woods slowly stirred in the bare tree tops.

'What did you do before the war, Albert?'

'I was in the rag-trade in Whitechapel, exporting and

importing to France and Italy.'

'Is that what you'll do when it's over?'

He shrugged. 'God knows. I never think about it. I can't imagine it ever being over.'

'What did the others do before the war?'

'Pauli was at the Sorbonne studying law. René you haven't met. I'm not sure what he did. He says he had a theatrical agency. My guess is that he was poncing for girls. Martin worked for a London merchant bank in Paris. And Beaucaire never worked, his father is a concert pianist and Beaucaire just played around.'

'What about the radio operator?'

'Her field-name's Rita, she was secretary to an MP. Just a kid. It was her first job. I think her old man was an MP too.'

'Will they talk?'

Albert smiled. 'We all talk, Jacques. Sooner or later.'

Then they saw Pauli walking slowly along the edge of the woods peering into the trees as he walked.

He had brought bread and cold sausages, and the three of them ate hungrily.

It was four in the afternoon before they rode over the Pont d'Issy and threaded their way through to Montparnasse and the café. They made wide diversions to avoid even the smallest villages, until they were on the outskirts of Paris itself. Pauli, who had travelled by train was waiting for them, his pale face flushed with excitement.

'There was half the bloody Wehrmacht at Evreux. Cranes, searchlights, two tank transporters and general pandemonium. People who got on the train at Evreux had to go through three check-points. Gestapo, Milice, Feldgendarmerie, the lot.'

'Did you hear any details?'

Pauli grinned. 'The accounts varied from six to ten locos

out of action and the guard patrol already in the *kaserne*, awaiting court-martial. It was easy.'

Harmer smiled. 'If it isn't easy you don't do it. We're not looking for medals. Go and tell the others. There were only three locos, by the way.'

Now he was back at the café Harmer was impatient to see the girl. He had cleared his mind of her while the operation was on, but sitting in the woods, and cycling back to Paris, he had thought of her. Thinking of what she had said about him, and thinking about her body. The way she sighed when his hands covered her breasts, and her grey eyes looking up at him as he moved in her. Harmer had had sex only with prostitutes. Not many times, and the visits had been spaced out like other men's visits to a dentist for a regular check-up. The women's lack of affection was matched by his own. His haste as great as theirs. But it dismissed the fiery thoughts that sometimes lurked at the edge of his mind and left him free again to think again of more normal things. Not for him the secret touching of hands, or stolen kisses; and the only words of praise he had ever had were from the people who used his war-time skills.

He walked slowly up the stairs to their rooms, his mind composed for indifference, but his heart beating as fast as any teenager's. He knocked and went in, dreading that for some reason she might not be there. But she was. Sitting in the tatty chair by the window, smiling as he closed the door.

'How did it go?'

'Fine.'

'Tell me what you did.'

'It's safer if I don't tell you.'

'I know. But tell me all the same. I'll know when you report to London anyway.'

'We went to Evreux and put three locomotives out of action.'

'And there were no problems?'

He smiled. 'I'm no hero, sweetie. If there are problems I keep well away.'

'You called me sweetie.'

For a moment he was going to apologize but he stood there awkwardly, silent until she smiled at him.

'I missed you, Jane. I was glad to be coming back to you.'

'I missed you too, Jimmy. Every minute.'

She saw the pleasure on his face and said, 'Let's eat out and celebrate.'

'Have you ever been to Versailles?'

'Yes.'

'Fontainebleau?'

'Yes.'

'Moret?'

'No. I've never even heard of it.'

'We'll wait until you've sent my stuff to London then we'll go to Moret for the night and take a day off tomorrow.'

'Where is Moret?'

'About 45 miles from Paris. It's Moret-sur-Loing and it's old-fashioned and pretty.'

She looked at her watch. 'You've got an hour to write out your stuff.'

He wrote out an appreciation of the situation of Seagull, how it was re-formed, and gave details of the sabotage at Evreux. He listed possible new targets and asked for recommendations, and an air drop of explosives.

She encoded it carefully, and then they waited for transmission time, which was set for 7.20.

London responded immediately and she tapped out the coded message. The signal was acknowledged and she was told to stand by. It was twenty minutes before London came back, and he watched as she wrote the five-figure groups on the pad. Then she switched off the set, took off the phones and went through the standard routine of packing the radio back into its case.

Then she sat at the bedside table and decoded the message. When she had finished she read it through before she handed it to him. And he noticed that her hand was trembling.

> archevêque figures 2019 you will break off all
> contact with seagull immediately repeat immediately
> stop you will desist from all action immediately
> repeat immediately stop you will be subject to court
> of enquiry in due course stop meantime you are
> severely reprimanded stop figures 2019 message ends

She saw the stricken look on his face as he turned to look at her.

'I don't understand. What the hell's it all about?'

'I don't know, Jamie. They don't even say what we are to do.'

'I'll ask them for instructions on tomorrow night's schedule.'

'Why do *you* think they're reacting like this?'

'Well, they did say that I shouldn't contact Seagull. And I didn't. They contacted me. And they can hardly expect me to leave the stupid bastards to rot.'

'What are you going to do if tomorrow's reply is on the same lines?'

'Sweetie, I've got a quarter of a million francs in my belt and that will keep the lot of us until they come over. The Côte d'Azur in March will be all mimosa and sunshine.'

'Let's go out for a meal.'

And to her surprise he agreed.

'Yes. Let's do that.'

They went to a local restaurant and although he was obviously disturbed by London's reaction she was surprised at his ability to stay cool and calm. He knew what had to be done and was doing it. For him SOE's curt reprimands were merely one more burden to carry.

The next day carried a hint of spring. There was a cold wind but the sky was blue and the sun shone as they walked down towards the Seine. But by mid-day as they stood on the Quai Saint Michel the wind dropped and the skies were overcast. He stood with his arm around her as they looked across the Ile de la Cité.

'D'you remember a Trenet song called 'La Chanson des rues'? This reminds me of the words.'

'Tell me the words.'

He turned half-smiling towards her and sang softly, *'Modeste musique, poésie d'un sou, mais c'est air mélancolique, me poursuive partout'*.

She looked up at his face, smiling. 'Why haven't you sung before, my boy? You've got a nice voice. Better than Trenet's. *Do* you feel melancholy?'

'Not with you.'

And he bent to kiss her cheek.

That night they ate in their room.

When the girl woke the following morning there was a note on the pillow beside her. It said, 'Sweetie, will be back about 11.30. Love J.'

She read it again and again, and eventually she folded the small slip of paper and put it in her handbag, before she snuggled down again in the bed.

It was almost mid-day before he returned, and he seemed relaxed, as if he had made some decision. They cycled to the Bois de Boulogne and ate at the restaurant by the Grande Cascade. And as proof that it was almost spring it was still light when they arrived back at the café.

It was an earlier transmission time that night, and Harmer

sat at the bedside-table writing and rewriting his message for London. There were twelve minutes to spare after the girl had encoded the signal, and she was glad that he no longer seemed under the tension of the previous evening.

After she had transmitted the message she switched to receive and waited. Minutes went by without an acknowledgement. She checked all the controls and looked at her watch. She turned to look at Harmer and shifted one phone from an ear.

'There's no reply, Jimmy.'

'Have you got a stand-by drill for that?'

'Yes. Stand-by for ten minutes. Then come back at the original start time plus sixty minutes.'

'We'd better do that then.'

There had been no response at the end of ten minutes. And no response an hour later. Harmer stood up and put on his overcoat.

'I'll phone Marcel in Chartres and get him to contact de Salis in Lyon. He can warn London that they're not coming through.'

He walked to the kiosk by the cemetery gates and rang the number in Chartres. He gave his instructions to Marcel Thomas, and checked that he knew the coded phone number of the café so that he could contact them as soon as possible.

It was ten o'clock when the patron came upstairs to fetch him to the telephone downstairs. It was Marcel Thomas.

'Something's gone wrong, Jacques.'

'Go on.'

'I contacted de Salis. London had already contacted them. They had an early morning schedule today. They were told to have no contact with you.'

'Who told them that?'

'London. It wasn't signed.'

106

'Was any reason given?'

'They wouldn't tell me anything more. They were very suspicious of me. And of you.'

'Listen. I'll send a man down to you tomorrow. His name is Albert. Take him to Lyon, to de Salis. Let him tell de Salis what we've been doing. And ask him to put London in the picture.'

'It won't do any good, Jacques. Whatever London have said, or implied, de Salis believes it. He hung up on me while I was speaking.'

'All the same you will go there with Albert. Understood?'

'Whatever you say, Jacques. I'm sorry about this. Maybe it will be cleared up quickly.'

'Maybe. *Soyez sage.*'

'Goodnight.'

Harmer stood by the telephone for a few minutes and then walked back up the stairs. The girl looked anxious as she turned to see his face.

'Is it OK, Jimmy?'

'More or less. We'll see what happens.' He sighed. 'I'm going up to the railway station for a few minutes to see the SNCF men and check if we can get tickets direct to Nice.'

'Will they help?'

'I think so.'

'Don't be long, love.'

He walked over to where she sat on the edge of the bed and kissed her.

There was only the red-headed man on duty. He was sure that there would be problems if they tried to go direct to the south. There were constant checks on all long distance trains. They would do best, he said, to split up and take different routes, and keep breaking the journey. If Harmer came back at eleven the next day, they would have checked. The man showed him on a railway map several suggested alternative routes but warned him that the Germans were carrying out more and more checks on all travellers on main lines even over short distances. When he left the station there were forty minutes left before curfew and he walked slowly back in the crisp night air. He stood silently and still in the shadow of a shop door as a police van raced by.

He went in the side entrance and climbed slowly up the stairs and he suddenly remembered and smiled as he touched the ring in its tissue paper in his jacket pocket. He had bought it for her that morning. Second-hand from a man in the Rue Mouffetard. She would be pleased. He was smiling as he walked in the room.

The man sitting in the chair by the window was wearing a black hat and a black leather coat, and he was pointing a Walther P38 at Harmer. The man who was standing behind the door touched him with the spout of a machine pistol. The bedside-lamp lay smashed on the floor and the case with the radio had gone from under the table. Harmer's heart was pumping madly near his throat as he said hoarsely, 'What the hell's going on?'

The man in the black leather coat nodded to the man standing alongside Harmer and Harmer saw the shadow of the uplifted arm on the curtains a split second before the blow landed behind his ear.

Eight

He could smell his own sour vomit as he came to, and slowly the two figures merged into one as his vision focused under the glare of the light. It shone straight into his face, and he could only just make out the figure of a man at the desk. He wondered how they had got the desk into the bedroom, and then the man spoke. Quite softly, but it was like a gong echoing in his head.

'We ought to talk, Archevêque. We've got a lot to talk about.'

And suddenly the room was flooded with light. He wasn't in the bedroom, he was in an office with white walls and a high ceiling. There were metal filing cabinets along one wall and a large-scale street plan of Paris and its suburbs on the wall. Marked out with narrow coloured ribbons and clusters of different coloured pins.

The man at the table had a nondescript face, he was half-smiling, his brown eyes amused as he watched Harmer trying to reorientate himself. As he waited he sorted through the documents and other oddments that had been taken from Harmer's clothes. He looked up, casually sucking his teeth, and when Harmer closed his eyes the man stood up, walked round his desk and shook Harmer awake.

'We've got to talk, my friend. It could save your friends a lot of distress. Especially the girl.'

Harmer opened his eyes and a sudden haemorrhage of bright red blood flowed from his nose as his head came forward. He could feel it warm under his chin as it seeped down inside the collar of his sweater.

The German sat perched on the edge of the desk, one leg swinging idly as he looked at Harmer.

'We knew you'd left Lyon and were back in London, but we didn't expect you here in Paris, with Seagull.'

The man laughed softly when he saw the surprise on Harmer's face at his knowledge.

'You've kept us very busy you know. We had written off the Seagull network.' He paused for a moment, then said quietly, 'Why did London send you back here, my friend?'

Harmer sat in silence and the man stood up, walked back to his seat and sat down. He leaned forward as he spoke.

'Archevêque, you've got enough experience to know what will happen if you don't talk to me now. We know so much already, but I should like to confirm a few points. You have nothing to gain by not talking. All the Seagull network is in our hands. Why cause them and yourself unnecessary suffering?'

The man reached for the telephone when Harmer didn't reply.

'Klugman speaking. Take him away.'

The two men who came in, untied his hands from the back of the chair, and then upended the chair so that he fell to his knees. He groaned as a boot went into his kidneys. A hand grabbed at his hair and pulled him upright, and seconds later they were hurrying him, stumbling, down a corridor to concrete steps that led down to the basement.

He was barely conscious as they stripped off his clothes, but he heard the water running and he knew what they were going to do. His head hit the wall as they threw him into the bath, and the icy cold water closed over his face as a hand shoved his head under. He struggled frenziedly but their hands kept him under. Big, revolving, blood-red circles turned faster and faster behind his eyes, and as a grabbing hand squeezed his scrotum his mouth opened and water rushed in. Then his head was pulled out of the water by his hair, and he was fighting to get his breath against the water in his wind-pipe. He could hear a terrible rasping noise, and he realized that it was his lungs fighting frantically for air. At his first breath fingers splayed into his hair, and slowly and methodically his head was beaten against the cast-iron side of the bath. Then thick fingers spread over his face and he was pushed under the water again. And for another twenty minutes, that seemed like a lifetime, they went through the same routine. But now he was unconscious, and the water was pink with his blood when they dragged him out.

When he came to he was lying on his back on the wet concrete floor, and as he opened his eyes a fist smashed into his face and he heard the crunch of his teeth as they were forced out of their sockets.

He was only half-conscious when they took him back upstairs and dumped him back in the chair. For several minutes his interrogator, Klugman, paced slowly up and down in front of his desk.

'What's your real name, Archevêque? What do they call you back at Baker Street? Why did they send you to Seagull? Why did they feed you into the mincing machine when they knew we had Seagull in our hands? Somebody in London must really dislike you, my friend.'

The room seemed to tilt slowly, the light in the ceiling seemed to go out, and Harmer slid sideways to the floor.

By the fourth day they knew he wasn't going to talk. His fingers had been broken at every joint, his thumbs pulled from their sockets, and his chest, back and arms were covered with weals that were open and suppurating.

There was one last interrogation when Klugman had only questioned him about London.

'Was it Carter or Pardoe who sent you to Paris?'

He smiled grimly as he saw the shock on Harmer's battered face.

'We probably know more about London than you do, Archevêque. You didn't stand a chance with those bastards controlling you. Their security just fell apart these last two months. We'd been after René for a year and then – bang. We'd got him. Careless radio procedures, and that was enough. Is there anything you want before you go?'

Harmer turned his head as best he could to look at Klugman.

'Where am I going?' he mumbled through his swollen lips.

'Have you heard of Buchenwald?'

Harmer shook his head.

'It's a camp for prisoners.'

'An Oflag for PWs?'

'Not really. You aren't a prisoner of war, you know. You're a spy. It's more for special prisoners.'

'Are the others going there?'

Klugman shook his head. 'I'm afraid I couldn't discuss that.'

'Can I have the ring back?'

'What ring was that?'

'A gold ring with a single diamond. It was in my jacket pocket wrapped in tissue paper.'

'I haven't seen it. I'll send it on if I come across it. No hard feelings about all this I hope. We are all only doing our various duties. You do yours, and we do ours.'

Harmer looked at him with his one good eye.

'It will be my turn soon, Klugman. We'll see how well you do when you're on the receiving end.'

The German smiled. 'The Americans are still stuck at Anzio and they'll find the Wehrmacht a tougher nut to crack than the Italians.'

'Have you given my details to the Red Cross?'

'Like I said, you're an enemy agent, my friend, not a soldier. No uniform, false papers, a transmitter, a pistol, what would Geneva want with you?'

Klugman reached for the phone and he guessed that he was telling them to take him away.

It was two days before they came for him from his water-logged cell, and with four other prisoners he was driven in the prison van to the Gare de l'Est in the early hours of the morning. The platforms were thick with Wehrmacht troops and SS, as long columns of prisoners were loaded onto the long train of cattle trucks. The doors of half the trucks were already closed and padlocked, and Harmer barely had the strength to heave himself up the three foot gap from the platform to the truck, and no hands reached out to help him.

Inside the carriage two small grilles let in a faint light from the platforms and as he stood at the double doors a soldier clamped an iron around each of his ankles. The irons were joined together with a heavy chain. There were forty or fifty men in the wagon when the doors slammed to.

It was another two hours before the train pulled out of the station, jolting slowly across the points. And in the darkness men groaned and cried out, in French and Italian, Yiddish and Polish. They called out their names and where they came from. But as the time passed there were only the groans.

After nearly four hours the train lurched to a stop and ten minutes later the doors were thrown wide, and the Germans shouted to them to get out. The sky was pink with the dawn, and the air was mild, and the word came back that they were outside the station at Châlons sur Marne. They were given pieces of dried ersatz bread that tasted much the same as acorn coffee. A tub was brought up for them to drink the slimy water with their hands.

The big Wehrmacht trucks pulled into line alongside the tracks and slowly the prisoners were loaded and driven off. All day the long convoy moved over the hills and along the valleys to Verdun. There, in the early evening, they were given a thin potato soup before they were loaded on to another train. The train halted just short of Metz and they heard the sirens sounding an air-raid warning in the city. Shortly afterwards they could hear the heavy beat of bombers going over, and minutes later they heard anti-aircraft guns firing and the earth-shaking thud of heavy bombs.

They were detained yet again at Saarbrucken and there was another issue of bread and water before they were transferred to another road convoy.

It was early evening as they drew up outside the camp. They were formed up into groups of twenty, the shackles taken off their ankles and thrown in a heap.

There was a high, wooden watch-tower each side of the wide entrance and in large letters on a banner between the two towers were the words *'Arbeit macht Frei'*. Harmer and his group were marched in twenty minutes later to the reception shed. Slowly the line of men filed through the processing line. Under a scalding shower before their heads were shaved, then their body hair was shaved and a white liquid was painted over their genitals in two deft strokes of a painter's brush. He slid his feet into the rough wooden clogs and followed the file back on to the wide, square, parade ground.

They were given numbers and marched off in groups to the long wooden huts at the far end of the compound. The bunks were three tiered and Harmer put his mess-tin on a

114

top tier and stood watching as other men were brought in. There were three low-powered bulbs in the ceiling, and it made their grim faces look even grimmer. He took off his jacket and, with great pain, used the pins he had been given to fasten his number tape and the red triangle to his sleeve. There were black and green triangles for common criminals and yellow triangles for Jews. There were other colours but he had no idea what they indicated.

A Kapo in his blue and white striped clothes, and his black armband, read out the camp rules in German and broken French, and when he had left the lights went out.

Harmer lay in the darkness as men shouted curses in several languages and prayed aloud in Hebrew, German and French. His body ached and burned with pain and he tried not to think of the girl. Hot tears leaked from his eyes and ran down his cheeks. His body shook as if with an ague and despite his utter exhaustion it was two hours before he slept.

It was dark when they paraded for the roll-call next morning, he guessed from the sky that it was about five a.m. A big man, a Pole, had been appointed *Blockältester* and as the SS officer came along with his torch the Pole had shouted '*Mützen ab*' and the men had snatched off their black caps. Two men in the hut had died during the night but were included in the roll-call, and when all the names had been called and checked they were sent back to their hut. There were two tubs of thin gruel on the long tables down the centre of the hut, and they were allowed ten minutes eating time.

The dawn was breaking as they were driven to the quarry and they worked without break until the late afternoon.

A French Jew who seemed to know the ropes had taken Harmer to the medical unit and they had taped the broken joints of his fingers into a rough splint. They partially

115

succeeded in forcing the thumb joints back into their cusps before they taped the whole of each hand until it was held like a solid glove.

By the time a week had passed the members in his group were beginning to be recognized by the SS guards, and were chased and beaten as indiscriminately and mercilessly as the rest of the prisoners.

Every man *was* an island, intent solely on his own survival, wary of all contacts, attempting invisibility. The news of the D-day landings did not filter through until the end of July and even then few believed that it was either true or significant. Survival of that particular day was their only hope and objective. For the war to end, or the Germans to be defeated, was neither a dream nor a wish. That was something for the world they had left, the world outside. The world that had become no more than a vague dream. Inside the camp, every hour was a lifetime. Where you saw the smoke from the squat black chimney of the crematorium but felt no grief for the bodies that were burning, just fear that your name might be on the next list.

In the autumn of 1944 a wave of typhoid swept through Harmer's hut. On the tenth day of the outbreak a medical orderly gave the survivors an injection. By then Harmer's weight was down to 130 pounds, his putty coloured skin hanging in folds on his gaunt frame like some obscene, ill-fitting suit. The broken joints on his hands had set so badly that they were virtually immovable. He no longer had even vague thoughts of his past life, or what had happened. He worked, was beaten, ate like an animal, and the nearest he ever came to the outside world was to whisper, to himself, his name. Sometimes on his bunk he awoke in the night because someone was screaming, and he would weep when he realized that it was himself. But he was never conscious of what he was dreaming about. Even the seasons went by unnoticed.

It was always winter in his mind.

By the spring of 1945 the ovens could no longer cope with their human load. The Einsatzkommandos had been brought in, and the Jewish prisoners were exterminated day after day, their bodies thrown into the massive deep pits that Harmer and his fellow inmates had to dig. There was an air of frenzy about the SS, gold teeth were left in corpses' jaws and only the most valuable and obvious rings were hacked off the hands of the corpses.

It was April when a US army infantry unit entered the camp. Harmer was sitting silently, his eyes unseeing as he held a dead man's hand. He had been dead for several hours but Harmer had stayed there, holding the dead man's hand for the rest of the day. It was a week before an American investigation team discovered from the camp records that he was possibly an Allied agent. They took him to a US field-hospital in Erfurt. A month later a French liaison team had failed to identify him. Both doctors and liaison teams were hampered by the fact that Harmer couldn't, or wouldn't, talk. They knew he could hear because he did what he was told. But when they asked him questions he just lay there, his eyes open, focused on something far away.

It was September before a nurse heard him whisper his name. They made him say it again and again, and then tried to persuade him to say more. But he didn't respond. They tried United States Missing Persons lists first, but it was late October before he was identified as British.

He was flown to England and taken to a military hospital on the Isle of Wight. They operated on his joints, broke them and re-set them so that they articulated properly providing he didn't use them with great pressure. He was treated both kindly and with understanding because he had been in Buchenwald. Slowly he eased himself back into the world and began to talk.

A lieutenant-colonel, Intelligence Corps, came down to see him from the War Office, and over a period of two weeks he was de-briefed without pressure. Most of the records of Special Operations Executive had been destroyed the previous September. SOE had been stood down with almost indecent haste. It no longer had a role to play. Churchill was no longer Prime Minister and SOE's rivals swept it briskly under the carpet. He was told that there was no record of the fate of any of the members of Seagull, nor of his own team. Pensions were being paid to dependants on the basis that they were all presumed dead. He was told sympathetically to consider himself absolutely blameless. It was a vague and half-lit area in which he and his colleagues had worked. All concerned knew the risks and the dangers, and the survivors must turn their minds to a new life and to earning a living. There was a substantial amount of back pay accumulated in his account at Glyn, Mills, and nobody even mentioned the francs which had been issued to him. His references from the War Office would be of the highest and there were opportunities for officers with his experience in the Control Commission in Germany. There was accumulated leave of at least seven months due to him, along with his clothing coupons and demobilization papers.

Part II

Part II

Nine

It would be unfair to describe the village of Marden as nondescript, even though its four-square church is its only real feature. It lies just far enough from Kent's county town of Maidstone to be within easy commuting distance, and still provide the benefits that come from living in a genuinely rural area.

Detective Chief Superintendent Harmer stood in his small back garden looking up at the dark blue sky. The moving glow was in the night sky exactly where the BBC news had said it would be. If all went to plan, they had said, it would circle the earth every ninety-five minutes. If all didn't go to plan, it would head off into infinity and timelessness. It was the fourth of October 1957, and he was watching Sputnik 1.

As he walked across the lawn to the open back door he thought about infinity. He had got to the bit about what happened at the edges, and then that there couldn't be any edges, before he shivered and closed the door behind him. He was not a man for philosophy. He saw no point in racking his brains over things that had no answers.

He switched on the radio and reached for his book before he sat down in the easy chair. It was John Braine's *Room at the Top*, the kind of story he enjoyed, about the sort of people he understood. He'd got a damn good idea of how it would turn out, but he was going to enjoy the journey getting there.

An hour later he grilled the fish-fingers, opened a tin of peaches, and plugged two holes in the top of a tin of sweetened condensed milk with the spike on the tin-opener. It was much the same as he would have had if he had been on duty and eating at the police canteen. Except for the chips. He could never be bothered with chips for one.

He had been Chief Super for only three months. When Ames had been promoted and posted to Leeds there had been a chance that the Chief Constable might have brought in an outsider, but Maidstone was the headquarters of the Kent Constabulary and the CC reckoned that a stranger might not have taken too easily to the peculiar patterns of crime that Kent provided. There were all the usual crimes that came from a mixed area of farming and industry, plus the problems of the Medway towns and the Naval base, and in addition the problems of tens of thousands of foreigners pouring in through Dover and Folkestone. Nuclear power stations, smuggling, and illegal immigrants, all provided their own special police problems.

When he had joined the police force Harmer had done his year on the beat like the rest of them but because of his SOE experience his path into CID had been assured. His promotions had been quicker than average, but at Detective Superintendent level even the best men stick. It's the point where establishments begin to count more than skill and experience. A question of waiting for dead men's shoes or transfer postings to other forces. He was held in high regard by most of his fellows. His intuition was combined with a respect for those administrative routines that solved serious crimes more often than flashes of inspiration. At the dinner they had given him to mark his promotion the toast had been to a 'detective's detective'. No more ornate compliment could have pleased him as much.

Younger detectives reckoned him as something of a disciplinarian, but he had a reputation as a fair man, and detective constables who had done a year or two with James Harmer were always welcome in other forces. Another obvious virtue to his contemporaries was his devotion to his work and his men. He despised those who sought the kudos for themselves from other men's work, and if he had personal ambitions they were at nobody else's expense. There had been times when he appeared to be passed over for promotion but he had never complained, either in private or public. He had just got on with his work.

At exactly ten o'clock Harmer checked the windows and doors, switched out the lights and walked up the narrow stairs. He lit a last cigarette as he lay in bed reading, and when it was down to the filter he stubbed it out carefully in the glass ashtray, switched out the light, and settled down for sleep.

Harmer's home was a typical small Kentish clapboard cottage, built in the late 16th century of oak boards fixed to a timber framework. Its four, square, wooden-framed windows that caught the sun at the front had only needed the sills replacing when he took it over, and the outside doors were still the originals, except for a board across the bottom where weather had rotted the original elm away. The outside of the cottage was painted white, and the window frames a dark brown. The small front garden was given over to roses, and the equally small garden at the back was half lawn and half vegetable and fruit patch. Harmer himself was no gardener but an old man from the village came in twice a week to keep it neat and tidy. The gardener's wife cleaned the house for him and cooked a meal on the few occasions when he had a visitor.

*

There were four of them round the table. Harmer, Detective Superintendent Phillips, and Detective Sergeants Fellowes and Morton.

Harmer looked down at his list and then looked up at Morton.

'What about the woman reported missing at Chatham?'

Morton shrugged. 'The locals have done the routine checks. Nobody unaccounted for in the hospitals, no corpses.'

'What's the family situation?'

'He's about thirty-five. An ordinary sort of fellow. A welder at the dockyard. She's not been to the doctor since Easter when she thought she might be pregnant. She wasn't. No history of domestic trouble. He earns reasonable money.'

'Anybody see her go?'

'There's an old biddy two doors down said she saw her leave about mid-day. Doesn't remember her carrying a case or anything, but described her as dressed-up.'

'What do the locals think?'

Morton smiled. 'They think she's gone off for a screw.'

Harmer's face showed his disapproval and his eyes were hard as he looked at his junior.

'And what do you think?'

'I think they're probably right.'

Harmer looked for a sign of defiance but found none, and moved on to the next item on his list. He looked at Fellowes.

'What was the Fire Service view on the fire at Mason's?'

'They're pretty sure that it was arson, but they are waiting for the final laboratory report.'

'Any suspects?'

'I've done you a report, sir. There are two suspects. Not acting together from the evidence. It could be one or the other.'

124

Harmer turned to look at Phillips.

'Anything you want to raise, Ted?'

'Any news of the replacements for Jones and Walters?'

'The Chief Constable's got a short list of six and I gather that he'll be interviewing next week. I'd say we've got to soldier on for another month. Is that all?'

'Yes, sir.'

'Right.' He turned to Morton. 'I'd like a word with you, Sergeant Morton.'

When the others had gone Harmer lit a cigarette and leaned back in his chair. But Morton took no consolation from these signs of apparent relaxation. He knew that Harmer used the outward signs of informality when he was at his most scathing.

'How long have you been a sergeant, Morton?'

'A year, sir. Thirteen months.'

'How many women-reported-missing cases have you been on since you were CID?'

'Quite a number, sir.'

'How many?'

Morton closed his eyes and his lips moved as he went through the motions of counting.

'About twenty, sir.'

'And how many had gone off for sexual intercourse?'

'I don't remember.'

'Half of them?'

'I shouldn't think so, sir.'

'So why do you think that was the reason for her going off?

'The locals seemed to think that. I thought they were probably right.'

'That woman, Sergeant Morton, is a member of the public who has been reported missing. She's somebody's wife. She could be dead or injured, she could be suffering from some mental illness, depression perhaps. But because you have no information of any kind as to why she is missing, you label her with your own oafish surmises. I can't stop what you think, Morton, but I can stop you repeating unfounded opinions in front of others. You will drop whatever else you are on and trace that woman. Understood?'

'All the usual . . .'

'I said, understood, Sergeant. Yes or no?'

'Yes, sir.'

'You're here to protect the public, not pass judgement on them. Canteen gossip is not investigation.'

He nodded dismissal and Morton stood up, opened his mouth to speak, changed his mind and walked out of the office.

Harmer pulled the pile of buff covered files in front of him and opened the top one, read the memo sheet and the papers, initialled it and put it to one side. Then, lighting another cigarette, he leaned back in his chair and looked towards the big windows. He knew that he would eventually get Morton moved. Probably back on to normal police duties. He wasn't quite sure that it was justified, but he knew that he would do it as soon as there was an opportunity. You could be a good policeman without being a cynic. Morton probably wasn't even mature enough to be classed as a cynic. Just a young man who assumed the worst in all human beings. When you were convinced that a suspect had committed a crime then you went for him, but until that point they were the public, to be defended by the police and the courts. He felt the cold fingers of depression touching the edge of his mind. He knew that he had only gone through the kind of justification for his feelings about Morton that he could give to others. Those weren't the real reasons be disliked him, and he knew it. When Harmer came back from the war he had closed his mind deliberately and totally to all that had happened. At least he had tried to. But there were things that people said, looks on faces that seeped round the edges of his mental curtain. Sometimes, in the moments before he slept, some ghastly scene would edge into his mind and he would leap out of bed, trembling, his heart thumping wildly, and he would walk downstairs into the peaceful darkness of the garden.

Harmer subconsciously judged the whole of humanity on one criterion. Which side would they have been on in Buchenwald. Would they be victims or could they look at a pile of corpses and not see them. Harmer hid his small nightmares as carefully as psychopaths hide their ghastly fantasies. He was aware of this subconscious sorting of humanity, but gave it no more thought than a man who had realized long ago that he preferred brunettes to blondes. There was nobody he could talk to about it, even had he acknowledged it to himself. At first, people had sometimes asked him what it was like in the camp, but there had been nothing to say. Nothing he *could* say. And he would push the question aside dismissively. He screamed sometimes, when he was alone and driving his car, and he heard the screams far away as he tried to ignore them and went on being Detective Chief Superintendent Harmer, Kent County Constabulary. If ever he screamed at night he buried his face in the pillows.

Harmer turned back to the stack of files, reading through them carefully, initialling the distribution slips and sometimes putting a file to one side.

He had lunch in the canteen and the shop talk cheered him up. Harmer liked policemen and the police force. To him it was a sort of club for like-minded men with a common aim. His experience and expertise were accepted, he didn't have to keep proving it.

That afternoon he drove down to Chatham with the Special Branch man for a meeting with the Royal Navy's

Intelligence Officer for the quarterly discussions of the general security of the naval dockyards.

In the early evening he drove to Ashford where a raid on a dairy depot had ended with a haul of £75,000 and a severely injured guard who was in intensive care at the hospital. It was almost midnight when he got back to the cottage. He listened to the forecast for coastal waters as he ate his porridge in the kitchen. He decided that if Sunday was reasonable weather he would spend it on the boat.

On the Saturday evening he drove up to London with two colleagues and their wives. There hadn't been time for a meal because they had to claim their tickets from the box-office half an hour before the show started.

It was Drury Lane, and 'My Fair Lady', and Harmer loved every moment of it, the songs, the costumes and the cast. He was a Julie Andrews fan. She wasn't just pretty, you could hear every word, and the lovely voice was always right on the note. He would have liked a girl like Julie Andrews to look after. He thought Freddie Eynsford-Hill was rather a drip, and he was humming 'On the Street Where You Live' as they walked to the restaurant in Covent Garden to have their meal.

They pulled his leg, as they ate, about his views on Professor Higgins and 'Why can't women be more like men'. One of the wives said that Higgins had sounded like Harmer talking about women police recruits. When Harmer, in a pained voice, said that in his opinion Higgins was absolutely right, he couldn't understand their amusement.

One of the couples was going to Hastings and they walked back together to Charing Cross Station. There was quite a crowd for the last trains and a small queue at Platform 5. Harmer left them to make a phone call from the station hotel, and learned that the stake-out in Sevenoaks had been a

128

flop. It looked as if there had been a tip-off. A report had just come in that a girl aged eight had been reported missing in Cranbrook. She hadn't been seen since four that afternoon. The usual story. Had gone to the sweet shop alone. Never got there. A team had gone down to help the locals.

As he walked through the swing doors and turned left towards the station forecourt a woman passed him and he swung round to look at her. It had happened before and he had always been mistaken. For a moment he hesitated, and then he hurried after her. As he caught up with her he said, breathlessly, 'Excuse me.' The woman glanced at him with a look of disgust. But the brief glance had been enough. This time it wasn't a mistake. 'Jane,' he said. 'It's me, Jimmy.' He reached out to touch her arm and she shook it away angrily, half turning towards him.

'If you don't go away I shall call a . . .Oh my God, my God.' She closed her eyes for a moment and then opened them slowly. The same grey eyes staring at his face. She shook her head as if in disbelief. She saw that he was trembling and she said softly, 'You're cold. Let's go in the hotel.' She hesitated for a moment, as if she regretted the impulsive reaction. Then she walked with him to the hotel entrance.

Ten

The bar was closed and he took her arm as they walked up the wide stairs to the first floor lounge. A waiter was switching out the lights and for the first time in his life he used his weight and gave the man his official card. He asked for glasses and a bottle of Red Burgundy.

As they sat at the small round table there was suddenly an air of constraint. Where did you link up with the broken chain? Two broken chains. One of war and one of emotion. He felt, too, that her eyes were avoiding him.

'Can we talk?'

She looked up and nodded. 'Of course.'

'When did you get back?'

'Where from?'

'I don't know what happened to you. Where did they take you?'

'They took me to Natzweiler.'

'Was that a concentration camp?'

'Yes.'

'Are you married or anything?'

The big eyes looked at his face. 'Why do you ask?'

'I wondered how long we could talk.'

'A good practical reason.'

130

'I suppose it is.'

The waiter brought the wine and the glasses. Harmer scribbled a note for the station-master, gave it to the waiter with the key of his car, and a pound note. He turned back to look at her.

'You didn't answer my question.'

'No. I'm not married. Or anything.'

'Where do you live?'

'In a little mews flat in Kensington.'

'Have you got a job?'

'Yes. I translate novels for publishers.'

'Where could we go to talk? It's kind of odd sitting here asking questions after . . . after all these years.'

'We can go to my place.'

'Will that be all right?'

'Oh James, don't be so Victorian. We used to . . .' She paused, then bit her lip as she nodded. 'Yes, it'll be all right.'

He paid the bill and they walked down to the hotel doors and along to the waiting taxis. Harmer was barely conscious of what he was doing or what was going on around him. It was like a dream with a strange, flat, slow dialogue between total strangers.

He held her hand in the taxi. She was wearing a glove and he could feel her warmth through the thin material. His hand covered the back of hers but she didn't turn it.

Her flat was at the bottom of Adam and Eve Mews. There was some sort of shop underneath. They went up the narrow wooden stairs and he waited as she unlocked the wooden inner door.

Inside, the rooms were bright and cheerful. White painted walls, comfortable furniture and a long desk in one corner with a typewriter and a pile of books. There was a big bowl of chrysanthemums on a low, round coffee-table encircled by easy chairs.

She bent down to turn on the gas fire, moved over to draw the curtains and then took off her coat.

'Give me your coat, James, and I'll get the percolator going.'

He gave her his coat and she walked through to another room. Harmer stood there awkwardly, his hands in his pockets to induce a relaxation that he didn't feel. His head almost touched the low ceiling and he felt over-large and clumsy in the very feminine room. He tried desperately to think of things to say. But it was all questions, like an interrogation. Embarrassing, as if they were meeting years after being divorced. He wondered why he had never been notified that she had survived.

She came back in, with a tray, and cups and saucers and a Cona.

'Milk and sugar, James?'

The crisp question echoed round the room and for a moment they were silent as their minds went back over the years. As if she were the ex-wife who no longer remembered her former husband's tastes.

'Both please, Jane.'

When she sat down she busied herself with the things on the tray.

'What are you doing now, James?'

'Guess.'

She smiled. 'I've no idea. Schoolmaster?'

'I'm a policeman.'

There was a pause and then she said softly, 'Of course. How right. You must be very good at it.'

'Maybe.'

'When did you get back, James?'

'In 1946. I was in hospital for some months. What about you?'

'I was back quite quickly. June 1945.'

'I wonder why they didn't tell me that you were back.'

'I expect they had their reasons.'

Harmer thought she looked at him oddly. As if she expected him to comment.

'I wonder what happened to the others?'

'Pauli is a *juge d'instruction* in Paris. Beaucaire plays the piano in a night-club. Martin works here in London at Rothschilds. Albert is in an asylum in Paris. He never recovered. You didn't meet René and his radio girl. They both died in Fresnes under interrogation. But you probably know that.'

'I've not heard a word about any of them. SOE had been closed down long before I got back. They said that there were no records of survivors.'

'Who debriefed you? Carter?'

'No. It wasn't an SOE man. I think they'd all gone. It was an Intelligence Corps man from the War Office.'

'Are *you* married, James?'

'No. Have you seen any of the Seagull people since the war?'

'Yes. I've seen them all.'

'Lately?'

'We meet if we can once a year.'

'How did you all get in touch with each other?'

'We were all debriefed in London. We kept in touch.'

'Who debriefed you?'

'Carter.'

'What's Carter doing now?'

'He's a director of Coulthards, the merchant bankers.'

'Does he go to the reunions?'

'No. He's not been invited.'

'Why wasn't I invited?'

'Nobody knew that you were still alive.'

'It was only a few days we were together but I'd like to meet them just once. Who should I contact?'

There was a long silence and Harmer looked at her face, waiting for an answer.

She said softly, 'I shouldn't contact any of them, James. It wouldn't be . . . wise.'

'Why not?'

'They think the network was betrayed to the Germans.'

'I think they're probably right.'

'But *they* think it was you,' she said quietly.

It took time before Harmer could absorb it, and his emotions went from disbelief to anger and then to mere confusion. His voice trembled as he spoke.

'Is that true, Janie? You're not joking?'

'No, I'm not joking.'

He took a deep breath. 'And what did you think?'

'I kept an open mind.'

'Was that the best you could do?'

'I'm afraid so.'

'But you were with me all the time. I was arrested too.'

'You disobeyed London's orders.'

'But you were there. I couldn't leave those people to be picked up by the Germans.'

'They were picked up after you took over.'

He stood up and took off his jacket and rolled up the lower part of his shirt-sleeve. He pushed his forearm towards her. She saw the tattooed concentration camp number just above his wrist. She looked back at his face and shrugged.

'What's a tattoo number, James? We've all got them.'

In anger his hands went to his tie to unknot it and throw it on the chair. Then he slipped off his shirt. He turned for her to see his broad back but she had already seen the raw wide weals across his ribs. They continued across his back standing out white, ugly and uneven against his sallow skin. He thrust his

134

hands towards her and she saw the misshapen knobbly joints.

'Can I ask you two questions, James?'

'Maybe you won't believe the answers.'

'I shall. One of them I ask solely because you always did speak the truth.'

'Go on,' he said, as he put on his shirt.

'On one of the last days, when London were being difficult I asked you if maybe the surveillance wasn't a cover for something else. You didn't answer in words, you just shook your head. Was that because you knew something the rest of us didn't know but you didn't want to tell me a lie?'

'I can remember you saying that. I don't remember shaking my head. Maybe I had something else on my mind. I meant exactly what I indicated. That it wasn't a cover. There was nothing it *could* cover. What's the other question?'

'On the morning of the day we were picked up you went out for about an hour and a half. You didn't tell me where you were going and when you came back you didn't say where you had been. Where had you been?'

She saw him look towards the gas fire and his face looked younger, less lined in the orange light. Then he turned to look at her directly.

His voice was barely audible as he spoke. 'I went out to buy you an engagement ring. I got it from a man in the Rue Mouffetard. Second-hand. Gold with a small diamond.'

He saw the tears well up in the big grey eyes. They collected, hung for a moment, then cascaded down her cheeks.

Then she was sobbing, her hands to her face and she cried out, 'My God, my God, what have they done to us all?'

He knelt down beside her chair and she put her head on his shoulder and her arms around him. He knelt there in silence, gently stroking her neck.

But it was a kind of catharsis, the strained formality had gone. They were people again.

She lifted her face to look at him, smiling despite the tears.

'It's wonderful to see you again, Jimmy. I thought about you so often.'

'I asked about you but they said you were untraced. No information available. I was in a pretty bad mental state anyway.'

'I think it's best if we don't talk about those days. Maybe some time, but not now.'

'I can't just leave it that the others think I betrayed them.'

'Does it really matter after all this time?'

'It matters to me, and maybe it does to them. It must have mattered to *you* to feel that you had gone through all that because the network was betrayed by me or somebody else.'

'Why didn't you try and trace them before?'

He sighed. 'I was in a bad state, sweetie, when I got back. A bit of a zombie. I think I just retreated. I was told there was no trace of anyone. You were all presumed dead. If they had told me that any of us was alive I would probably have done something. I would certainly have contacted you. In a way I just wanted to escape from the nightmare.'

'I felt like that, too. It was several years before I went to the reunions. And I didn't know them all that well.'

'Why did they suspect me?'

'I think as people talked and compared notes they felt that the Germans seemed to know too much. So somebody had betrayed us.'

'Why not René or the WT operator? They were arrested days before.'

'They both died under interrogation. If they had talked that wouldn't have happened. They would have sent them to camps. There were all sorts of unexplained bits and pieces. You were at loggerheads with London. That seemed odd.'

136

'But only you and I knew that.'

'Oh, Carter hinted at it in the debriefings. It was implied that if you had not disobeyed orders all would have been well. It sounded as if Carter suspected you too. He didn't say so. It was just vaguely implied.'

'They're bastards. But the Germans *did* seem to know far too much. Maybe there *was* a traitor. Did they all go to camps?'

'Yes.'

'Maybe I should contact Carter and see what he knows.'

'Don't do that, Jimmy. He won't help you.'

'Why not?'

'My impression was that he did think it was you. It was a bloody mess and that was the only explanation. And they were glad to leave it like that. An unsolved mystery that was best forgotten.'

'Where did you have the reunions?'

'In Paris. At the café the first time. But it upset me, and we went to Le Lapin the other times.'

'I've never been back.'

'I haven't either except for the reunions. It's strange. I was so in love with Paris and France, but it's got no pull for me now. But tell me about you.'

He stood up and sat back in the other chair.

'There's not much to tell. I joined the police. I've got on pretty well.'

'Do you like it?'

He shrugged. 'You know, I've never thought of it like that. I just get on with it.'

'And not married. What happened?'

He laughed. 'Nothing happened, sweetie.'

'No loves? No girl-friends?'

'No. I just keep to myself. I think being in a camp changes you. It hangs over you and nobody else would ever

137

understand. How about you?'

'There were a couple of nice young men in the early days. But like you said. Camps do things to you. What they do to girls makes you afraid of men. All men.'

'Of me?'

She looked at him for a long time before she answered. And when she spoke she spoke very quietly.

'No. I'm not afraid of you. But I couldn't go to bed with you, and that won't ever alter. But only you could understand why. I tried to explain to others. They were sympathetic at first, but after a time they wanted to prove that they were the exceptions. When they weren't, they were angry. I don't blame them. How could they possibly understand? I look at men's faces and wonder if *they* could do those things to me, and my conclusions are always the same. Yes, they could.'

'It's not true, sweetie.'

She said softly, 'They were like wild animals, Jimmy.' She shuddered and shook her head to drive away her thoughts, and he recognized the gesture.

'It's late, sweetie. I'd better find somewhere for the night.'

'Just stay here. It's a nice comfy sofa, I've slept on it myself sometimes. I'll get you some coverings.'

When she came back with sheets, pillows and blankets, he said, 'Can I go on seeing you, Janie?'

'Of course. Any time you want.'

'Frequently?'

She laughed. 'Just as frequently as you like.'

'I don't remind you of bad things?'

'No. Not at all. I shared with you the last good days of my life.'

'I'll make more good days for you, sweetie.'

'We'll see.'

Eleven

The Chief Constable was a dry old stick. A neat little man whose navy background showed in his alert blue eyes and the crow's feet alongside them.

'You don't need to ask *me*, you know. I've told you often enough that you should take some leave. A chap can't just keep slogging on. We all need to have our batteries charged from time to time.'

'It'll be about ten days, sir.'

'You're not going to try and take that damned boat of yours across the Channel, I hope.'

'No, sir.'

'What are you going to do?'

'I'm going to France, sir. Paris.'

'Ah well. At least I don't have to give you any lectures on *that* subject. Some little bird told me you'd got yourself a girl friend?'

'We were in the army together, sir.'

'Ah yes. You were in one of those private armies weren't you?'

'I was in SOE. Special Operations Executive.'

'She going with you?'

'Yes.'

'Excellent. Pop in and see me when you get back.'

Harmer went back to his office to hand over and tidy up his desk. It took him a couple of hours but he lingered on, walking across to the windows to look out across the town. He felt uneasy about what he was going to do despite his determination to do it. He had been single-minded about his duties and responsibilities in the SOE days. There was a war on. Now he was single-minded in the same way about his police work, but peacetime was different. It was not so solitary. You did your own part with single-mindedness but others took over. Magistrates and judges. The machinery of the State. What he was intending to do would take him back into the old days. Picking scabs off old wounds. The girl had said that it wasn't worth it. Maybe she was right, but he was sure it had to be done.

He switched off his desk light, the main lights, closed the door behind him, picked up his case from the front office and walked to the station. The girl met him at Waterloo.

They had a late meal at a restaurant in Wardour Street and went back to her flat. By then Harmer had become a frequent visitor. He kept a suit, bathrobe and shaving gear permanently there. They were as close in their present lives as they had been in Paris, except that they didn't sleep together. He never kissed her, and he never held her hand unless she was wearing a glove. But they cared for each other at least as much as any other couple cared. And they were happier than most.

Back in the flat she made them coffee, and as she sat down she said, 'Are you worried, Jimmy? You seem tense.'

'Not worried. Tense maybe. Like waiting to make a drop.'

'You won't be disappointed if they're sceptical or don't believe you?'

'Yes. I'll be disappointed. It's a difficult thing to prove or disprove. I don't expect it to be easy.'

'I think you should speak to Pauli first.'

'Why?'

'He's got a legal mind. He's used to sorting out evidence.'

He sighed. 'I haven't got any evidence. Let's not talk about it. How are your parents?'

'They're fine. They were delighted that I'd met you again. They sent you their love.'

'Did you tell them about Paris and the rest of it?'

'I told them a little when I first came back, because they had to see me in hospital. Later on they were worried about me not wanting to marry either of the two men. I had to tell them much more at that time. My father was very angry. Wrote nasty letters to the War Office, Ministers, and all and sundry. There were acknowledgements but no replies. My mother was angry, too, but she was more practical than daddy. She was a great support. They were very upset that you were "missing presumed dead".'

'Did they remember me?'

'Jimmy, you've gone all the way back to when I first knew you. Of course they remembered you. Why the hell shouldn't they? They liked you. The Seagull people admired you. They said you had been overloaded. Even Carter said that very few people could have coped with what you had to deal with.'

'I thought sometimes about contacting your parents.'

'Why on earth didn't you?'

He shrugged. 'It seemed selfish.'

'How could it be selfish?'

'I'd just be a reminder of you, and they'd have to make the effort to talk to me while they were thinking about you.'

'How is that selfish, Jimmy?'

'Because part of my motive in contacting them would have

been to remind myself of you, and them, and that nice Christmas.'

'But that isn't selfish. They would have understood.'

'I'm sure they would have but we should carry our burdens ourselves not pass them on to other people.'

She smiled. 'That's what friends are for.'

Harmer shook his head. 'Not to my way of thinking.' He looked at his watch. 'We'd better sleep, sweetie. We've got an early start.'

They took a taxi from the airport to the small hotel in the Rue des Capucines. The girl phoned Pauli who said that he would be delighted to come and have a drink with her at four o'clock. In two hours' time. His real name was Jean-Paul Moreau.

It was just after four when he phoned from reception and she asked him to come up to her room.

He came in smiling and kissed her cheek. He nodded at Harmer as he stood back; and then he recognized him. The smile faded, there was surprise and distaste on his face but he bowed politely.

'I didn't recognize you at first. How are you?'

'I'm fine thank you. And you?'

Moreau shrugged. 'Not bad. A little tired of policemen, thieves, and courts, all day.'

The girl stepped in. 'Jacques's real name is James Harmer. He is a policeman.'

Moreau raised his eyebrows and half-smiled as if his point had been made for him.

'How stupid of me. My apologies. It's all rather sudden and surprising. What are you both doing over here?'

'I came over to see you,' Harmer said.

'Me? About what?'

'About what happened in '44.'

Moreau's eyes showed his anger but he shrugged and said, 'Those days are best forgotten.' He turned to the girl. 'You always look so young you know.'

She laughed. 'Stop playing the Frenchman. We *do* want to talk to you. Sit down and have a drink.'

Moreau sat down reluctantly, trying to avoid looking at Harmer. When the girl had poured the wine she sat down too.

'I've told James what we suspected, Jean-Paul, that's why he's come over. Please listen to him.'

'But really, my dear, this is all past history. That was thirteen years ago. It's all over.'

'It was for me, too,' Harmer said. 'Until I met Jane again and she told me what you all suspected.'

'Mr Harmer, I met someone five or six years ago who had been part of your *réseau* in Lyon. He was full of praise for you. You were the hero. So I know you were a brave man. But there comes a point when brave men disintegrate. The SOE man in London said the same.'

'We could at least talk.'

Moreau shrugged. 'OK. We talk.'

'Tell me why you all suspected somebody had betrayed Seagull to the Germans.'

Moreau leaned forward. 'We were all arrested on the same day, yes? Almost the same hour?'

'I don't know. Jane was arrested before I got back to the café.'

'We checked, Mr Harmer. It was so. They knew all our field names, and our real names, the old safe-house addresses and the new ones. They knew your wavelengths, and they knew about the locomotive sabotage at Evreux. They knew everything.'

'Who interrogated you?'

'The same man dealt with all of us. His name was Walther

143

Klugman. He was Gestapo.'

Harmer sat for long moments in silence. Then, looking at the girl, he said, 'I think somebody *must* have betrayed us.' He turned to look at Moreau. 'They knew about far more than you have said. They knew who was controlling me in London. Nobody except me knew that.'

'And me,' the girl said quietly.

'How long did they interrogate you?' Harmer asked, looking back at Moreau.

'Two days.'

'Did they beat you up?'

'Of course. But that was routine sadism. There was very little they asked me about. They obviously already knew all they wanted to know. They seemed to be doing a double-check, as if they couldn't believe their luck.'

'What camp were you sent to?'

'Natzweiler. We were all sent there except you.'

'I was sent to Buchenwald.'

Moreau didn't respond and Harmer said, 'Maybe you don't believe that.'

'That could have been a cover for a collaborator.'

'And the weals on my body. And these.' Harmer thrust out his hands. His fingers splayed out. Moreau glanced at the misshapen joints, shrugged and looked back at Harmer.

'That could be why a man talks, my friend.'

'Why should I do it?'

'That's not the question. There's a hundred reasons why men talk. *Somebody* betrayed us. Who else could it be?'

Harmer leaned back in his chair. 'I don't know. I really don't know.'

'So why don't we leave it at that. One of the great unsolved mysteries of our time. Another "Marie Celeste".'

'Jane told me that Albert was so badly treated that he's still in an asylum.'

144

'That's true. For a few years we went to see him but there's no point now. He doesn't recognize us.'

'What did they do to him?'

'God knows. Whatever it was it was too much.'

'But why Albert?'

'He did the sabotage at Evreux with you. We put it down to that.'

'Was there ever an enquiry?'

'No. We were "F" section. De Gaulle and RF section didn't give a damn about us.'

'Was Klugman prosecuted at Nuremburg?'

'Not at Nuremburg. A few years later. He was prosecuted for other war crimes. Nothing to do with SOE or us. We offered evidence but it was refused. By the British. He served three years. He was out long ago.'

'What was he before the war?'

'God knows. He's a business man in Amsterdam now.'

'What kind of business?'

'I think it's cars. He imports luxury cars. Cadillacs, Jaguars, Rolls-Royces, that sort of stuff.'

'Would you take me to see Albert?'

'He won't be able to help you. He's in another world.'

'I didn't expect that he could help me. I'd just like to visit him.'

Moreau shrugged. 'When do you want to go?'

'That's up to you.'

'OK. Tomorrow morning. I'll come here at ten. I'll drive you there. It's outside Paris.' He stood up. 'Now I really must go.'

He kissed the girl, bowed to Harmer, and left.

When they were alone she said, 'I'm sorry it was like that, Jimmy.'

He half-smiled. 'You warned me, sweetie. I suppose I couldn't really expect much more. But it was a bit depressing

145

to actually experience it. I guess I'm used to dishing it out, not taking it.'

'What are you going to do?'

'I'm going to sleep on it, and decide after I've seen Albert.'

'It doesn't sound as if he could help.'

'Seeing him might help me decide what to do, sweetie. Let's go out and eat.'

The asylum was a beautiful old house in the woods near the aerodrome at Villacoublay-Velizy. A long, low, stone building. Mainly 17th century with a modern administration block at the rear.

The journey was virtually silent. Moreau asked no questions and responded curtly to all Harmer's attempts to make conversation.

The sisters who ran the Hospice St Clair were both kindly and efficient, and they were led down the white echoing corridors to a small room that was used for such meetings.

There were two chairs, a small table with a bible, and a copper jug full of late dahlias. And a red button marked *Alarme*.

A sister with a calm, apple face wheeled in the invalid chair and said, 'We're much better today, really. Yesterday was not so good.'

Harmer looked at the man in the wheel-chair. He wore an old-fashioned striped woollen shirt without a collar, and a pair of baggy grey trousers. He sat motionless with his arms hanging down, and his head lolling on one shoulder. His face was smooth like a baby's but the flesh was grey. The lips and eyelids were a bright red as if they had been painted; and long beads of saliva trailed from his mouth to his chin. From time to time his thin chest moved as he sighed. The way a child sighs in its sleep.

It didn't seem possible that this was the tough, stocky man

who had crept into the loco sheds with him, and then sat with him in the woods; elated and talkative because of their success. The man who had said that he couldn't imagine the war ever being over.

He reached down and took the thin hand in his.

'Albert. It's me, Jacques.'

The washed out blue eyes didn't move, they stayed focused on something far away.

Harmer looked up at the sister. 'Does he ever talk?'

She smiled and shook her head. 'No, he can't talk. And he can't hear.'

'Is he in pain?'

'Not so far as we can tell.'

'What is wrong medically?'

'It's only partly clinical. It's the end stage of total withdrawal and there is severe impairment now of the whole nervous system.'

'Will he improve?'

She shook her head. 'There's maybe another year. Not more.'

'Is there anything he needs? Any help I could give?'

She smiled. 'We always need help, m'sieur. There is a box in the hall. Is that all, gentlemen?'

'Yes, thank you.'

She leaned down and lifted both of Albert's arms clear of the wheels and put them in his lap. Moreau opened the door as she pushed the wheel-chair away. She turned and smiled.

'God bless you both.'

Harmer put money in the box and then they walked in silence back to the car.

The journey back was totally silent, and when the car pulled up outside the hotel Harmer said, 'Thank you for taking me, Jean-Paul. It was a help.'

Moreau raised his eyebrows and shrugged. 'Good. Give

my regards to Jane.'

Harmer knew now what he must do and he hurried up the stairs at the hotel to their room. Eager to tell her his plan.

The room was empty and he gritted his teeth to hold back the nausea as he stood at the door.

When she came in she was smiling. Two books in her hand and a gramophone record. She stopped as she saw him slumped in the chair.

'What on earth's the matter, Jimmy? You look ill.'

She threw the books and record on the bed and hurried round to him.

There were beads of perspiration on his forehead, and his face was white.

'Was it terrible at the asylum? Tell me.'

He shook his head and said quietly, 'I thought you would be here. It was like that other time.'

She sat on the edge of the bed, holding his hand, stroking it gently. And at that moment she felt no inhibitions.

'Let's go back to London and forget all this.'

'No. I'm going to Amsterdam. I'm going to find Klugman.'

She sighed. 'Without me?'

'No. With you, if you'll come.'

'Of course I'll come.' She smiled to encourage him. 'It'll be like the old days when we were at Beaulieu.'

He shook his head and stood up unsteadily.

'I'll check the flights.'

They took a taxi from Schiphol to Amsterdam. The driver gave them the names of two small hotels near the museum. The first one was full, but the second, *Het Vlaamsche Leeuw*, had found them a suite that looked over the square.

He checked in the telephone directory. There was no entry

148

for a car-dealer named Klugman, but there was a private address entry under Klugman, Walther.

At the reception desk the clerk called for the manager.

'American cars. Well there's Hooft and Geel in Dam Straat, and Heijermans in Spui Straat. They're both good companies with their own service departments. There's a quite new one opened in Rembrandt's Plein but I don't really know anything about them.'

'I was given the name of a Mr Klugman in London. He was highly recommended.'

The manager smiled. 'Of course. He is the owner of Hooft and Geel. He bought them out in – let me see . . . ' He turned to the clerk and spoke in Dutch. They exchanged a few words. '. . . we're not exactly sure, but it must be five or six years ago.'

'Thank you very much.'

He had been given directions and he walked across the canal bridges at Oude Hoogstraat and saw the showroom on the right hand side of Dam Straat.

As he walked in a young man came towards him. He smiled amiably and, with a good salesman's instinct, he spoke in English.

'Was there any particular car you had in mind, sir?'

'Yes. The grey Cadillac.'

It was the only car Harmer could identify.

'It's a good choice, sir. One year old but with full air-conditioning.'

He opened the door. 'It's a right-hand drive, sir. If you'd like to get in I'll go over her history.'

Harmer sat in the driver's seat and the salesman slid in beside him.

'We've had it in the workshops. It's in perfect condition. It's done forty thousand kilometres which means with this size of engine it's barely run-in. We only took it in two weeks

149

ago, it belonged to the United States Military Attaché in The Hague. He has been posted back to Washington. We have a full service history and all documents of importation and taxes.'

'How much is it?'

'Are you English or Irish, sir?'

'English.'

'The car as it stands is five thousand pounds sterling. To transport to London would be approximately one hundred fifty sterling and British taxes would be about one thousand fifty.'

'I'd like to try it, anyway.'

'Of course. I could take you for a run now.'

Harmer turned to look at the young man.

'I had been recommended to see Mr Klugman personally. Is he here?'

'No, sir, he is in The Hague.' He smiled. 'Buying a Rolls, as it happens. I could make an appointment for you tomorrow.'

'Fine. How about ten-thirty?'

'May I check in his diary, sir?'

'Of course.'

The salesman came back with a large red diary.

'That's OK, sir. What name is it?'

Harmer searched for a name and said, 'Frazer.'

'Right, sir. Tomorrow morning. Ten-thirty. Trial run, the grey Cadillac.'

Klugman looked bigger than he remembered. Dressed in a well-cut dark blue suit with black brogue shoes he could have been any nationality, he spoke English fluently, and from somewhere he had acquired an American accent. There was no trace of a German accent.

'My assistant tells me you're interested in the Cadillac.'

150

'I'd want to argue about the price.'

Klugman smiled. 'Of course, but let's make sure first that it's the right car for you. Let me take you for a run.' He turned and snapped his fingers. 'Piet. The keys.' It was the only German gesture he made.

'Are you working in Holland?'

'No. Just a visitor.'

'We can arrange all export documentation for you in forty-eight hours. Depending on the country.'

'It would be England.'

'Ah yes. I was in Coventry two months ago at Jaguars. We carry full spares for every car we handle. Right. Let me get her out of the showroom first.'

Harmer stood watching as Klugman skilfully drove the big grey car between a Jaguar and a Rolls Royce to the opening where the big plate-glass windows had been pushed apart, and then on to the cobbled street.

As Harmer slid into the passenger seat Klugman said, 'D'you know Amsterdam well?'

'Hardly at all.'

'Are you in a hurry?'

'Not at all.'

'Right, we'll head towards Hilversum and then we'll get a nice mix of highway and some country roads. A car like this needs to warm up before she can show her paces.'

Klugman chatted away. Ferreting around to find out what he could of the potential purchaser's background. He drove with great skill and style. Taking no risks, but using the car to its full, pointing out its virtues as he drove.

He turned off the main road at Bussum and when they were on a minor road in the flat countryside Harmer asked him to stop.

'Sure. Would you like to take over for a kilometre or two?'

'No. I want to talk.'

Klugman let the big car roll to a standstill with only a final touch on the brakes. He switched off the ignition and turned to look at Harmer.

'So. Let's talk. The price *is* negotiable but only . . .'

Harmer interrupted. 'It isn't the car I want to talk about.'

Klugman smiled, his eyebrows raised; he was well used to the vagaries of wealthy men.

'You go right ahead, sir.'

'You don't remember me?'

Klugman looked at Harmer's face with only mild interest. He shook his head. 'We do have a lot of English and Irish people interested in our cars. The embassies in The Hague both recommend us to their nationals. I try to remember faces but I'm afraid that I don't always succeed.'

'I'm thinking of way back. Say 1944.'

Klugman's head came round sharply to look again at Harmer. For a moment there was fear in his eyes, fear that changed to anger. And then the moment passed. Klugman was under control again. But it was obvious that he had no idea of what Harmer was actually referring to.

'That would be very unlikely, Mr Frazer. I was in the army at that time.'

'Not quite the army, was it, Herr Klugman?'

Klugman reached for the ignition key and Harmer's hand clamped round his wrist.

'We're going to talk, Herr Klugman. If you answer my questions truthfully there will be no problems for you.'

'Who are you? Your name's not Frazer is it?'

'No, it's Harmer, but when you and I met in 1944 you knew me under another name.'

'And what was that?'

'My code name was Archevêque, my field name was Hubert. Jacques Hubert. You interrogated me at the Gestapo building in Paris.'

152

Klugman's eyes narrowed as he looked at Harmer's face and after a few moments he said, 'I remember the names, but I don't remember your face.' He paused and went on. 'I make no secret of being a German, Mr Harmer. There's no room for blackmail in my situation in Amsterdam.'

'I've no intention of blackmailing you, Klugman, but I doubt if your business would survive very long if your customers knew your real background. The Wehrmacht is one thing, the Gestapo is another.'

Klugman looked at him with contempt, and a show of self-righteous defiance.

'I stood trial, was convicted, and served my sentence. I was found guilty of administrative offences only. The Dutch authorities are fully informed.'

'I'm not interested in what you did, Herr Klugman. I'm only interested in what I did.'

'I don't understand.'

'Do you remember the Seagull network?'

'Of course. I was responsible for the arrests. It was the most successful operation we had in 1944.'

'Would you talk with me about that operation? How you traced us? I would pay for your time.'

Klugman smiled. 'You know, I told my assistant that you weren't a Cadillac man. I just knew it.'

'I don't look rich enough.'

'No. Nothing to do with that. Rich men seldom *look* rich. No, it's a question of matching cars to personalities.'

'What would my car be?'

'A Rover. You're a Rover man.'

'Will you talk with me?'

'Why not?' Klugman shrugged, lifting his hands from the steering wheel.

'How about you find somewhere where we can eat and talk in peace.'

Klugman drove them to a small, old-fashioned country inn. They were the only guests in the small restaurant and when they had ordered their food Klugman folded his arms, his elbows on the table. His confidence back.

'Tell me what you want to know.'

'What sort of information did you have on Seagull before you arrested René and the radio operator?'

Klugman closed his eyes, trying to recall those far off days.

'I can remember that we knew of one safe-house in one of the small streets off the Rue de Varenne. I can't remember its name. We had a good description of René. Nothing much beyond that. But in the two weeks before we picked up René and the radio operator the signals traffic was very insecure. Our signals people had broken the code about nine weeks before that, so we were reading the traffic between London and Seagull without much difficulty. But in the last few weeks they were ridiculously insecure.'

'In what way?'

'Addresses given instead of code names. A couple of references to operations that were sufficiently explicit for us to work them out. Our signals people said it indicated unusual pressure.'

'*Were* Seagull under that much pressure?'

Klugman looked surprised. 'It wasn't Seagull who were insecure, it was London.'

'You mean signals from London gave actual addresses of safe-houses?'

'Yes. We spent hours and days trying to work out what London were up to. We thought it must be a trap. That they were trying a radio game like we had done in Holland with Nordpol.'

'What did you do?'

'We put a surveillance on all the addresses and watched. We referred the whole case to Berlin and they instructed us

154

to pick up René and the operator, and interrogate them. We must have started picking up your radio traffic the day we took in René and his radio operator. We didn't break your code for a couple of days and even then we weren't sure. You were having some sort of hassle with London about Seagull. The D/F vans were heavily booked so we weren't able to pinpoint you. We knew you were somewhere up near the railway station.'

'How did you find out where we were?'

'I don't remember.' He closed his eyes for a moment. 'I think the first lead was when we broke your code and we picked up your code-name. Archevêque. We knew you had left your group in Lyon and gone to London. We thought maybe London had given your code-name to some other agent. It didn't seem possible that you hadn't gone back to Lyon. Then somebody, I think maybe one of the cryptographers, did a check on the signals traffic of your old network. What was it called?'

'Curfew.'

'That's it. And that was the break-through. There was a signal from London warning them to have no contact with you. And it gave your location at the café.'

'You mean its code-name or the actual name?'

'The actual name, and the *arrondissement*. I don't think it gave the street. But that was no problem.'

'I don't believe it, Klugman.'

'What don't you believe?'

'That they gave away my location.'

'*We* all thought it was a bit odd. But everything had got a bit odd about Seagull. What were you supposed to be doing? They were sending you rockets for contacting Seagull. If not that, what *were* you up to?'

'That's when you raided the café.'

'I think we delayed it for twenty-four hours for some

155

reason. Yes. I remember. We got the D/F vans and set them up to check your radio traffic. You tried two or three times to contact London but they didn't come back to you. We checked that they were responding to other networks, and they were. That made us a bit suspicious.'

'What did you suspect?'

'God knows. But the whole Seagull affair had become suspect. Nothing added up. It looked like London were deliberately throwing them all away. And you too.'

'What did you decide?'

'We left it to Berlin. They came back in about two days and told us to round up Seagull and you and the girl.'

'Did René or his radio girl talk?'

'Very little. Nothing that we didn't know already.' Klugman looked at him. 'This is all off the record, yes?'

'Absolutely.'

'You're not investigating officially, or writing memoirs or anything like that?'

'No. I just want to know out of personal interest. When you interrogated me you seemed to know a lot about London.'

Klugman laughed. 'Did I? I must have been bluffing. We knew some things of course, which we had picked up from interrogations. And as you know, one or two SOE people turned over to us after they were arrested.'

'Are you telling the truth when you say that René and his operator didn't talk?'

'They didn't talk, I assure you.'

'Was there a traitor?'

'Absolutely none. In fact we were rather sorry for you all. Everybody held out, more or less, but you got no support from London. If it hadn't been for their insecurity we probably wouldn't have got any of you. Seagull were being reasonably successful until a couple of months before you arrived.'

Harmer looked across at Klugman. 'Do you regret what you did in those days?'

Klugman paused only for a moment. 'No. I carried out my orders. You will have done the same to our people.'

'You mean torture them?'

'Sure. You were enemy agents. Killing Germans. Sabotaging. You will have done the same to our people.'

'We didn't torture prisoners even if they *were* agents.'

Klugman smiled. 'How do you know?'

'I just know.'

'You bombed Hamburg and Dresden and killed tens of thousands of people in a night. Mothers and children. And in Occupied Germany your counter-intelligence people were as rough as we were. I can give you names and incidents if you wish.'

'One of the Seagull men went into an asylum after your people had finished with him. He's still there. He'll die there.'

Harmer saw the tense muscles around Klugman's mouth as he looked across the table at Harmer.

'My wife divorced me. I've not seen my children for ten years. We've all paid some sort of price. Berlin would have sacrificed me without a second thought. Just as London sacrificed you and your people.'

'Is that how you saw it? That London sacrificed us?'

Klugman nodded. 'No doubt about it. They threw you away, my friend. The only thing we didn't know was why. Their lack of elementary signals security in the last two weeks would have got them court-martialled if they'd been on our side.'

'Will you take me back?'

'Where are you staying?'

'Can you drop me at the market near the museum?'

157

'You mean Nieuwmarkt?'

'That's it.'

They both sat silently with their own thoughts on the journey back and when Harmer got out of the car in the market place he bent down and said to Klugman, 'Thanks for your help. How can I pay you?'

Klugman half-smiled. 'A kind thought once in a while.' And he started the engine.

It was snowing as they walked across the tarmac at the airport and when they were airborne Harmer ordered two whiskies. It was the first time the girl had seen Harmer drink any spirits. She wondered why, because he seemed more buoyant, more self-confident, after his meeting with Klugman. He had gone over with her again and again the things that Klugman had said. But after that first talk he had never mentioned the subject again. She thought that it had settled the affair in his mind.

He saw her back to her flat and then caught a train to Maidstone.

They spent Christmas in Edinburgh with her parents and on the way back they visited his father in Seahouses. His mother had died in 1948 and his father now lived alone on his pension, and the interest from the capital that came from selling the boarding house. His small cottage looked over the harbour. A small brownstone two up two down that was typical of the town and the man. The old man asked no questions, almost pointedly indifferent to his son's life. Half-amused at what must have seemed even to him a successful career, but handing out no praise or affection. More concerned with the price of tea and fruit-cake. They took a taxi down to Newcastle, and the train to London.

There had been no great difficulty in tracing Carter. He was in 'Who's Who' and the Directory of Directors. He had even found a blurred photograph of Carter in a back copy of the *Financial Times*. Alongside a piece speculating on the possible merger of Coulthards and a smaller merchant bank.

Over a period of three weeks he checked out the Coulthard offices, Carter's club, his house in Wimbledon, and a small flat that was in Carter's name in Notting Hill. A young girl lived at the flat.

By the second week in February Harmer had established that Carter visited the flat most evenings on his way home to Wimbledon, and it was obvious that the girl was Carter's mistress. Between the office in the city and Notting Hill, Carter abandoned his bowler hat and tie, always stopping his car at the same place in Hyde Park to effect the transformation. And a few casual enquiries had told him that Carter was well on his way to his first million.

He said nothing to Jane Frazer about his enquiries, and after they had got back from Amsterdam they never talked of their visit to Paris. She felt that he had coped well with a difficult situation. She hoped that it was because of their close friendship that he had been able to shrug off his initial determination to prove his own integrity.

Harmer chose a Tuesday evening for his first encounter with Carter. As always Carter had gone up the short flight of stone steps two at a time, the key to the pale blue door already in his hand. As he watched, Harmer saw a pale pink glow on the steep stairs inside the house before the street door closed.

Carter usually stayed about an hour and Harmer sat quietly in his car, waiting and watching the house. After thirty-five minutes he released the bonnet catch of his car, got out, and after lifting the bonnet, pulled off one of the clips from the distributor head.

As he walked across the road and up the stone steps he

pulled out his warrant card. He pressed the bell and waited. It was two or three minutes before he heard footsteps coming down the stairs inside, and it was the girl who opened the door. He showed her his identity card.

'Good evening. I'm sorry to disturb you. Chief Superintendent Harmer. I wonder if I could use your phone to contact my headquarters. I've got a problem.'

For a moment she hesitated, then she shrugged. 'OK. Come in.'

He followed her up the stairs and she opened the door to a room that was lit only by a pink-shaded standard-lamp. Carter was sitting in an easy chair, a drink in his hand, his jacket on the floor beside him.

Harmer smiled a friendly policeman smile.

'So sorry to disturb you, sir. I won't be a couple of minutes. The young lady kindly said I could use your phone. Chief Superintendent Harmer, sir. Kent Constabulary. A small problem with my car.'

Carter obviously didn't recognize either him or the name, but looking slightly shifty he pointed to the 'phone that stood on a small desk in the corner of the room. He said, 'It's over there. Help yourself.' But he glared angrily at the girl.

Harmer stood at the desk dialling the Yard's number.

'Transport please. Chief Superintendent Harmer, Maidstone . . . yes please . . . hello, hello . . . Sergeant Hacker please . . . ah Bill, Chief Superintendent Harmer . . . a problem with the car . . . won't start . . . yes, yes I've checked that. No it's full . . . if you could I'd be much obliged . . . about how long . . . fine. Thanks, Bill.'

He hung up and turned to look at Carter.

'That's been a great help, sir.'

And he saw the stir of recognition on Carter's face. It was time to get his word in first. He frowned as he stared at Carter. 'Don't I know you, sir? Now where have we met –

are you a barrister by any chance?'

Carter smiled a superior smile. 'No. We met a long time ago. I thought your name rang a bell. Baker Street. SOE.'

'My God, yes.' Harmer's recognition sounded genuine enough.

'And now you're a senior policeman.'

'Well, I wouldn't say that.'

'Modest as ever.' Carter turned to the girl. 'Mr Harmer was one of our best men in Special Operations.' And Carter said it with an air of self-approval as if such a compliment from him was only just short of a knighthood.

The girl looked at Harmer. 'It must have been terribly exciting.'

'Not really.'

And then Carter stood up, reaching for his jacket. 'Well, my dear, I'll be getting on my way.' He turned to Harmer. 'I'll take a turn with you until they've fixed your car.'

The squad car was parked alongside Harmer's car and as he and Carter walked over towards it the constable standing on the pavement said, 'It's OK now, sir. A loose distributor cap. That's all.'

'Thank you, Constable. Goodnight.'

The policeman saluted and got back in the squad car.

Carter stood there, rocking slowly on his feet as he looked at Harmer. 'My God. All that seems a long time ago.'

'It is a long time ago. How are things with you?'

'Oh not bad. I'm at one of the banks, you know.'

'Barclay's or something like that?'

'No. A merchant bank. Coulthards. Earns me an honest penny.'

Harmer showed no recognition of the name. And Carter said, 'I clean forgot to introduce you to Miss Watkins. Does a bit of freelance work for us now and again.'

'Seemed a nice young lady.' And he saw the reassured

161

look at her being called a 'young lady'. It had the old-fashioned air of casual formality that a long-serving butler might use. It implied that she had hardly been noticed. 'Have you got time for a drink?'

Carter looked at his watch. 'Why the hell not? There's a nice little bar round the corner.'

As they walked together Harmer knew that Carter had taken the bait. He had a new and genuine alibi. The old friend from army days. What sort of wife could cavil at that sort of excuse?

In the bar Carter paid for the drinks. He gave at length the history of his successful banking career, the problems of seventy per cent tax, and the arduous duties of being next Lord Mayor but two. It seemed that City life was very demanding of time and energy.

'Why don't you escape down to the country for a weekend's relaxation? I could put you up, or you could use my boat on the Medway.'

Carter turned to look at him, his glass half-raised to his mouth. Relaxation and boats rang bells in Carter's mind, as Harmer knew it would. Carter had few excuses to be in town at weekends, so for two days he was not only wasting his investment, but leaving his girl-friend free for the other liaisons he feared and suspected. An old army friend, a middle-aged senior policeman was a perfect alibi. And a boat on a river was out of touch with telephones and telegrams. Out of touch with everyone, because it was mobile. Who would know where it was? It could be anywhere. And Harmer was obviously well-disposed. Probably quite impressed by hobnobbing with a leading light in the City. He'd be no problem. He could even find out the name of his Chief Constable and put a good word in for him. Never did any harm. Cast your bread on the water and all that.

'You know, that's a damned good idea. I'd like to take

162

you up on that. Must be a bit cold on a boat, though, at this time of year.'

'There's gas heating, and boats are always very cosy.'

Carter filed away this information, especially the word 'cosy' and turned the clock back for the first time.

'I understand you got back long after SOE had been folded.'

'Yes. I was in dock for a time.'

Carter's eyebrows raised. 'All well now, I hope.'

'Oh yes.'

'Well, I'd better be on my way. Have you got a card you could scribble your number on?'

Harmer gave him his official card and Carter held it far out to read it.

'Detective Chief Superintendent, eh? I'll have to mind my p's and q's with you, what?' And he gave a hearty, shoulder-heaving, officers' mess type laugh.

Harmer reckoned on it being three weeks before he heard again from Carter, but he had the call after only a week. Carter would like to spend the weekend on the boat in two weeks' time, if that was possible. And on the Thursday of the week before he was due down on the following Friday afternoon, Carter phoned again. Miss Watkins, he may remember Miss Watkins, needed a breath of fresh air, was looking a bit peaky, and if Harmer agreed, he had invited her down too, just for the Friday night. Were there separate cabins? They would be driving down independently, could he perhaps give Carter a map reference? He gave Carter explicit instructions for getting to the boatyard at Yalding.

Jane Frazer had suggested that they had their meal at the small French restaurant they often used in Dean Street, but Harmer was insistent. He was taking her to the Mayfair. That's why he was wearing his best blue suit.

163

Half way through the meal Harmer called over the waiter and gave him an envelope. The waiter read the name on the envelope and smiled as he walked off.

They were drinking their coffee and she was glancing casually round the restaurant as the band played the first few bars. Then she turned quickly to look at him.

'Jimmy. Listen to what they're playing.'

The orchestra were playing 'The Last Time I Saw Paris'.

'How about we dance?'

She smiled. 'I never thought I'd hear *you* say that. But yes. What a lovely coincidence.'

His dancing was no better and no worse than that long-ago night on the parachute course, but she smiled up at him with obvious pleasure. When the orchestra leader raised a champagne glass to her and bowed to her partner she looked back at Harmer's face.

'Why all that for us?' Then she saw his smile. 'James Harmer, did you do this? Is that what the mysterious envelope was all about?'

And for a few minutes her body was not stiff with tension because a man's arm was round her. And her hand in his squeezed it tightly.

The taxi dropped them in Kensington High Street and she slid her arm in his as they walked slowly down the mews to her flat.

The night sky was a deep blue, and the moon was full. The kind of moon there was on the night they had been dropped in France. Harmer still, subconsciously, noticed full moons.

She made them coffee because there was no hurry for him to catch a train. Harmer had come up in his car because he would be too late for the last train.

'I won't be able to see you for a bit, sweetie.'

'A special case?'

'Kind of.'

164

'Will you phone me when you can?'

'I will.'

He reached in his pocket and then held out his closed hand to her.

'It's not nicely wrapped, but it's for you. Better late than never.'

He let the small tissue-paper wrapped object fall into her cupped palm, and he watched as she opened the paper carefully. Around the thin gold ring were four diamonds and at the crown a small ruby. She looked at it for a long time and then looked at his face. He saw the faint edge of fear in her eyes.

'It's not an engagement ring this time, sweetie. But it *is* to say I love you.'

She sighed as she looked at him. 'It's beautiful, Jimmy, but you ought to be giving it to a real girl. A normal, uncomplicated girl. Not a neurotic.'

He shook his head. 'You're not neurotic, my love. Just wounded. We're a pair, you and I. We're just a bit clenched-up but we understand one another without talking about it. I think I always was a bit clenched-up. Long before the war. Until you came along. You nearly got me out of it, but one way and another the war just made it final. I'm grateful for all you've done for me. You gave me one of my nicest memories.'

'What's that?'

'It isn't romantic.'

'Tell me.'

'It was walking out of the black-out into your parents' house that first Christmas in Edinburgh. Your mother looked at you so lovingly as we went in, and then she turned and looked at me. Just the same look. She didn't know me from Adam. But I was welcome because I came with you. And by the next day I was welcome because I was me. It may

165

not be true, but to me all the lights in that house have an orange sort of glow. I think of it often. And for me – all that – is you.'

'It's always there. It's still the same. For both of us.'

'It's not, my love. Let's not kid ourselves. When your father looked at you this time he looked sad, and your mother chatted on to try and occupy his mind with other thoughts. They've probably looked in an atlas to find where Natzweiler is. They'll have seen the pictures, and we'd be kidding ourselves if we thought it hadn't made a difference, even to them.'

'Don't spoil our nice evening.'

'You don't mind about the ring?'

'Of course I don't. I shall wear it.'

'You don't have to.'

'I know. But I shall.'

She slid the ring slowly on to the third finger of her left hand, looked at it for a moment and then looked up at his face. For a moment he thought she was going to kiss him. But she didn't. He knew it was in her mind, he had seen it in her eyes. But he understood.

He stood and looked around the room because he knew that he'd almost certainly never see it again.

As she let him out he turned and kissed her forehead, and when he was at the bottom of the stairs at the street door, she called out. 'Don't forget to phone me when you can.'

He drove quite slowly back to Marden and the cottage.

Twelve

Harmer left Maidstone just after lunch on the Friday, and bought food and milk for the boat. The Calor gas cylinders were both full, and he took the plastic covers off the bunks and seats. After he finished he lit a cigarette and poured himself a coffee from the Thermos.

The girl arrived first in a mud-spattered Morris 1000 and Harmer showed her where to park it, carrying her bag back to the boat, lifting the canvas hood so that she could jump down on to the after deck.

She looked around the saloon. 'Say, this is great isn't it?'

'Would you like a coffee?'

'You bet.'

'Milk, sugar?'

'Both.'

With the steaming coffee in front of them she sat opposite him at the saloon table. She sipped slowly at her coffee.

'Christ. It's hot.' She put the mug down. 'He phoned me to say that he'll be two hours late. Probably merging ICI with GEC.' She grinned at him. She really was very pretty. 'What was he like when you knew him in the war?'

'He was very efficient.'

'He thinks a lot of you. Great hero and all that stuff.'

167

He smiled. 'You don't like heroes?'

She laughed. 'It isn't that, but he's got this kind of power complex. He's happy to say you're a hero provided it's recognized that that means he was an even bigger hero. Like being late tonight. It gives him a kick to be the big man doing deals on Friday night, while his young mistress waits with hot pants for her lord and master.'

'*Are* you his mistress?'

She smiled. 'You bloody well know I am. You're a detective. I expect he gave you the part-time secretary story. But you didn't believe it, did you?'

He half-smiled. 'Maybe not.'

She stood, struggling out of her anorak, and he was conscious of the full breasts in her thin cotton sweater. As she sat down she said, 'Have you met his wife?'

'No.'

'She's quite nice, actually. All twin sets and pearls. But she fits in well with his business and entertaining. I think she was in Special whatever it was, during the war.'

'Do you mind?'

'What?'

'Just being his mistress?'

She shrugged. 'I'm not even that. It's a business deal. He wants what I've got and he pays for it.'

'Don't you like him?'

'I do in a way. He's a kind of grown up kid in some ways. All cricket bats and Eton. But he doesn't really give a damn for people. They've all got a price, and if they're useful he pays the price, uses them and then, when they've served their purpose, he throws them away. I met him at a party and he drove me back to my place. It was obvious that he wanted to screw me, but he sat there working out a deal. How much? Could he do this, would I let him do that? It was like a bloody menu. You could see his mind working out whether it was a good deal or not. He wrote out a cheque and two minutes later we were in bed, and he was like a kid in a toy-shop.'

'How old are you?'

'Twenty.'

'What will you do when it ends?'

She smiled and shrugged. 'There are plenty more where he came from.'

Then they heard car doors clunking expensively, and when Harmer looked through the saloon windows he could see the lights of Carter's Bentley as Carter unloaded his bags.

He went up to the after deck and helped him on board. He was wearing a blazer and grey flannels, and looked cheerful and excited. There was an air of buckets and spades and sandcastles about him.

'Hello, James,' he said, and nodded to the girl. 'Sorry if I've held you up. Got involved with a delegation from the Treasury.'

Harmer showed him round the boat and then left them to it.

He went back the next day, Saturday, straight from his office to the boat. The girl was alone, listening to the radio. She seemed pleased to see him.

'Hi. My lord and master's in Maidstone. Phoning the little woman.'

'And how are you?'

'Fine. Fine. He's enjoying himself. You're the perfect alibi.'

'Is it today you go?'

'It was supposed to be, but he wants me to stay tonight. I'll be leaving about nine on Sunday morning. *He's* not leaving until the afternoon.'

'Tell him I'll call over and see him mid-morning on Sunday, will you? I'll bring him a Sunday paper.'

'OK. I'll tell him.'

She came up on deck and waved to him as he got into his car. And he waved back.

He drove straight back to Maidstone and checked the reports on his desk. There was nothing that really needed his attention. He ate in the canteen. It was almost deserted, but Phillips was there and they sat at a table together.

'What brings you in tonight, Jim?'

'Just thought I'd see what was going on, Frank.'

'You saw the suspected murder at Sevenoaks?'

'Yes. Who've you got up there?'

'Andrews and Barker. Looks like the corpse has been there a long time from the first path. report.'

'What are you doing tonight?'

'Just holding the fort.'

'D'you want me to take over?'

Phillips looked at his watch, and then back at Harmer's face. 'That would be nice, Jim. I could take the old girl to see Marilyn Monroe at the flea-pit.'

'OK. Sign off, and I'll sign on when I go up.'

There were the usual Saturday night incidents but nothing that wasn't better left to others, and at two o'clock he signed off. They knew his number if they needed him.

At the cottage he made himself a glass of Ovaltine and carried it upstairs to his bedroom. He undressed slowly and put on his flannel pyjamas. And for some reason he knelt down at the side of his bed, and put his hands together to pray. He hadn't said any prayers since he was a child. He said the Lord's Prayer as well as he could remember it, then, with his head still bowed, he tried to think of those he should pray for. Jane and her parents, Albert, himself, the people who died in the camps, his mother, Carter, the survivors from the camps. And then he stopped, and his mind went back to Carter. He could pray for all the world, but he couldn't pray for Carter. If there *was* an all-knowing God then he'd know already what his thoughts were about Carter. He would know that his prayer was spurious. He felt sure it was some sort of sin, mortal or otherwise, to pray a lying prayer. Harmer was neither religious nor given to philosophy so he stood up, his prayer abandoned, his feet cold on the sticky linoleum. After he got into his bed it was some time before he actually slept.

He left his car at the caravan site and, *Sunday Times* in hand, walked down to the river. The girl's car had gone, but Carter's grey Bentley was still there. Harmer put his hand casually on the radiator as he passed. It was cold.

Carter was drinking a whisky and soda, the bottles in front of him on the saloon table.

'Help yourself, James.' He waved a magnanimous hand. And Harmer sat down.

'You know I never knew your christian name, Carter.'

'Monty. Montague Rayner Carter. That's what it is.'

'It's a dull old day, isn't it?'

'You know, on a boat it's different. Kind of snug. You can forget the world outside.'

'Why did you send me to Paris, Carter?'

For a moment the question didn't sink in. Carter's hand was on its way to the whisky bottle and it hesitated before his fingers finally closed round its neck. He slowly filled his glass with whisky, then looked up at Harmer's face.

'What was that you were saying?'

'Why did you send me to Paris?'

'What the hell are you on about, Harmer? What is this, an interrogation?' He saw the anger in Harmer's eyes and he shrugged. 'If you want to play games, we'll play. You know damn well why you were sent to Paris. You had orders, you were briefed, you had documentation.'

'Go on.'

'There ain't no more, my friend. They picked you up and that was the end of it.'

'Why did they pick me up?'

'God knows. You must know better than I do.'

'I don't think so, Carter.'

'What do you mean?'

'What exactly did you send me to do?'

'What did your orders say?'

'To keep the Seagull network under surveillance and report to London.'

'Exactly.'

'Why did you close down the radio on me?'

'Because you were endangering Seagull, and your own team, and you were disobeying orders.'

'Seagull's radio-operator and leader were arrested before I got to Paris. The rest would have gone in a week.'

'They were in in a matter of days anyway. Even with you in charge.'

'Who told them where we were? Who gave them the safe-house addresses?'

'How the hell should I know? You were there. Who do *you* think told them?'

Harmer looked at Carter's washed-out blue eyes.

'I think *you* told them.'

'My God, this is ridiculous,' and Carter put his hands on the table to get to his feet. There wasn't much room between the foam seat and the table, and Carter was only half standing when he saw the pistol in Harmer's hand. It wasn't pointed at him but he subsided back on to the seat.

'I'll have to report all this you know, Harmer. You're sick

172

or ill or something.'

'Why did you give safe-house addresses instead of code names in your signals?'

Carter frowned, his weak mouth pouting.

'We didn't know *where* you were, Harmer. So we couldn't have done that.'

'I'm talking about the Seagull safe-houses. Not mine.'

'You never saw Seagull radio traffic. Their operator was arrested the day after you arrived.'

'Answer me, Carter.'

Carter shook his head in feigned despair. 'Tell me how I can help you, Harmer. How can I put your mind at rest?'

'Don't bullshit me.'

'Why, oh why, should I do that?'

'You did do it, Carter. The Germans told me so.'

'They were bluffing. Trying to break you down.'

'They didn't tell me then. Their case officer told me a few weeks ago.'

'What's his name? I'll see that we take action against him. Its outrageous.'

Harmer looked at Carter's podgy hands on the table. There were ginger hairs curling from under his watch-strap. He looked up at Carter's face.

'You never used a gun during the war did you?'

'I did a small arms course.'

The pistol lay on Harmer's open palm.

'This is a Walther. Let me show you that it's loaded.'

He pulled back the slide and a cartridge flew out and one from the magazine clunked into the breech.

'There's six more, Carter. But across the table it won't take more than one.'

'You're mad. You're raving mad.'

'You may be right but that won't help you.'

Carter looked frantically out of the window. It was

beginning to get dark. There were no lights except a faint reflection of the moon on the Bentley's radiator.

'There's nobody for at least a mile, Carter. It's winter. Only enthusiasts and men with young mistresses use boats in winter.'

'How dare you.'

And the nose of the pistol smashed down on the back of Carter's hand. He snatched it away, moaning softly, sliding it into the warmth under his arm. And then the pistol was pointing at his chest.

'I'm going to shoot you, Carter, unless you tell me what I want to know.'

'For Christ's sake!' Carter shouted. 'It was policy. Nothing to do with me.'

'Go on.'

Carter sighed. 'There was a vital network working between Paris and Cherbourg. They were a special team sent over to prepare for D-day. Right in the landing area. We had to keep the Germans off their backs. We shoved the Krauts a bit towards Seagull to keep them occupied and away from the others.'

'You mean you threw Seagull away?'

'Yes, if you like. But there were hundreds of thousands of lives at stake.'

'How many lives did betraying Seagull save?'

'God knows. I'm not a bloody soldier.'

'So why did you send *me*?'

'To check what was happening. We should have withdrawn you after the Seagull people had been taken if you hadn't interfered.'

'And because I interfered you threw me and the girl to the Gestapo along with the others.'

'Nobody was thrown away. You all came back for God's sake. You're alive. You've done well.'

'Who worked all this out?'

174

'I was told to give protection to the Penguin circuit. That was the only way.'

'Have you ever thought about what happened to all of us?'

'Of course I have. It's very much to be regretted. But it was a necessity of war.'

'D'you remember a man with the field-name Albert?'

'No.'

'He's in a French asylum. Been there ever since the war. He's a vegetable, not a human being.'

'Terrible.'

'And René and his operator died under interrogation in Fresnes prison.'

'I know.'

'And Jane Frazer?'

'She's OK. I've seen her since the war.'

'Are you sure she's OK?'

'Of course I'm sure.'

'And me?'

Carter shrugged. 'You seem perfectly all right apart from this obsession.' He was still holding his damaged hand. 'I can understand your annoyance at all this, Harmer, but you mustn't let it get out of proportion.'

Harmer looked at him with disbelief and contempt. Carter was being the oil-on-troubled-waters man, the man who could always smooth the feathers down when the negotiations for another quarter per cent caused raised voices.

'The Germans rumbled that you'd thrown us away.'

'Maybe they did. But they never found out why. And they were not so stupid as some of our people liked to make out.'

'Too bloody true. It was only people like me who were that stupid.'

Carter smiled, a rather lip-trembling smile.

'Come on. Let's have a drink together. It was all a long time ago and I'll have to be going.'

175

Harmer slid the pistol into his pocket and stood up. For a moment he looked at Carter, and then, the hesitation gone, he reached out both hands for Carter's head. His right arm crooked across Carter's face, the thumb of his left hand sliding up his jaw line to the point where his jaw bone met his ear. He pressed in his thumb with all the strength of his arm and the weight of his body. Carter's body lifted and arched and Harmer heard one hinge of the table crunch free of the hull as Carter's legs threshed wildly. Then after a few seconds of convulsion Carter was still, his inert body half off the seat, his head and torso bent back towards the cabin floor. The instructors at the course in Scotland had maintained that it should only take ten seconds' pressure on the nerve point to kill a man. It had taken a little longer, maybe a total of fifteen seconds, before Carter had died. But like the instructors had said, it was both infallible and silent.

Harmer looked around the cabin and then turned and dragged Carter's body from behind the table to the floor. He looked at his watch. It was 5.14, and outside it was already dark.

He went up the three steps to the wheelhouse and turned both ignition keys to warm the engines. When the two indicator lights glowed red he turned the keys further, and both diesels thumped into life.

The warps had been looped round the bollards without being knotted. He had done this deliberately so that he wouldn't need to trample the banks. He swung the stem warps free and the boat's head came round slowly from the bank. Then the stern warps, and the boat was shifting with the current. He put the starboard engine into low revs and the boat's head swung out towards the river. A touch forward on the port control and she was away from the moorings and heading down river.

The slow thump of the diesels increased and he switched

on the navigation lights and the searchlight on the coach-house roof. They went very slowly down river and then he saw what he was looking for. He put the engines into neutral, then into reverse, and the boat was close to the far river bank. He stood waiting, both warps coiled in one hand, an iron stake in the other. Two feet from the bank he swung the boat's head towards the shingle and jumped. He heard it touch and grind as he stamped in the stake and knotted both ropes into the circular loop. The boat swung uneasily on the single mooring until finally her nose scraped and grounded on the loose shingle at the foot of the bank. He felt the shingle grating under the hull as the boat tilted when he stepped back on board.

It took all his strength to lift Carter's body and haul him up to the deck. He rested there, for a few moments, taking deep breaths of the cold night air. Then he lifted the body, shoving it over his shoulder in a rough fireman's lift, and as the boat's stern swung towards the bank he half jumped, half stumbled onto the bank. His knees buckled under the load and then, straightening up he walked to the edge of the wood. A few yards inside the trees he threw the body to the ground, standing there panting, wiping the sweat from his eyes. Then he turned and went back to the boat. Half an hour later he edged the boat back on to her moorings. He left her exactly as she was and walked slowly back to his car at the nearby caravan site.

At the cottage he shivered in the darkness as he stripped off all his clothing and laid it on the concrete path below the kitchen window. Inside, he ran a bath and soaked in the warm water, scrubbing his nails and toenails and thoroughly washing his hair.

He dressed slowly, and when he had finished he picked up a brown paper bag and his police torch. In the darkness he pushed the discarded clothes into the bag and briefly flashed his torch to check that nothing had been missed. With the paper bag and the torch on the floor of the car he headed for the coast.

When he eventually got to the marshes the moon was up and he turned off the main road to the network of tracks that threaded across the marshes themselves. Between Dungeness and New Romney he stopped the car and wound down the window. He could hear the roll and hiss of the incoming tide on the long sloping beach. Switching off the car lights he got out and stumbled across the rough grass. The beaches were empty as far as he could see. There were sometimes anglers sea-fishing at night. But there was no one there.

He walked back to the car and took the paper bag, carrying it carefully back to the beach. Twenty yards from the edge of the sea he piled the clothes on top of the paper bag. He threw two small gelatine petrol fillers in the centre and lit the bag. The clothes burned quite slowly until the gelatine melted and the petrol caught. Half an hour later there was just a small heap of ashes, and the white-fringed, incoming tide was already eating away at its outer edges.

He walked back to a rock and lit a cigarette and waited until the tide was almost lapping his feet, and the heap of ashes washed away.

It was just past three in the morning when he got back to the cottage at Marden.

Part III

Part III

Thirteen

Carter's body was discovered ten days later. Harmer was off duty when the message came through, and Phillips took a team up to Yalding. They put up the canvas screens and waited for the doctor to arrive. Phillips roped off a wide area, and the photographer had almost finished by the time the doctor finally came. A reporter from a local news agency had followed the doctor. He was kept off the site and refused any information.

An hour later the doctor reported to Phillips that the man was aged somewhere between 48 and 54, had been dead for at least a week, and that he had no idea, from his superficial examination, as to the cause of death.

When Phillips used a public telephone by the river bridge to ring Harmer's Marden number there was no reply. He then phoned the police headquarters at Maidstone, but Harmer was not there either, and Maidstone had no contact number where Harmer could be reached, other than his cottage at Marden.

The two sergeants were taking earth samples while they waited for the van from the mortuary, and Phillips looked across the bleak spring landscape as he tried to make up his mind. Instinct and experience told him that it was murder, but there was generally some obvious physical evidence of murder or manslaughter that meant that the case would eventually hang on forensic evidence as much as on routine enquiries. There was something about the way the body was lying. It wasn't a natural fall, that was certain. The arm was too far bent under the body for it to be a fall leading to concussion, and then death from exposure. On the other hand there was no obvious medical evidence of violence of any kind. The Police Surgeon would have examined the corpse more thoroughly, but he was in court giving expert evidence in a case at the Old Bailey.

Harmer would be annoyed if he called in the Yard without reference to him. But putrefaction had already set in and despite the season there were already bloated blue-bottles on the face and neck. The weather forecast at one o'clock had said a mild night with some rain. Without quite knowing why, he made up his mind and walked back to the call-box. He had to check the Chief Constable's number in his notebook before he made the call. He explained the position and the Chief Constable hadn't hesitated. If he had doubts he should call in the Yard immediately. Ruffled feathers could be smoothed down later.

Detective Chief Inspector Hayles drove from Scotland Yard and picked up the Maidstone Police Surgeon from the Old Bailey and took him directly to the site. A generator and lights had already been installed, and Dr Keating got to work straight away. Without his secretary to make notes it took Dr Keating two hours before he could give his instructions for the body to be wrapped and taken to the mortuary.

After he had seen the body loaded into the van Keating took various soil temperatures again and when he stood up he took Phillips and Hayles to one side.

'I'll go straight back to Maidstone. I'll have to do an autopsy. I'll need to have a bite first because I haven't eaten all day. It's going to be one of those long drawn-out jobs. There's a small wound on the back of his left hand, a cut, with some internal bruising that must have been sustained before death. It could be the result of a defensive gesture against an attack. I can't say yet. And there's a massive discoloration and bruising under the left ear. My guess is that there has been some kind of paralysis of the central nervous system immediately before death.'

Hayles said, 'Is it definitely murder?'

Keating shrugged. 'My instinct says that it isn't natural causes, but I couldn't go further than that until I've done the autopsy.' He looked at his watch. 'I'll be starting about ten and I'd say I'd finish about midnight; if I'm lucky.'

When Dr Keating had left, Hayles said to Phillips, 'Where's Jimmy Harmer?'

'He's off duty. I couldn't raise him at his home.'

'Let me have a word with my chaps and then you can take me into Maidstone. We'd better see if we can contact Harmer and put him in the picture. When are you off duty?'

'About an hour ago. I'll stick around until we know whether it's murder or not. I'll see if we can put your chaps up in the section house for tonight.'

'If we're staying I'll want a hall or something, and some clerical help.'

The corpse was taken from the mortuary to the hospital for the autopsy, and Hayles and Phillips had put up a trestle table at the police station to lay out the things that had been removed from the clothes of the dead man.

Phillips took down the details as Hayles examined each item.

'Driving licence valid until 30 November 1958. Name, M. R. Carter. Address 49 Kings Avenue, Wimbledon SW19. Membership card. Same name. Special Forces Club, valid to 31 December 1958. Membership card Cockatoo Club no dates no name. Pigskin wallet, worn. Containing two five pound notes, one . . . no two . . . ten pound notes, twenty-two one pound notes, three ten shilling notes. Photograph of man and woman in garden. Receipt for meal at Berkeley Buttery dated 3 January 1958. Two joined half tickets numbers 0943 and 0944, the Aldwych Theatre. Nine visiting cards M. R. Carter. Director, Coulthard's Bank, London and Singapore. Photograph approx two and a quarter inches square of naked girl. First class train ticket London-Glasgow return, uncancelled and unclipped. Membership ticket ''Times'' lending library. Valid until 31 December 1960, name M. R. Carter. No address.

'One white handkerchief, folded, unused. Initial C. Pocket diary. Embossed MC. Prudential Insurance Co. High Holborn. Wrist-watch Rolex Chronometer. Black leather strap. Plain card with various notes in pencil and ink. Looks like directions. Finger ring, one diamond, 18 carat gold. One packet cigarettes. Fifteen unsmoked. Passing Cloud. Damaged. One gold lighter, initial C. A six pack Durex sheaths. Two missing. Imitation tortoiseshell comb. Hold on. As you were. Tortoiseshell comb. Parker 51 pen, metallic blue. Gold propelling pencil. Cheque book. Barclays Bank Account number 09417432, two cheques used. Wimbledon High Street Branch. Marked on cover, No. 4 account. And that's it.'

'Do you want me to check the address in Wimbledon?'

Hayles pursed his lips. 'Check it in the phone book but don't contact anybody as yet.'

Phillips was back five minutes later.

'It's in the book. I phoned Wimbledon and he was reported missing nine days ago. Mrs Judith Carter made the report.'

'Did they read you her statement?'

'They can't get at it until the civilian clerk comes in tomorrow morning. They said she seemed calm and collected. Didn't want a lot of publicity or it could damage the bank.'

'Send Fellowes up to interview her first thing tomorrow morning. Tell him to check her original statement before he sees her. And tell him to check what action Wimbledon took about her report. I'm going to the hospital to see what Keating has found.'

Keating was pulling off his surgical gloves, flexing his fingers, as Hayles walked over to him.

The incision was from the throat to the pelvis and the body lay open like a fish that had been filleted. And small pieces of flesh and bone were in marked specimen jars like goldfish in a bowl, small trails of blood winding and curling in the preserving fluid. Hayles had seen too many autopsied corpses to be either sickened or impressed.

'What did you make of it, doctor?'

'Almost certainly murdered.'

'How?'

'Ah. That's why I said *almost* certainly murdered. He was almost certainly murdered elsewhere. There is a whole series of broken blood vessels down the right side. That occurred after death. Probably when the body was thrown down. There are typical signs of asphyxia. Pin point haemorrhaging in the eyes and under the scalp.'

'Strangled?'

'No. There are no marks of strangling. But what there is is a massive bruising under the left ear. Someone has applied enormous pressure there. More than just normal pressure from a finger or a thumb. It's a nerve pressure point and I'd say he died in five to fifteen seconds. Certainly not longer.'

'Could the pressure have been applied by a blow from something?'

185

'No. A blow from anything would have had to break open the skin to apply that kind of force. It was definitely pressure, not a blow. A blow there might have paralysed him for a few minutes but it couldn't have killed him. I'd say it was pressure from a thumb or a knuckle applied by a very powerful man. And a man with special knowledge.'

Hayles's eyes were alert. 'What kind of special knowledge?'

'He'd need to know that pressure applied at that precise point, could kill a man.'

'You mean a doctor?'

'Could be. A doctor, a surgeon, an osteopath, a vet even. A wrestler.' He shrugged. 'A professional killer.'

'When shall I get your report?'

'Preliminary report mid-day today. Full report in about three days. There's unlikely to be much more that's positive in the full report. Most of my tests will be negative checks to confirm my opinion.'

Detective Sergeant Fellowes stood in the pale morning sunlight reading the statement by Mrs Judith Carter. He noted the times and dates that she mentioned, and put the report back on the counter. He looked at the sergeant and then at his watch.

'Where's Kings Avenue?'

'Up the hill. Fork right at the top just past the row of shops and then third on the left.'

'That's where I'll be if Maidstone want me.'

'OK.'

Fellowes was 30, and although the more unpleasant sights that were the background of his job never affected him, he didn't like emotional scenes. And this was undoubtedly going to be one of those scenes. Telling wives that the last time they saw their husbands really was the last time, was, he reckoned, a job for men with grey hair, solemn voices, and silver stars on their shoulders. At first they never believed it. 'I spoke to him on the phone at his office.' And then the facts would sink home. In a few days' time it would be the panic of insurances and mortgages, but on that first day, and for those first few hours, you could see what happened when people's minds collapsed. He remembered what the elderly inspector had said to him the first time he had witnessed the breaking of the news. As they walked down the garden path he had said, 'When you get married, lad, live every day as if it were your last. Because one day you're gonna be right.'

He rang the bell on the blue door and the gentle chimes rang in the hall.

The woman who answered the door had one of those neat well-boned faces that change with age but are always beautiful.

'Mrs Carter?'

'Yes.'

'I'm Detective Sergeant Fellowes. Can I have a word with you?'

She opened the door for him to come in and he could smell lavender floor polish as he waited for her to shut the door.

For a moment she leaned back against the door, her eyes closed. And then she led him to a large living room and pointed to an armchair.

'Do sit down.'

As he sat she stood for a moment, and then sat down slowly on the long settee.

'Is it about my husband?'

'I'd just like to go over your statement to the station at Wimbledon.'

She said nothing but he saw the tension in her clasped hands and white knuckles.

'You said that your husband told you that he would be

187

away for the weekend, staying with an old army friend?'

'That's right.'

'Did he give you an address?'

'There wasn't an address, they were staying on a boat on the river.'

'What was his friend's name, Mrs Carter?'

She closed her eyes to think then she looked up at him.

'I think it was Harper. A name like that.'

'And where was the boat?'

'On the river.'

'The Medway?'

'I don't remember. I don't think it was mentioned.'

'What did he take with him?'

'A case.'

'What size case?'

She shrugged. 'A weekend case. Medium size I should say.'

'And you've not heard from him since?'

'Yes. As I said in my statement he phoned me on the Saturday about mid-day.'

'Did he say where he was phoning from?'

'No. But it was a reversed charge. The operator said a call-box in Maidenhead.'

'In Maidenhead?' The surprise in his voice made her look at his face.

'Is that wrong?'

'Could it have been Maidstone?'

'Yes. It could.'

'What did he say?'

'Nothing much. He was having a pleasant restful time with his friend and he would be back about eight or nine on Sunday evening.'

'And that was the last you heard from him?'

The pale, grey eyes looked at his face.

188

'You've found him haven't you? He's dead.'

'I'm afraid it's possible.'

'Where is he?'

'He's at the Maidstone hospital.'

'Does that mean he's still alive?'

'There's been an autopsy.'

He reached for the buff envelope and took out the photograph that showed the head after it had been cleaned up, and before the flaps of skin had hung down over his face.

'Is that your husband?'

She looked at it, her hand to her mouth, as she slowly nodded. She was shivering from shock. Trying hard to get herself under control. She nodded and gave him back the photograph.

'Yes. That's my husband.'

'Are you alone here, Mrs Carter?'

'Yes.'

'Have you a relation or a good friend who could come over?'

'Only my sister.'

'Where does she live?'

'In Putney.'

'Have you got her telephone number or her address?'

'Yes.' She looked at him. 'My phone book is on the hall table. Her name is Fielding. Mary Fielding.'

'You sit there and I'll call her.'

It was half an hour before her sister came over. A squad car had picked her up and she looked worried but efficient.

Back at the Wimbledon police station he phoned Phillips, who, after speaking to Hayles, ordered him to go to the bank and interview Sir Peter Woolmer, chairman of the board. Had Carter got work problems, or money problems? Fish around, were the instructions.

*

Sir Peter Woolmer was not impressed by detective sergeants and he kept Fellowes waiting for twenty minutes.

When he was finally ushered into the ornate office Sir Peter waved him to a chair in front of his massive desk. He was a big, handsome man. He made no move to shake hands or stand up.

'What is it, Sergeant?'

Fellowes decided to go straight in.

'I've come about one of your fellow directors. Mr M. R. Carter.'

The eyes that had put Grenadier Guards in their place didn't show surprise or interest. So Fellowes carried on.

'He's dead. Possibly murdered and we . . .'

'Hold on. Hold on.' A big, well-manicured hand was held up to silence him. 'Are you telling the truth, Sergeant?'

Fellowes prayed that his silence would anger Sir Peter as much as the remark had angered him. Sir Peter reached for one of the three cigars that were ranged side by side to attention on his desk. His other hand reached for a gold cigar-cutter. He slowly and carefully clipped the end off the cigar before he looked back at Fellowes.

'Tell me exactly what's happened.'

'Mr Carter was found dead in a wood yesterday. It seems likely that he was murdered and . . .'

'Who found him?'

'. . . and we should like to know if Mr Carter had any financial worries or business worries.'

'Are you suggesting he'd been dipping his hand in the till?'

Fellowes glared. He remembered his police-school training and longed to ignore it.

'Could you answer my question, Sir Peter. Do you know if Mr Carter had any financial or business worries?'

'No more than the rest of us.'

'He was successful?'

'Very.'

'A stable man?'

'Of course, or he wouldn't be a director of the bank.'

Fellowes stood up. 'Thank you for your time, Sir Peter.'

'Is this going to be in the papers?'

'That's up to the investigating officer. It's entirely at his discretion.'

'Who's the Chief Constable?'

Fellowes half-smiled. 'Rear-Admiral Connors. His number's in the book.'

As Fellowes went down in the lift he smiled to himself. 'Sailor-boy' would go through all the courtesies and then Sir bloody Peter would get the broadside. 'Sailor-boy' didn't like outsiders telling him what to do and what not to do.

A brief report of the finding of the body and the possibility of foul play was in the London evenings' last editions that evening. It was only two paragraphs. The smudgy photograph didn't flatter him.

Fourteen

Penny Watkins was a little piqued at not hearing for so long from Carter. It was part of their arrangement that she never contacted him at his office or his home. But there was a small tobacconist's near his offices where she could address letters to him or, if necessary, leave written messages. She had written to him three times and had gone there once to check. Her letters had not been collected, and that had never happened before. But if that was how he wanted to play it she would go along with it. But she'd keep the catch down on the street door lock so that when he *did* come he'd have to ring, not just turn the key and walk in, monarch of all he surveyed. There were plenty of other men who were happy to pay their way into her bed.

The man who now lay with her on her bed was younger than Carter, he was about forty-five, and she thought that he was a bit of a creep. Unlike Carter, who never said anything critical of his wife, this one gave her the saga of his domestic unhappiness. He hadn't got the courage just to have sex with her, he had to establish justification. Whenever he visited her he had her with hot, urgent lust, and then he would detail his wife's latest misdemeanours as he lay there gathering strength for a final onslaught on her body. He talked as garrulous women talk, giving verbatim, both sides of the encounter. He was an utter bore, but he paid her generously. His hand gently stroked her spine as he talked.

'So I said to her, it was only yesterday when you claimed that you never had . . . '

'Would you like a drink, Jacko?'

'What? Oh. A drink. Yes. That would be nice. Have you got a gin? Gordon's if there's a choice.'

She stood beside the bed pulling the lacy black briefs up her long legs.

He giggled. 'I say, old girl. I hope that doesn't mean you're shutting up shop for tonight.'

She gave him a smile that was perhaps not professional but it *was* contrived.

'Of course not. I'll be back.'

When she came back with the drinks he was lying there naked, smoking and reading the evening paper. He turned to smile at her, his eyes glancing at her naked breasts. He turned to the paper.

'I reckon the Liberals are going to take Torrington, what do you think?'

'I've no idea, Jacko. If *you* say they will, then I'm sure they will.'

'I say. Isn't this the old buffer I bumped into the first time I came here? The one who asked me what the hell I was doing coming out of your place.'

He pushed the paper towards her and she looked at his pointing finger. She saw the picture and she saw the name and for a moment her heart seemed to stop. Then she shook her head.

'No. It's nobody I know.'

He let the paper fall at his side of the bed and as he turned towards her she helped him pull the lacy panties down her legs.

By the time he left it was well past midnight and she stood in the small bathroom watching the water rising in the bath. When she was lying in the warm comfort of the water she tried to work it out. It hadn't taken her long. She didn't want to be involved. Her parents thought she was a secretary. Not that she was scared of *them*. But she knew what the newspapers would make of it. Banker's blonde mistress. Young enough to be his daughter. Love nest in Notting Hill Gate. The nice gentlemen who now beat a path to her bed wouldn't come near her. In fact she'd better even tear out the page in her little red book that listed Carter's name. She looked at the condensation on the glass of brandy that stood in the soap-tray at the side of the bath, and wondered what had happened to him. What had he been up to? Thank God the lease was in her name and paid for to the end of the year. She wasn't moved by Carter's death. He was her number one client but she wasn't the tart with the golden heart. She had always given him what he wanted, what he paid for. But that didn't include being involved with the police.

It was in the middle of the next afternoon when she had the horrible thought, and she checked a name and a telephone number in her little red book. He was younger than the rest of them, and when he booked her he booked her for the night. He wasn't married, and he needed no alibis. He'd even taken her out for meals a few times. And there were things he wanted to do with her that she'd never allowed. Perhaps this was the time to relax her scruples.

She waited as the number rang.

'Alcott, Stamford & Rose. Can I help you?'

'Mr Rose please.'

'Who shall I say is calling?'

'Just put me through, please.'

There were the usual clicks and clatter, and then she heard his voice.

194

'Rose speaking.'

'David, it's Penny. Penny Watkins.'

'Ah, yes. What've you been up to, kid?'

'I want some advice.'

'What about?'

'About something that's happpened to a girl-friend of mine.'

'Go on.'

'Will you come and see me, David? Tonight?'

She heard him chuckle. 'That's a new ploy for you, sweetie.'

'I'm serious, David.'

'OK. I'll be there about . . . five . . . no, make it five-thirty. OK?'

'OK.'

When he arrived she was wearing a peach-coloured peignoir and he grinned as she gave him a drink.

'You're a cheeky little bitch. I thought you really did want advice.'

'I do, Dave.' She sat opposite him, smiling. 'I'll pay your fee afterwards.'

'What is it all about?'

'A girl-friend of mine is friendly with a man who's wanted by the police. She knows they want him, but she doesn't want to give him away. If she doesn't tell them can they say she's part of the crime?'

'What's the crime?'

She hesitated. 'A big robbery.'

'Is she harbouring him?'

She hesitated longer. 'I think so.'

'How does she know the police want him?'

'She read it in the papers.'

'Was she party to the crime?'

'She doesn't know anything about it.'

He looked at the long slender legs that were revealed by the peignoir. Then back at her face.

'You'd make a bloody awful witness, Penny.'

'Why? What do you mean?'

'This is like one of those interviews that doctors have with girls who have girl-friends who desperately want to know if you can get clap off lavatory seats or have babies if he takes it out before anything happens.'

She didn't answer but she leaned forward a little so that her cleavage revealed substantially more of her firm young breasts.

'Help me, Dave.'

'Tell me the truth then.'

'I went for a dirty week-end on a boat with one of my men friends. He stayed on after I came back. He's been found murdered.'

'How do you know?'

She reached down, handed him the folded newspaper and pointed to the photograph. He read the piece through and then handed it back.

'You'd better tell them what you know, Penny.'

'Do I have to?'

'You could hang on for a few days pretending you haven't seen it in the papers but you'll have to talk to them in the end. They'll get on to you sooner or later, and then they'll want to know why you kept quiet.'

'Could they make me an accessory or whatever they call it?'

'Not unless you were.'

'I swear I know nothing about it.'

'Did anybody see you there with him?'

'Yes. An old friend of his.'

'Jesus. You really fix it, kid, when you get in trouble. That doesn't leave you any choice. You tell 'em straight away.'

'Then I'll be in all the papers and I'll lose all my clients.'

'It won't necessarily get in the papers. And you might be inundated with new clients. What you've got isn't going to be any less attractive than it is now. With all due respect, kid, they come for what you've got between your legs, not for your beautiful soul.'

'Would you do it for me?'

'I can act for you, but I can't tell your story for you.'

'It's true. I swear it on my mother's grave.'

'She's not dead, you silly bitch, you told me she lives in Pinner.'

She shrugged, unabashed. 'It was just a...you know.'

'Figure of speech?'

'Yes.'

'Well don't try those on the police. They write 'em down and you have to sign them.'

'Will you help me?'

'Yes. But you'll have to see me in my office tomorrow morning.'

'Why can't we do it here?'

'I'm a solicitor, my love. An officer of the court. And my partners are solicitors. I can't say –"I was lying on this beautiful girl...just resting before I did it again...and she briefed me to act for her..." '

He fell silent, because she was smiling and naked and she said, 'Take me to bed first.'

Detective Superintendent Hayles was getting a bit touchy with his team as they sat round the trestle tables in the church hall with Phillips.

'That's great. We don't know which boat he was on. We don't know how he got down here. We don't know who the hell his army pal was. We aren't *exactly* sure how he was

197

killed. And we haven't got the foggiest idea of *why* he was killed.'

Phillips said, 'If it would help we can take details of every boat five miles up and down stream from the bridge at Yalding. Check their owners and then check the boats.'

'We'd better do that but we need another line. And, by God, we need a motive. No money troubles. No domestic trouble. His money wasn't taken. There was no attempt to remove identification. It just doesn't make sense.' He looked at Phillips. 'When's Harmer back?'

'I heard that he's on sick leave.'

'What's the matter with him?'

'I'm not sure but he does get gastric trouble from time to time. He was in a concentration camp in the war.'

'Poor sod. I'll nip down and see him as soon as we've got this moving.'

Hayles looked across at Fellowes. 'No indication of another woman when you talked to his missus?'

'I hinted at it at the second interview but she said he wasn't that kind of man.'

'Jesus,' he said dismissively. 'Everybody's that kind of man. I tell you what, Sergeant. Have a snoop around the staff at the bank. Typists and secretaries. See what you can find out. Take 'em for a drink and look at them with those big brown eyes of yours.' He paused. 'Another odd thing is that although nobody says anything but good about him, everybody's under control. There ain't many wet hankies and red eyes.'

Hayles gave a general nod and stood up. He stood there thinking, then turned slowly, and as he got to the door the WPC on the temporary switchboard called out to him. There was a call for him from Chelsea police station.

As he put the phone to his ear he said, 'Detective Superintendent Hayles.'

'Station Sergeant Maclean, sir, Chelsea Police Station. I've got a gentleman here would like a word with you about your investigation.'

'Who is he?'

'He's right beside me, sir. Shall I put him on?'

'OK.'

There was a pause as the phone was handed over.

'Is that Superintendent Hayles?'

'Speaking.'

'Are you the officer in charge of the investigation into the death of a Mr Carter?'

'I am.'

'I have a client who might be able to help you with your investigation.'

'What's his name?'

'It's a young woman. She'll give you her name when you interview her.'

'Where is she now?'

'Let me explain, Superintendent. My name is David Rose and I'm the young lady's solicitor. I suggest you interview her in my office.'

'Where's that?'

'49 Kings Road, Chelsea.'

'When would it be convenient for her?'

'Shall we say four this afternoon?'

'That's fine, I'll be there. What's your telephone number, Mr Rose?'

'01 890 4040.'

'Thank you.'

Hayles had been a detective a long time, and a policeman even longer. He had a theory that if you grafted away remorselessly on all the obvious leads in a baffling case, then the good Lord would send you a piece of the jig-saw. Instinct told him that this was one of those pieces.

A driver from Maidstone drove his car up to London and it was 3.45 as they drove over Battersea Bridge.

Rose's offices were over a hairdresser's salon. They were modern offices, and well, but not luxuriously, furnished. As soon as he gave his name to the receptionist she phoned through to Rose and he came straight out to take him to his office.

There was no sign of a girl as Rose sat down.

'My client is in another office, Superintendent, because I wanted a word with you first. I have advised her to speak to you absolutely frankly. There is no reason why she shouldn't. She is not in any way involved in the alleged murder but she can give you valuable information. What she is concerned about, and what I am concerned about, is unfavourable press comment about my client.'

'Why should helping the police lead to unfavourable press comment, Mr Rose?'

Rose looked Hayles in the eye. 'Let us hypothesize for a moment, Superintendent. Let us suppose that my client had a relationship with the murdered man. A financial and sexual relationship of long standing. It would harm her for this to be known.'

Hayles nodded. 'You know as well as I do, Mr Rose, that I can make no promises. Especially as I have no idea what your client is going to tell me. She has volunteered the information to help our enquiries and I have no interest in causing her any embarrassment.'

Rose nodded and picked up the internal phone and pressed a button.

'Ask Miss Watkins to come in, please.'

Rose shoved a paper across his desk.

'Her full name, address and telephone number, Superintendent. And a brief preliminary statement. Unsigned.'

'Thank you.' Hayles read quickly through the statement.

As she came in and Rose gave her a seat alongside his Hayles had a fleeting thought of her naked, instead of in the brown jersey suit that she was wearing.

'Miss Watkins, this is Detective Superintendent Hayles who is in charge of the investigation into the death of Mr Carter. I want you to answer all his questions as accurately as you can.'

She nodded and Hayles gave her a friendly smile.

'You say in your statement, Miss Watkins, that you knew Mr Carter over a period of nearly three years. How old were you when you first met him?'

'Seventeen.'

'Right. Now your statement ends where he invited you to stay for one night with him on a boat. Can you describe the boat and where it was?'

'It was near a village called Yalding, and it was moored near a caravan site. I could take you there. The boat was quite big. Wooden. The main part was painted white with a blue line.'

She stopped and looked at Hayles, who said, 'You say in your statement that the boat did not belong to Mr Carter. Do you know who it belonged to?'

'It belonged to a friend of his.'

'Do you remember his friend's name?'

'No. But I'd know it if I heard it again.'

'Can you describe him?'

'He was a big man. Heavily built. About six foot tall. A reddish sort of face. A nice man.'

'Were they both together with you on the boat?'

'No. His friend was there on the first evening for about ten minutes. He came the next day for about the same time.'

'Were they on good terms?'

'Oh yes. They were very friendly.'

201

'They knew one another well?'

'Yes. From the war.'

'Did the friend make any kind of sexual advances to you?'

'No. He wasn't that kind of man.'

'No verbal advances?'

'No. Nothing like that.'

'Where did the friend live?'

'Somewhere round about Maidstone.'

'How do you know that?'

'He said so.'

'But you never saw his home?'

'No.'

'Did he work in London, d'you know?'

'No. He worked in Maidstone.'

'Any idea what sort of job he had?'

'He was a policeman.'

Hayles looked up sharply from his notepad and looked at the girl. He said very quietly, 'How do you know that?'

'He said he was.'

'What exactly did he say – "I am a policeman" – something like that?'

'They hadn't seen each other for years and the policeman's car broke down near my flat. He used my phone and he phoned Scotland Yard for help to put it right.'

Hayles looked at Rose. But it was obvious that this was the first time he had heard this information.

'How old was he – approximately?'

'A bit younger than Monty – Mr Carter.'

'Between say forty and forty-five?'

'Yes.'

'Did he say what rank he was?'

'Can you tell me some?'

'Constable, sergeant, inspector, superintendent . . .'

'That's it, superintendent.'

202

Hayles sat very quietly for several moments and he could hear the tapping of a typewriter down the corridor.

'You're quite sure that when he phoned Scotland Yard he said superintendent?'

'Yes.'

'Did any help come for his car?'

'Yes. I saw a squad car from the window after he left.'

'Did he say what he was doing to be near your flat?'

'I don't think so. I can't really remember.'

'Miss Watkins. I want you to think very carefully back to that phone call to Scotland Yard. Try and remember anything you can. Don't hurry.'

She closed her eyes and Rose and Hayles exchanged grim looks. When she opened her eyes she said, 'I can't remember any more.'

'Fair enough, Miss Watkins. Now I just want to go back to the name. You're sure you can't remember the name?'

'No. I can't remember it. But I think I'd know it if I heard it again.'

Hayles said very softly, 'Was it Phillips?'

She shook her head. 'No.'

'Harmer?'

Her eyes lit up. 'Yes. That was it. Harmer. Jimmy Harmer.'

'You're quite, quite sure that was the name?'

'Yes, absolutely sure.'

'I see. Is there any chance that in fact he was not a superintendent but a *chief* superintendent? A detective chief superintendent?'

'I don't remember that part.'

Hayles looked across the desk at Rose. 'Mr Rose, would you have any objection to your client making a signed statement now, at Chelsea Police Station?'

'Provided that no information on her statement is given to

the media, I would have no objection.' He turned to the girl.
'Would you object, Miss Watkins?'

'Not if you say it's OK.'

'Yes. It's quite OK.'

At the police station Hayles sent the girl with a WPC to
the canteen while he phoned Phillips at Maidstone.

'Frank?'

'Yes, sir.'

'Take two of my men on one side and put them on a
continual surveillance of Detective Chief Superintendent
Harmer. Full time. D'you understand?'

'No, sir.'

'Well, just do as I say. Do it with all the discretion you
can. But do it right away. Keep the two men completely
separate from the rest of the team. Say you've sent them
back to the Yard. I'll explain when I see you.'

'You're sure about this, sir?'

'Yes. I wish I wasn't. But there's still a long way to go.'

'Right, sir.'

The girl dictated the statement, read it twice after it was
typed, and then signed it. Hayles had four photocopies made
before he left. He posted one addressed to himself at
Scotland Yard.

As the police driver turned the car on to the main road
south, Hayles, on the back seat with his feet up, closed his
eyes. But not in sleep.

Fifteen

It had not taken long to check the ownership of all the boats moored near the caravan site. There were moorings on only one bank of the river.

It was raining when they went on board Harmer's boat. Carter's weekend case lay open on the double bunk for'ard. There were initialled shirts and handkerchiefs, and two empty envelopes addressed to him in a jacket pocket. They were careful to avoid unnecessary touching of the boat and its contents.

When they had sealed the canvas hood and the door to the saloon they got back into Phillips's car. Hayles turned to look at Phillips's face.

'It just doesn't fit, Frank. Jimmy Harmer's an experienced detective. If he wanted to knock somebody off he wouldn't leave all this stuff around. He's made no effort to conceal anything, not even the body. He'd know that it was only a matter of time before it was found. He'll know that the girl can witness that he knew Carter, and that Carter had been on his boat. All Carter's things are there which indicates that if he left the boat for some reason he expected to come back. No valuables were taken. It wasn't sexual jealousy about the girl. He hadn't even seen Carter for years. He only met him by chance. What the hell motive is there?'

'Maybe we'd better ask Jimmy Harmer himself'

'Not bloody likely. I'm going to talk to the Chief Constable and the Yard before I go near him.'

'The evidence against him doesn't amount to much. You can prove opportunity but that's all. No evidence of motive or anything to connect *him* to the killing. It could have been somebody else.'

'When I talk to him we shall get more. And, now that we've got a suspect, Keating can start looking it over again.'

The Chief Constable listened to Hayles without comment but wasted no time. He phoned the Assistant Commissioner at Scotland Yard and asked him for an urgent meeting. The AC said that he would come down himself.

Assistant Commissioner Oakeshott had brought one of the police legal advisers with him. Rooms had been taken for them at the Castle Hotel and that was where they had all met.

Oakeshott listened in silence as Hayles reported his findings. When he finished Oakeshott stayed silent for several minutes.

'I don't think you'd stand a chance in court, Chief Inspector.'

'It's the only real lead I have, sir.'

Oakeshott pursed his lips. 'Too bad.'

'But if I could question him I could probably get a lot more.'

'You mean charge him, and then question him?' The amazement was rather exaggerated but it made the point.

'No. Just ask him to answer a few questions to assist my enquiry.'

Oakeshott turned to his legal man. 'What do you think, Grover?'

'There's no reason why the Chief Superintendent shouldn't answer questions to help an enquiry. But he'll probably say that he knew him all right. He lent him his boat, and that's it. There's nothing to connect him further.'

'There is, sir.' Hayles was leaning forward.

'What?'

'Harmer will have seen the papers or listened to the news. He must know about Carter's death. Why hasn't he contacted Maidstone?'

'Maybe he doesn't read the papers or listen to the news. You said he was off sick so he may be confined to his bed.'

'And why hasn't he been to the boat since the Sunday morning visit? Surely he'd want to check that they'd left it shipshape and safe. They could have left lights on or gas on. And surely he'd contact Carter about the weekend. Did he enjoy himself and all that.'

'I agree. That would be the normal pattern. But it doesn't mean anything in court terms. And like I said he may still be confined to bed.'

'We could soon find out if he knows Carter is missing or not.'

'If he says he doesn't know, shows surprise? Then you haven't done anything except alert him.'

Hayles looked up quickly. 'Does that mean you suspect him, sir?'

'It certainly does.'

'I wasn't thinking of me asking him.'

'Who, then?'

'I thought we could brief one of the WPCs to phone him, pretending that she's Mrs Carter asking where the hell her husband is. We'd get something from his reaction.'

Oakeshott thought for a moment and then said, 'A good

idea, Hayles. I'm glad that I didn't hear you say it.' He stood up, half-smiling. 'Let me know if there are any further developments.'

The Chief Constable stayed on after Hayles left.

The girl sat with the phone in front of her on the small table, and Hayles sat opposite with an interconnected phone.

'What if he says he's never heard of Carter?'

'You express surprise. Your husband phoned you on the Saturday to say he had seen him and was having a good time. No panic on your part. Just that you want to know where he is. His office wants to know. You just talk like you *are* his wife.'

She nodded, and as he lifted the receiver she looked at the pad again, and dialled the number. Hayles could see the pulse beating fast in her neck as she waited while the phone rang at the other end. Maybe Harmer wouldn't answer. But he heard the phone being picked up at the other end.

'Marden 074.'

'Is that Mr Harmer?'

'Who is that?'

'It's Judith Carter, Monty's wife, Mr Harmer. I was wondering where he can be. I haven't seen him since he came down a couple of week-ends ago to your boat. His office has been . . .'

The phone at the other end was hung up. There was just the sound of the dialling tone.

Hayles said, 'Right, find Inspector Phillips for me, love.'

When Phillips came he told him what had happened.

'What are you going to do now?'

'I'm going out to see Harmer, and you're coming with me.'

They stopped the car well short of Harmer's cottage, and as

they walked towards it they saw that there were lights on downstairs.

Harmer opened the door himself after they had knocked, peering at them in the dim light from the room behind him.

'Who is it?'

'It's me, Jimmy. Frank Phillips. Are you any better?'

Hayles saw the door closing and stopped it with his foot, pushing it open and walking inside past Harmer. He saw Phillips closing the door and waited for Harmer to join him in the small sitting room.

'I'm Hayles. Detective Inspector Hayles from Scotland Yard. You know me, and I know you. I'd like to ask you some questions. OK?'

Harmer didn't reply but he sat down in the armchair that he had obviously been sitting in before they came. There was a glass of milk and two biscuits on a plate near the reading lamp on the small antique table. And beside the leg of the chair Phillips saw an open paperback lying face down. It was Pascal's *Pensées*.

There was only one other armchair and Hayles sat down in that and Phillips stood watching awkwardly.

Hayles looked at Harmer's face and then said quietly, 'Tell me what happened, Jimmy. Was it an accident?'

Harmer made no reply.

'Jimmy, you're a policeman same as me. Don't make it difficult for us both. When did you last see Carter?'

Harmer moved in his chair as if to make himself more comfortable. But he said nothing.

'Jimmy. I don't want to do it but if you don't answer my questions I'm going to have to take you in to Maidstone and question you there. Formally.'

Harmer reached down for the book and, spreading the pages flat, he started to read.

For a moment Hayles was nonplussed and then he spoke

again. Coldly and formally. 'James Harmer, I am a police officer, and I am making enquiries into the death of Montague Carter. I believe you can help me with my enquiries and I must ask you to accompany me and Detective Inspector Phillips to Maidstone police station.'

Harmer put down the book and looked at Hayles. But he didn't speak. He made no move to resist when Hayles's firm grip on his arm forced him to stand. Phillips switched out the lights before he left and Hayles sat in the back seat of the car with Harmer as they drove to Maidstone.

There were some surprised looking faces as the three of them walked into the last interview room at the far end of the corridor.

Hayles put a series of questions to Harmer but he remained silent. Phillips asked similar questions, with the same lack of response. Hayles finally contacted the Assistant Commissioner and the Chief Constable. They both walked over to the police station.

Harmer was taken up to the more comfortable atmosphere of the Chief Constable's room. The Assistant Commissioner was there too, but Hayles and Phillips were asked to wait outside.

The Chief Constable announced to Harmer who the AC was, and then sat down at his desk looking across at Harmer.

'Would you sit down, Chief Superintendent.'

Harmer reached for a chair almost as if he was unable to see. When he was sitting the Chief Constable said, 'Is there anything I can do for you, James? Would you like to see a doctor? Would you like to talk to me off the record?'

But Harmer didn't speak.

'The Detective Inspector is investigating a murder, and it seems that you know the man, and that he was last seen on your boat. I'd like to ask if you would tell me if anything untoward happened that you know of.'

When Harmer didn't reply the Chief Constable had pressed the bell on his desk and Hayles came in alone. He looked at the Chief Constable, who nodded. And then at AC Oakeshott, who also nodded.

With his eyes on Harmer's face Hayles said his piece.

'James Harmer, I arrest you on suspicion of the murder of Montague Rayner Carter on or about the twenty-eighth of February nineteen fifty-eight. Anything you say may be used in evidence at your trial.'

He walked over to Harmer and took his arm. He walked stiffly with him to the cells.

By the next morning the atmosphere at the station was tense. The thought of their Detective Chief Superintendent in his own cells, on a charge of suspected murder, had much the same electric charge as prisoners in jails are said to experience on the morning of a hanging. It seemed both incredible, and yet a visible fact at the same time.

At Scotland Yard the Deputy Director of Public Prosecutions was creating a different sort of tension. Assistant Commissioner Oakeshott was on the receiving end.

'Of course I understand, Assistant Commissioner. All I am saying is that there is a vast difference between understanding and approving. You no doubt remember the old joke about "the pleasure's yours, the baby's mine". Well, you've landed us with a very wet baby, and unless I'm much mistaken it's not going to win any beauty prizes.' He paused. 'If it's not asking too much I should appreciate just one piece of evidence connecting Harmer to the murder. Just one, Mr Oakeshott.'

He stood up, brief-case in hand. 'We're going to have problems making it stick in the magistrates court, let alone in front of a judge and jury. You'd better tell Hayles to start fishing very quickly.'

'You think he's not guilty?'

'Of course I don't. He's got all the signs of guilt, but looking guilty isn't a crime. As yet.'

When Hayles was alone he was glad that the Chief Constable and the AC had been in on the decision. Not that that would help him if the case was thrown out of court.

At Maidstone he sensed that feelings were running against him, and reluctantly he asked for more men from the Yard, until eventually there were twenty-five men pursuing enquiries that sounded like dead-ends even as he briefed them.

It was a week before their enquiries paid even the smallest dividend. They found a couple who had been walking along the river bank the night of the murder, who had seen a boat heading slowly down river. A white boat. And there had been a big man at the wheel. They weren't sure if they could recognize him again. There had only been a faint light from the instrument panel.

They were taken to the moorings and had walked up and down the nineteen boats that were tied up there. Hayles breathed a sigh of relief when they identified Harmer's boat as the boat they had seen.

He was in direct touch now with the Deputy Director of Public Prosecutions. Nobody was anxious to stand between him and his fate. When he phoned, the DDPP had listened, and his response had been helpful enough. If Hayles felt there were reasonable grounds for an identity parade he should go ahead irrespective of the outcome.

It had taken two hours to find a suitable number of men of Harmer's build, and the couple had seen them separately. The man had picked out Harmer, and the girl had said that it was either Harmer or the man at the far right of the line; who was, in fact, the deputy Town Clerk.

The DDPP sounded only mildly pleased with the outcome.

The next day in a thorough search of the area from the river bank to the woods the iron spike had been discovered; it matched three similar mooring spikes found in the locker in Harmer's boat.

Angus Maclean, the DDPP, telephoned the clerk to the magistrates and asked for a second adjournment. When there was some demurring at the other end he suggested that it might also be wise of the bench to appoint a solicitor to act on Harmer's behalf if he still refused to speak to anyone. He reckoned that he might as well point out to them that they were going to have their problems too.

It was budget day, 15 April, when Harmer appeared before the magistrates at Maidstone. The court was crowded with both press and public. The newspapers had trodden a careful path in the preceding weeks. There was little room for speculation without committing contempt of court, but most national newspapers had commissioned some barrister or other to write a piece on the law affecting accused who refused to answer questions put by the prosecution. In pieces discussing the finer points of 'mute of malice' or 'mute by natural causes' a few articles had included medical opinions on being 'mute by natural causes' that caused the office of the DPP to give mild hints to a couple of newspapers' legal advisers that they were sailing very near the wind.

The bench had been lectured on the law covering accused who 'stood mute'. It had been decided by the prosecution that Angus Maclean himself would put the case to the magistrates. It might indicate, without saying it of course, that the DPP was in a very determined mood over the case.

Angus Maclean was a handsome man who had had a very successful career at the bar before joining the DPP's team.

Not given to courtroom theatricals he presented his case quietly and slowly. Letting each point sink home before proceeding to the next. Harmer had not responded to the local solicitor who had been asked to defend him, but the prosecution had not been tender-hearted on that score. There were a few things said, a few lines crossed, that would not have been tolerated in an Assize Court, but on the whole the case was presented fairly. Witnesses' statements were not expanded when they gave evidence.

It took three days, mainly because Angus Maclean felt that three days of evidence looked better than two. The magistrates didn't retire but conferred briefly together. They found that there was a case to answer and Harmer was committed for trial.

Maclean asked that bail should not be granted, and suggested that unless the defence had strong views against it, the case should be tried at the Old Bailey rather than in Maidstone. Not, he emphasized, because of any possibility of local prejudice, but because the great majority of those concerned with the trial would find it more convenient for the trial to take place in London.

The chairman of the magistrates asked Harmer if he had any objection. And receiving no answer he gave the court's agreement to the transfer.

At a pre-trial hearing the judge had instructed the court to appoint a defence counsel as *amicus curiae*.

The court administration had given some thought as to who they should appoint to defend Harmer in the hope that the right personality might even, at this late stage, persuade him to talk and defend himself. Accused 'standing mute' were no problem to either the courts or their practitioners, but it left the public uneasy. And it could turn a trial into a spectacle.

*

214

Martin Palmer, QC, had taken silk the previous year, and when the court office decided that he would be appointed *amicus curiae* he was in Gamages' store. An unexpected 'refresher' allowed him to be standing in the toy department trying to decide whether a Hornby 'Duchess of Atholl' was a better buy than two Hornby tank engines. He decided for the 'Duchess' class locomotive, and looked forward to a quiet examination of his purchase in his room before he went home. There were a few letters to be signed and then the package could be opened, and all that beautiful valve-gear admired at close quarters.

It was for that reason that he showed some irritation when the chambers' managing clerk stopped him as he headed for his room.

'Mr Palmer.'

'Yes, Mr Cartwright.'

Cartwright had been a managing clerk of the chambers for many years, and he was used to a touch of asperity from his charges at the end of the day.

'The Old Bailey have appointed you as *amicus curiae* for this chap Harmer, sir. The Detective Chief Superintendent.'

'When's he up for trial?'

Cartwright was a little disappointed at the rather cavalier, down-to-earth question. There was going to be a lot of publicity on this case. That would be good for Mr Palmer, good for the chambers, and therefore good for Mr Cartwright.

'Third or fourth week in May, sir.'

'Tell the girl to get me the Court Administrator's office, will you?'

Jane Frazer was disappointed as the days went by, after the night when Harmer had given her the ring, without hearing from him. Several times she was tempted to ring his number but their unspoken arrangement was that he always rang her. She was loath to change it.

When she read in the newspapers of Carter's murder she was even more tempted to phone Harmer in case he hadn't seen the report. But no vague thought or premonition had made her connect Harmer with the death. When she read of Harmer's arrest and refusal to speak to anyone, it had been a physical as well as a mental shock.

After two days of doubt and misery she phoned her father and asked him to come to London to see her. Sensing her distress, but with no knowledge of what had caused it, he agreed without asking her reasons.

When he arrived the next day he sat listening as she told him about her days in Paris with Harmer, and what had happened to them both during the war. She told him how they had met again, accidentally, and the journey to Paris that led them both to the conclusion that they and the network had been betrayed. It had never entered her mind that Carter could be the traitor, and the betrayal, perhaps, official. But now that Carter was dead and Harmer was to be tried for his murder it all seemed to fall into place. What tormented her was what she should do.

She was relieved that her father had not come up with an instant answer but she wept that night as she made up the settee for him to sleep on, as she had so often done for Harmer.

The next day they talked, and her father's quiet voice and understanding soothed her. He would go down to Maidstone and see if Harmer would talk to him. See what help he needed. See what could be done.

Hamish Frazer was used to prisons, and Maidstone jail was an improvement on Barlinnie, but he felt on edge as he waited in the interview room to see Harmer. The warder said that when Harmer was told Frazer wanted to see him he hadn't replied. Frazer had persuaded him that this could be as much an expression of willingness as of dissent.

He stood up as Harmer was shown into the room and waited until the warder had closed the door and left. He held out his hand. For a moment Harmer hesitated and then he took it.

'It's good to see you, Jamie. Even in this God-forsaken place. Let's sit down for a few minutes.'

Harmer sat opposite him at the tiny table.

'First of all, let me tell you about Jane. She only discovered what had happened a couple of days ago. She was very distressed because she thinks the world of you. She sent for me to see what could be done. Would you talk with me?'

He saw Harmer's mouth say 'yes' but no sound came out. He saw him try again and heard the croak that eventually became 'yes'.

'Jane thinks she knows why this happened. I'm not going to talk about it in any detail in this place. I'm sure that it's private here but we'll take nothing for granted. But I *can* say that I think there would be an excellent defence if Jane's theory were correct. You understand what I mean?'

Harmer nodded, and Frazer reached out and put his hand on one of Harmer's misshapen hands on the table.

'Jane told me most of what happened both recently and back in the war days. I understand your feelings and I think others would understand too. Mother and I were always very fond of you, right from that Christmas way back. Money for top counsel would be no problem. I've got far more than I shall ever need. And Jane is already well provided for. So, please, can I help you?'

Harmer sighed deeply and licked his dry lips.

'We could never prove what they did. There will be no records. They will have destroyed them long ago. Nobody would admit what had been done to us.'

'We could subpoena anybody you felt might have information.'

Harmer shook his head. 'They wouldn't talk. They'd just sell me down the river again.'

'All of them?'

'There was probably only one other involved.'

'Do you know who he was?'

'I've no idea. But whoever it was he wouldn't talk. They wouldn't let him.'

'A good cross-examiner could prise it out of him.'

'They'd hide behind the Official Secrets Act.'

'That would make your point for you.'

'No. They'd see to that. They threw us all away once, and they would throw me away now. They don't really have any choice.'

'Why did they do it, Jamie?'

'To distract the Germans from another SOE network that was preparing for the landings.'

'Why not say this in court?'

Harmer looked at him. 'Who would believe me? I haven't any evidence. I wouldn't have known myself if I hadn't forced it out of Carter.'

'He must have felt terrible when he had to do that.'

Harmer shook his head. 'He didn't care. He tried to justify it. It was an order. He just carried it out.'

'What can I do for you?'

'Take care of Jane. Tell her I cared. But I couldn't bear to think of what he had done to all of us.'

'There's still a chance they may acquit you.'

'I don't care what they do. I squared things off, and that's what mattered. But in the end I couldn't bring myself to run away.'

'Would you like Jane to come and see you?'

'No. She'll understand why not.'

They clasped hands for a brief moment then Frazer left. Harmer went back to his silence again, and Frazer went back to London.

He took his daughter back with him to Edinburgh. To his surprise she did seem to understand, and that only confirmed Frazer's own realization of the terrible things that must have been done to his daughter. The girl they had once worried about in case she was too fond of too many men, and who now shuddered if a man accidentally brushed against her in a crowd.

Hayles came up with the one piece of evidence that Angus Maclean had prayed for. A link between Harmer's boat and the murder.

In checking out the comparison of the mooring spikes Hayles had called in a sergeant from the river police who had pointed out the marks on the shingle at the foot of the bank where a boat had grounded. Samples of the shingle and the surrounding soil were taken and a frogman had brought up samples scraped from the bow of Harmer's boat. Forensic confirmed that they not only tallied but were different from typical river-bed samples taken at the moorings.

Sixteen

Martin Palmer took the papers home for the weekend. He read them through twice and then put them to one side. There was an old copy of Archbold's 'Criminal Pleading, Evidence and Practice' in his study, and he walked upstairs to get it. He refreshed his mind on 'standing mute of malice' and then sat in his rickety wicker chair, thinking.

He guessed that the prosecution must have hopes of finding new evidence. With a little bit of help from the accused he could rip a few holes in the Crown case without too much trouble. But Harmer wouldn't be keeping silent for no reason, and if he got him to talk he'd have to put him in the box. And then the other side could do what they really wanted to do. Go on a full-scale fishing expedition. He would apply for Harmer to be moved up from Maidstone jail to Wormwood Scrubs.

When Harmer came in to the interview room Palmer waved him to the wooden chair at the other side of the scarred and battered table. His open brief-case took up half the available space, and he pushed it to one side, more for something to do than because he needed more room. He looked across at his client.

220

'Mr Harmer, I know you haven't been talking to people. I hope that you might decide to talk to me. But before that I'd like to talk to you. About the law and the case against you.'

He didn't wait for an answer but went on to discuss the law concerning accused who refused to answer questions. And then he outlined the prosecution's case.

'Now, you're a senior policeman, so I don't need to explain the significance of what I've said. You know it already. What you probably don't realize is that your colleagues are anxious that you should be given all the help you need. And the court has shown its wish to protect your interests by appointing me. Whether you help me or not, whether you like it or not, I shall defend you as best I can. At the moment I shall go into court with both hands tied behind my back. I'd be a lot happier with just one hand tied.'

He smiled as he looked across at Harmer's face. The brown eyes moved to look back at him but that was all. He sighed and pushed the thick file into his brief-case, and as he stood up he said, 'If you change your mind and want to talk to me I shall be leaving my work number and my home number with the office here, and they can call me at any time. Day or night. Understood?'

He deliberately tacked on the easy question at the end to lure an answer, but there was no response. In the taxi going back to his chambers he realized that it must be difficult to stay mute week after week. There would be times when the mind cried out to give an answer. But he spent little time thinking about Harmer's silence. If that was what he wanted then he'd have to get on with it. There would be no tears for Harmer from the court or from him on that account. It was Harmer's choice and he would have to live with the outcome.

Palmer applied for an adjournment and was granted

fourteen days. He was working hard on his unrewarding case, but there was a lot more to be done. He studied every line, every word, of the prosecution witnesses' statements and the indictment itself. But he knew that the Crown would have been meticulous in its presentation of such a cobweb of circumstantial evidence. They had all they could need in terms of opportunity, but little to connect the policeman with the murder. And not a shred of evidence concerning motive. They didn't *have* to establish motive but, if they had been able to, it would have provided some support for their ramshackle structure of circumstantial evidence. In the early stages he gave much thought to what Harmer's motive could be if he were guilty, but it had been fruitless thinking. After the report that a warder at Maidstone thought he had heard Harmer actually talking to his one and only visitor, Palmer had checked on the visitor. When he found that he was a retired Scots solicitor he thought it was worth a telephone call to see if it could help. He received a very frosty reply. A total refusal to discuss either the man's connection with Harmer, or whether they had actually talked.

Palmer refused all interviews with the press, but the photographers had haunted him, so that most of the nationals had carried pictures of him leaving the High Court or the Central Criminal Court from other trials in which he was appearing.

The case was to be heard by Lord Justice Hacker, a man whose absolute insistence on the letter of the law was renowned. He was often chosen to hear those cases where there appeared to be a possible conflict between the Establishment and the public interest. A testy man, but much respected by his colleagues and the bar. Under Lord Justice Hacker nothing could be taken for granted. No matter how well-trodden the precedents, you established them from the ground up, or they would be ignored, or put aside. Hacker

222

gave no hints or guidance, and was as sharp with fledgling barristers as he was with established war-horses. And if he were sharper with one group than another it was with those QCs of his own age who, once upon a time, had carried him back to his home from rugby club celebrations. There were some who still maintained that he was the best full-back the London Welsh had ever had. And there were grey-haired men who stood in the well of his court adjusting their wigs who hoped that he didn't remember that lifted knee or the hack on his shins.

Three days before the trial was due to begin Palmer spent an hour with Harmer in the interview room at the prison, explaining the case and the defence he had constructed. He wasn't sure that Harmer even listened. He didn't respond in any way, but it was a courtesy that Palmer felt that he owed this eccentric man.

The case was set down to start on the Monday and Lord Justice Hacker would be sitting in Court Number One.

Seventeen

Palmer went straight into court, laying out his books on the long front table, checking the sequence of his pile of documents, and then the maps and diagrams that were held in a spring clip.

Angus Maclean and his junior stood conferring in the corridor with Hayles and the witnesses. The press seats were already full and there was a queue of hopefuls for the already crowded public gallery. Then Hayles went into the court to sort out his papers on the oak table that ran along the right-hand side of the court. The police legal adviser sat to his left at the table, the pile of signed original statements in numbered box-files in front of him. His maps and diagrams were the originals, and there were separate piles of copies on the court bailiff's bench behind, for the judge and members of the jury.

Maclean and his junior were already at the front table as the usher called out, 'The court will rise,' and Lord Justice Hacker came through the side door behind the jury seats, nodded briefly to the court, and sat down. With a shuffling of feet the court settled back in its places.

Harmer sat in the dock between two policemen, his big frame dominating the trio, his eyes looking straight ahead, avoiding all other contact.

The jury had been sworn in, neither Maclean nor Palmer challenging any of them. There were eight men and four women. The clerk nodded to the police escort and they stood up with Harmer between them. Warned in advance of what to expect he had not asked Harmer his name but posed the alternative.

'Are you James Harmer?'

Harmer, still looking straight ahead, said nothing. Lord Justice Hacker without looking up from his notes said sharply, 'Read the indictment.'

'Yes, My Lord.' He turned to look again at Harmer. 'James Harmer, you are accused of the murder of Montague Rayner Carter on or about the twenty-eighth day of February in the year of our Lord nineteen fifty-eight. How do you answer?'

Harmer stayed silent. Hacker let the silence establish itself and then he looked towards the jury.

'Ladies and gentlemen of the jury. I am afraid that at this point it is necessary for me to explain a point of law to you. When a defendant does not reply to questions that are legally and correctly put to him, the court has to decide between two issues. Is the defendant what is called in law, "mute of malice"; that is to say, able to speak, but refusing to do so? Or is he "mute by visitation of God", that is to say, temporarily or permanently unable to speak? When there is any doubt it is normal practice for a jury to be sworn to try the issue. In this case I do not propose to ask you to give a verdict on this point. There is no doubt in my mind that the defendant stands "mute of malice". The second point that I want to draw to your attention is that the court has appointed learned counsel to act as what we call "amicus curiae" – the friend of the court – to act on behalf of the defendant. And the learned counsel who has been appointed raised no objection to my finding that the defendant stands "mute of malice". The defendant has not spoken or responded to questions from the moment of his arrest. This leads me to my final point. I want you to know that it is a matter of law that a defendant has the right to remain silent. During the trial, and when you retire to consider your verdict, you will not read into the defendant's silence any implication of guilt. Guilt is for the prosecution to try and establish, and for you alone to decide.' He turned from the jury to look at Maclean and nodded.

Maclean stood up slowly, two foolscap sheets in his left hand. He turned towards the jury.

'Ladies and gentlemen of the jury. It is the prosecution's intention to put before you evidence that will convince you that the defendant committed the act of murder on the deceased Montague Carter. But before I come to that evidence there are two points that I want to bring to your attention. The first is the occupation of the accused. He is a police officer. A very senior police officer. A detective chief superintendent of the Kent County Constabulary. It is my duty to point out to you that that has no bearing on this case. You may feel that a senior police officer is either less or more likely, to commit the crime of murder.' Maclean lowered his papers and glanced briefly at his Lordship as he turned towards the jury again. His Lordship was busy making notes. 'The defendant in any murder trial is a man or a woman – nothing more. He or she may be titled, eminent, famous or otherwise virtuous, but when he stands in the dock in this court he has to be considered as innocent until you decide that he is guilty. You may feel that where the crime of murder has been committed a senior policeman . . . '

'No, Mr Maclean. Not in this court.'

Maclean nodded. 'Of course, My Lord. Let me put it another way . . . '

'No, Mr Maclean. I shall not allow you to wander down that route. Not in your opening speech, anyway.'

'Right, Milord.' And Palmer, who had half-risen, sank back on his chair.

Maclean turned over a page. 'The second point that I want to make, ladies and gentlemen, is the question of the defendant's silence. Lord Justice Hacker has already explained to you that the defendant is entitled to remain silent. It is his right under our laws. And not the slightest element of guilt should be adduced because of the exercise of this right. However, I consider it my duty to point out that this is not only a question of "standing mute" in this court but, as His Lordship has already informed you, the defendant has remained silent from the moment of his arrest, even so far as my learned colleague, the "amicus curiae" appointed by this court, is concerned. I say this because the prosecution will not be presenting evidence to you to suggest what motivated this act of murder. It is not necessary for the Crown to establish the motive for you to bring a verdict of guilty. Just as it is not necessary to produce a body to establish that a murder has been committed. Turning now to the evidence that the prosecution will put before you I start with the finding of the body.

'On the afternoon of the tenth of March, a sales representative came upon a body lying in a wood near the village of Yalding, in Kent. It was subsequently identified as the body of Montague Rayner Carter, a director of a merchant bank. During the enquiries that followed certain facts emerged which I shall now . . . '

With a lunch-time break of an hour Maclean took until 4.10 p.m. to complete his opening speech, and the court was adjourned until ten a.m. the following morning.

Palmer went down to the Old Bailey cells to see Harmer before he was sent back to Wormwood Scrubs but he answered no questions, just sitting there stolidly. But Palmer sensed a tension in the man and wondered if the rituals and panoply of the court room had had some effect. It seemed unlikely in a senior police officer who would be used to such things, and well aware of the tattiness behind the scenes when you were on the investigating end, but it was very different when you were actually at the sharp end of all the ritual yourself.

The next morning Maclean introduced his first witness. When he had been sworn in Maclean started.

'Please tell the court your name.'

'Peter Lovegrove.'

'Right. Look at His Lordship when you're speaking, Mr Lovegrove. What is your occupation?'

'A sales representative for Lane Chemicals Limited.'

'You sell agricultural chemicals to farms, yes?'

'Yes.'

'And your sales territory includes Kent?'

'Yes.'

'Now will you tell the court what happened on the afternoon of March the tenth.'

'I pulled up my car at the side of the road just past the bridge over the Medway, down-river from Yalding. I ate my lunch and read the paper and then got out of my car and walked a short way into the woods to relieve myself. It was then I saw the body.'

'Right, Mr Lovegrove. What did you do then?'

'I drove back to Yalding village and phoned 999. I told them what I had found. They told me to go back to the woods and wait for them.'

'Did they say anything else?' Maclean smiled amiably.

'I don't think so.'

'Did they tell you not to touch the body or walk near it?'

228

'Yes. Sorry.'

'Was this the body you found, and was this the position of the body when you found it?'

Copies of the photograph were handed to His Lordship, the witness, and the jury. It was a colour photograph and Lovegrove looked at it, frowning.

'I don't remember seeing these stripes.'

'Ah, no. Those are a colour reference, Milord. For accurate colour comparison. So apart from the colour chart was that the body you found?'

'Yes.'

'And it was in that position?'

'Yes.'

'Thank you, Mr Lovegrove. No. Stay there please. My learned friend may have a question for you.'

Martin Palmer stood up, looking at Lovegrove, bending slightly as he mentally rehearsed the question he was going to put.

'Mr Lovegrove. Am I right in suggesting that you know the Yalding area very well?'

'Yes.'

'Do you make calls there regularly?'

'Yes.'

'Roughly how often?'

'It depends on the farming season.'

'You were in Yalding according to your evidence on March the tenth. When were you last there before that date?'

'The week before.'

'On the same day. A Wednesday?'

'Yes.'

'Do you usually take your lunch at the same spot when you make your calls in Yalding?'

'Yes.'

'And you ate your lunch, and read the paper as usual?'

'Yes.'

'At the same spot?'

'Yes.'

'How do you know it was the same spot on both occasions?'

'There's a gate there.'

'And did you, on the third of March, walk into the woods to relieve yourself?'

'Yes.'

'How can you be so sure?'

'Because I always do.'

'I see. And on that occasion, the third of March, did you see a body?'

Lovegrove hesitated, he wasn't sure what his chap wanted him to say. He looked towards Maclean but he was pointedly reading his notes.

'Well, Mr Lovegrove. Did you see a body or did you not? Answer, man.' His Lordship's voice was sharp and he cupped his hand to his ear encouragingly.

'No, sir. Milord.'

His Lordship, addressing nobody in particular, said, 'Either you saw a body or you didn't. It doesn't need working out.'

'Yes, sir.'

'That's all, Milord,' said Palmer, and sat down.

Sergeant Mouncey of the Kent County Constabulary, the next witness, described finding the body and taping off the area. He too identified the body as the one in the photograph. He described what he had done on Detective Inspector Phillips's instructions.

Palmer looked at his notes instead of at Sergeant Mouncey as he asked the first question.

'Sergeant Mouncey. When you looked at the body what was your first impression?'

'That it had been dead for some time, sir.'

'I expect that during your time in the police force you have seen a considerable number of dead bodies. Yes?'

'Yes, sir.'

'How many would you say, just roughly?'

'Somewhere between eighty and a hundred.'

'And how many of those had been murdered?'

'Including bodies in the morgue, sir?'

'Yes.'

'Eighteen or so.'

'Quite a number.'

The policeman, hearing no question, didn't reply. For the next question Palmer looked at him directly.

'When you first saw this body, were you under the impression that the man had been murdered?'

'I'm not qualified to say, sir.'

'I know you're not, Sergeant. I didn't ask you if the deceased *was* murdered, I asked you if your first impression was that he had been murdered or had died naturally.'

Sergeant Mouncey wasn't at all sure what garden-path he was being led down. He couldn't see the end of the line.

'I formed no opinion, sir.'

Palmer raised his eyebrows. 'As far as you were concerned he could have died from natural causes?'

'Yes, sir.'

'Murder did not come immediately into your mind?'

'No, sir.'

'That's all, thank you, Sergeant.'

Angus Maclean stood up again. 'Sergeant Mouncey, you told the court that you immediately contacted Inspector Phillips of CID. Why?'

'That's the usual procedure when bodies are found in suspicious circumstances.'

Maclean smiled and sat down. 'Thank you, Sergeant.'

Palmer was surprised at Maclean's next witness. Not surprised that he should be called, but at the order in which he was called. He had expected the forensic stuff next. The Crown hadn't even established yet that a murder *had* been committed, let alone who had committed it. The witness was Arthur Clagg who owned and ran a chandlery in Folkestone. Clagg's eyes wandered round the court from the witness box. Interested in what was going on, he was not embarrassed or uncomfortable. Almost too much at home, Maclean felt, as Clagg's eyes examined His Lordship at his note making.

'Yes, Mr Maclean.' Hacker didn't look up as he spoke.

'Mr Clagg. I want you to look at this object marked nineteen on the label.'

Clagg's big hand reached out.

'No. Don't touch it, Mr Clagg. Just look at it.'

Maclean waited for a few moments and then continued. 'Would you tell the court what that is, Mr Clagg?'

'It's a mooring spike.'

'A mooring spike. And what would it normally be used for?'

'For mooring craft temporarily on river banks.'

'When a boat is moored temporarily how many of these spikes are generally used?'

'Two. One for'ard. One aft.'

'They're used in pairs then?'

'Yes.'

'Are you the main distributor for these spikes in south-east England?'

'Yes.'

'And you generally sell them in pairs?'

'Yes.'

232

'That's all, Milord.'

Palmer rose, his hand settling his wig as he looked down at his notes.

'Mr Clagg. As well as your distributing agencies you have two retail chandleries selling to the public. Am I right?'

'You are, sir.'

'Do you remember the present price of a single spike?'

'About three shillings, sir.'

'About three shillings. So you do sell single spikes?'

'Oh yes. Plenty.'

'Why not in pairs?'

Clagg smiled. 'They forgets 'em, sir, in a hurry to cast off maybe. They often leave one behind.'

'So there is no particular significance in a boat-owner having three rather than four spikes in his store-locker?'

'I wouldn't say so, sir.'

Palmer looked up at the bench to check that His Lordship was taking notes. He wasn't. He was looking back at Palmer.

'The point you are making, Mr Palmer, is that people with boats may have odd numbers of these spikes rather than even numbers or pairs.'

'Yes, Milord.'

Hacker looked at Maclean who half stood up.

'No further questions, Milord.'

At the lunch-time adjournment Palmer had taken his coffee over to Maclean's table.

'When are you bringing your medical evidence in, Angus?'

Maclean smiled. 'Towards the end.'

'You haven't even established that Carter is dead yet. Let alone murdered.'

'You've seen the medical reports?'

'Of course. But the jury haven't.'

'They will, in due course.'

'I think I'm going to raise the point.'

'Are you bringing in a forensic witness?'

'I've taken advice but I wasn't proposing to put anybody on the stand.'

'Do you want to go and see Hacker?'

'It might be as well.'

Hacker always took a Churchillian nap after his sparse lunch but he showed no hesitation when the clerk came in with the request from Maclean and Palmer.

'Sit down. How long will this take?'

'About fifteen minutes, sir.'

Hacker turned to the bailiff. 'Tell the jury that we are adjourned until 2.20.' He turned back to the two counsel.

'Right. What is it?'

'I am concerned, Milord, at the order that evidence is being presented. We have not yet established death or that murder has been committed.'

'What do you say, Maclean?'

'I can only state that I am entitled to introduce evidence in a way that presents the matters clearly. I've got a host of circumstantial evidence that is the foundation of the Crown's case. I'd like to establish that first.'

Hacker looked at Palmer.

'I would submit, Milord, that the Crown is presenting its case in a manner that dilutes the significance of the medical evidence. We are getting a string of witnesses testifying in a way that takes the establishment of murder as a foregone conclusion. And it is not.'

'Are you contesting the Crown's medical evidence?'

'No, Milord, but I shall be contesting the inferences they draw from it, which moves towards the defendant.'

Hacker pursed his lips. 'I see no point of law involved in

234

this. Do you?'

'No, Milord. I shall touch on it in my closing speech, but by then the damage is done.'

Hacker straightened up his denture with his tongue as he reflected.

'Have you any feeling for Palmer's point, Maclean?'

'Feeling, yes, Milord. But I intend to present my case as I planned.'

Hacker's lips twitched towards a smile. 'Right, gentlemen. I am of a mind to address the jury myself on this point. Not at length. I'll just point out that the Crown has not yet established murder.'

Maclean had done his best to keep Mrs Carter well away from Penny Watkins before the trial opened. But Maclean underrated the virtues of the middle class, and the universality of women, when there is no longer anything personal at stake. Judith Carter's life would go on much as it had done before Carter's death. He had been by no means a bad husband but he had played no real part in her life. Only a man of great vitality or talent would have affected that. It was a life of background and evenness. There were no figures in the foreground or middle distance. Monty Carter had been just another part of the background. Like a tree masquerading as a wood in a Mozart opera. His escapades with Penny Watkins were the kind of things men did, it went along with nannies and nurseries, buckets and spades, and tittering at the sexy bits in the Bible. She and Penny Watkins were not rivals and never had been, so there was no need to be unpleasant. They had had tea together several times, talking quite freely of the pluses and minuses of the dead man; and men in general.

They sat together now in the gloomy corridor outside the court-room, chatting desultorily as they waited to be called.

Judith Carter was called first. She had repeated the oath as if there might be marks awarded for good elocution.

'You are Mrs Judith Carter, and you live at 49 Kings Avenue, Wimbledon?'

'Yes.'

'How long were you married, Mrs Carter?'

'Twelve years.'

'A happy marriage?'

'Yes.'

'Before he went away for the week-end on the boat, did your husband have any business worries that you know of?'

'None.'

'Any health problems?'

'Nothing serious. He had a tendency to bronchitis in the winter months.'

'Did he say anything about the proposed week-end before he went?'

'He said that he had recently met a friend of his from army days, and that they were going to take a week-end together on his friend's boat.'

'To do what?'

She shrugged and half-smiled. 'He said to talk about old times.'

'Nothing more than that?'

'No.'

'And you agreed to this?'

'Of course.'

'And when did you next hear from your husband?'

'On the Saturday, he phoned me from Maidstone.'

'How did you know it was Maidstone?'

'It was a reverse charge call. The operator said it was from Maidstone.'

'And what did your husband say?'

'He said he was enjoying the break and asked if the man

236

had been to repair the washing machine. I told him he had.'

'No hint of any problems?'

'None.'

'One final question, Mrs Carter. Did you love your husband?'

'We got on well together. It wasn't a romantic relationship after twelve years.'

'Thank you, Mrs Carter.'

Palmer half rose. 'No questions, Milord.'

There was a stir in the public gallery as Penny Watkins was sworn in, and a couple of younger policemen moved casually but rather too obviously to get a better view of the pretty girl.

'You are Penelope Margaret Watkins and you live at 27a Bedford Street, Notting Hill. Is that correct?'

'Yes.'

'How long had you known the deceased?'

'Nearly three years.'

'You had a very close relationship with him. Yes?'

'I slept with him.'

'Ah yes. And you and the deceased went down to Yalding on the evening of the 26th of February, a Friday?'

'We didn't go down together. We met at the boat.'

'Right. And you also met another man at that time. The owner of the boat?'

'Yes.'

'Can you see him in this court?'

'Yes. He's the man sitting between the two policemen.'

'I see. Did you see much of that man during the weekend?'

'No. He was there for a short time when I arrived until Monty came, then he left. He called in on the Saturday for about ten minutes or so.'

'That was the only time when you saw the defendant with

the deceased at that week-end?'

'Yes.'

'What was their relationship?'

'They seemed friendly enough.'

Maclean then went through the first meeting with Harmer in London at her flat. Her views on Carter's possible worries and the question of Carter objecting to sexual advances to her by Harmer. When Maclean had finished Palmer stood up.

'Miss Watkins, my learned friend asked if there was any sexual rivalry, centred on you, between the defendant and Mr Carter. Did the defendant make even the slightest advance to you in either word or deed?'

'No.'

'Would I be correct, Miss Watkins, if I suggested that you are quite used to men making sexual advances to you . . . '

Maclean was on his feet. 'Milord. I must object to . . . '

Hacker shook his head. 'You opened that door yourself, Mr Maclean.'

Palmer said quietly, 'I don't want to embarrass you, Miss Watkins. Let me rephrase my question. I suggest that as you are an extremely attractive young woman you are well able to recognize a sexual approach from a man if it takes place?'

'Yes. I am.'

'And there was no such advance by the defendant?'

'None whatsoever.'

'Did you feel that, perhaps mistakenly, Mr Carter imagined that such an advance had been made?'

'I'm sure he didn't. And if he had he would have been amused.'

'Why do you think that?'

'He thought Mr Harmer was rather old-fashioned.'

'Thank you, Miss Watkins.'

*

The next day Maclean presented the maps and diagrams showing where the body had been found, the relationship with the road and the river. The place where the mooring spike had been found. The place where the shingle had been rutted by the bow of a boat. The relationship between the moorings and the wood, and the relationship of Carter's car to the boat.

Chief Inspector Hayles gave evidence of his arrest of Harmer and his meeting with him at his cottage. Palmer asked no questions of the police officer witnesses until Phillips had given his evidence.

'Inspector Phillips. The defendant was a colleague of yours, was he not?'

'My immediate superior, sir.'

'You've worked with him on a number of enquiries, then?'

'Yes. Very many.'

'Any murder enquiries?'

'Yes.'

'How many?'

'A dozen or so.'

'Did he ever express to you any opinion about the crime of murder?'

'He was for bringing back hanging, sir. So was I.'

'You mean he saw murder as a heinous crime?'

'I don't understand, sir.'

'Did he see murder as a shameful and terrible crime?'

'This isn't really relevant, Mr Palmer,' Hacker said.

'As you direct, Milord.'

Hacker noted the word 'direct', and recognized the trap. 'Are you bringing character witnesses, Mr Palmer?'

'Yes, Milord. Several.'

'Leave this matter until then.'

'Certainly, Milord.'

*

Thursday morning started with the couple who had seen a boat moving down the river. Maclean put the girl on the stand first so that he could reinforce her evidence with the man's positive identification.

'You are Mavis Eileen Couper and you live at 4 Lime Cottages, Yalding?'

'Yes.'

Mavis Couper was 20. A pleasant-faced girl with fine hair that seemed hard to control. She smoothed errant strands into place while she looked around the court as Maclean leaned over his notes. She was not overawed by the court any more than she was overawed by the audiences at the theatre in Canterbury where she appeared with the Maidstone Amateur Players once a year.

'Now, Miss Couper. On the evening of the twenty-eighth of February this year, a Sunday, you went for a walk with a friend of yours, Mr Michael Chapman. About what time was this?'

'When we started off, you mean?'

'Let us say, at what time were you at the river bank?'

'About six o'clock.'

'Was it dark then?'

'Yes.'

'Nevertheless you saw something on the river. Would you tell us what you saw?'

'We saw a boat that . . .'

'Just what *you* saw, Miss Couper.'

'I saw a boat moving down the river towards the small bridge.'

'Can you describe the boat?'

'It was white and there were lights. A red one, a green one and an ordinary one on the top of it.'

'Did you notice anything else?'

'There was a chap steering it. A big chap.'

240

'How did you see this man in the dark?'

'There was a light coming up where he was standing and it was on his face and arms.'

'Was this a bright light?'

'No. It was quite faint.'

'But bright enough for you to see the man's face?'

'Yes.'

'Would you look at this diagram, Miss Couper, and tell us if you agree that the arrow marked fourteen shows accurately where you first saw the boat.'

She looked at the diagram frowning and the usher showed her the arrow. She looked up and back at Maclean.

'I don't understand this.'

'I see. Now address all your remarks to His Lordship and the jury if you please. Was the boat you saw, when you first saw it, beyond the line of moored boats?'

'Oh yes.'

'About how far beyond them?'

'About as far as from here to that wall.' And she pointed at the far wall of the court.

'And some time after this, you attended an identification parade and you were asked if one of those men was the man you saw steering the boat. Tell us what happened.'

'I saw two men who looked like the one in the boat and I couldn't decide which one it was but I'm sure . . .'

'Just a moment, Miss Couper. Do you see anywhere in this court a man who looks like the man on the boat that night?'

'Yes,' she said. 'The one over there.' And she pointed across the court at Harmer. 'The one in the middle,' she added.

'Thank you, Miss Couper.'

And Maclean sat down.

Palmer looked at the girl. He had seen the faint pink line

across the bridge of her nose. 'Do you wear glasses for reading or working, Miss Couper?'

'For reading.'

'Thank you, Miss Couper.' He looked up at His Lordship. 'I've no more questions, My Lord.'

Michael Chapman worked in an office in Maidstone. A tall, thin young man who mumbled as he took the oath.

'You are Michael Chapman of 9 Alma Terrace, Horsmonden?'

'Yes.'

'Speak up, Mr Chapman,' Maclean said, smiling amiably. 'His Lordship and the jury want to hear what you say.'

Chapman fidgeted in the box, touching his hair and smoothing his clothes.

'On the evening of the twenty-eighth of February this year you were walking with a friend of yours, Miss Couper, along the river bank at Yalding. Is that so?'

'Yes, Your Honour.'

Maclean ignored his elevation and continued. 'About what time was this?'

'Just after six,' Chapman mumbled.

'Was it dark then?'

'Yes.'

'But you saw something on the river. Would you tell us what you saw?'

'I saw a boat. A white boat with navigation lights. It was going slowly down towards the old bridge. I saw a man in the wheel-house.'

'Tell us how you saw him in the dark.'

'The lights from the instrument panel were shining on his face.'

'And subsequently you attended an identity parade and identified the man?'

242

'Yes.'

'Are you quite certain that he was the man?'

'Yes.'

'Can you see that man in court?'

Chapman looked at the jury benches, then at the dock, and he pointed. 'That's him.' He was pointing at Harmer.

Frank Vaughan, fair-haired and in his thirties, was technical adviser to the Medway River Board. Dressed in a Harris Tweed jacket with leather-patched pockets and elbows, he looked exactly what he was. A man who spent most of his time out of doors. When Vaughan had taken the oath, Maclean stood up and turned towards the jury.

'Ladies and gentlemen of the jury. I should like you to refer to the enlargement of the river map marked 27A.' He paused for a few moments while they sorted themselves out. 'You will see an arrow in red ink and an arrow in green ink. They mark two different locations on the river bank. The red one on the northern bank indicates the place where the mooring spike was found. The green arrow on the southern bank is the permanent mooring of the boat *Donna Tomara*, owned by the defendant. Those are the two places that I shall be referring to in my questions to this witness.'

Maclean turned to the witness box.

'You are Mr Frank Vaughan and you are employed by the Medway River Board as technical adviser?'

'I am.'

'Could you tell the court what qualifications you have?'

'A degree in geology and a degree in botany, both from Newcastle University.'

'And your duties, briefly, with the River Board?'

'I advise the Board on all scientific matters concerned with the non-tidal area of the Medway. I advise on pollution, riparian ecology, water analysis and conservation.'

'You were asked to examine the two places marked with

the red and green arrows and the hull of the motor vessel *Donna Tomara* to check whether there was any evidence that that particular boat had at some time temporarily moored at the place on the river bank marked with a red arrow.'

'Yes.'

'Would you tell us what you found?'

'At the place with the red arrow I took a cast of a channel that seemed to have been made by the bow of a boat grounding in the gravel there.'

'Just a moment, Mr Vaughan. Is this the cast you made?'

Maclean handed the cast to the usher who took it over to the witness stand.

'Yes. This is the cast. My initials are here.'

'Milord, the photographs of the cast are marked 27B.' Maclean turned back to Vaughan. 'Go on, Mr Vaughan.'

'I then examined the bow of the *Donna Tomara*, particularly below the water line.'

'And what did you find?'

'The boat's hull is wooden and painted white. I examined microscopically the gravel where I had made the cast. From a representative sample of twenty ounces I found white paint deposits on 7.5% of the pebbles. I analysed the paint and a small sample of paint from the boat. They were both made by the same manufacturer of the same formula.'

'What else did you find, Mr Vaughan?'

'In sampling the paint from the boat I found small deposits of felspar and quartz which corresponded with granite chips at the red arrow site. This site is slightly concave and tends to accumulate material from up river. There is no concavity of the bank at the green arrow mooring. I took representative samples at all levels down to the river bed at the permanent mooring and there were no examples of any igneous or metamorphic rock.'

'What does that mean in your opinion?'

244

'That the deposits on the boat came from the grounding of the boat at the red arrow site.'

'Thank you, Mr Vaughan.'

Palmer sat for a moment with his hand to his mouth. He knew the question he wanted to put but he wasn't sure that the jury would see the point. He took a deep breath as he stood up.

'Mr Vaughan. How long would deposits of paint remain on the shingle at the red arrow site?'

'Quite a long time.'

'How long?'

'A year, perhaps eighteen months.'

'I see. So those deposits of white paint could have been there for a year before you checked them?'

'They could have been.'

'Is the paint concerned quite commonly used?'

'Yes.'

'So the deposits on the shingle could be from any boat that used this commonly-used paint?'

'Yes, but...'

'Thank you, Mr Vaughan.'

Vaughan looked appealingly at Maclean who ignored him. Palmer continued.

'You told the court, Mr Vaughan, that you had found the paint in the shingle at the red arrow site and the paint on the boat were of the same make. Yes?'

'Yes.'

'Did you check any of the other white painted boats at the moorings to see if they had been painted with the same paint?'

'No. I wasn't asked to do that.'

'That's all, Mr Vaughan.'

Maclean stood up and asked with slightly overdone patience, 'On the point of the white paint deposits on the

245

shingle at the red arrow, can I confirm that you said you felt there was a connection between the two sites not only because of the paint deposits but because of minute deposits of felspar and quartz in the paint on the boat?'

'That's right,' said Vaughan, glaring triumphantly at Palmer now that he had been allowed to make his point.

Palmer half-rose and then subsided. He had made his point and another question could dilute its effect, so he stayed silent.

Dr Keating was a handsome man. His beard gave him a Victorian air which, combined with his longish nose and brown eyes, added up to a rather sad but calm face. At Maclean's suggestion he had gone through his academic qualifications, the posts to which he had been appointed and his published works.

His statement had been copied and circulated, and Maclean merely picked out those items which needed to be explained in lay terms, and supported the supposition that the deceased had been murdered.

Palmer had gone over Keating's report with a police surgeon and a pathologist from Guy's. From that conference he had arrived at a list of questions. The advice that he had been given was that there was virtually nothing to dispute in Keating's analysis, and that all he could do was to cast some doubt on the Crown's assumption that what had happened was murder rather than accidental.

When he stood up, Palmer turned first to the jury.

'Ladies and gentlemen of the jury. I am not a medical expert, and the questions I shall put to Dr Keating are not intended to dispute his findings. The defence accepts his report and his conclusions. However, the defence does not accept the interpretation which the Crown puts on Dr Keating's report.' He turned to Dr Keating in the witness box. 'Dr Keating, you describe the cause of death in your summing up as – I quote – "a massive insult to the brain". Would you enlarge on that?'

'I don't think I can. That statement was already an enlargement, a generalizing of what had been a series of almost simultaneous occurrences.'

'Let me get at it another way. The pressure applied to that one place on the neck, the extensive damage to the vagus, the hyoid bone – could that have been caused by a blow?'

'Not in practical terms. The pressure applied to that one spot was concentrated and extreme. To achieve that by a blow would be impossible to apply to such a small area. The same force applied a few inches away from that particular place would not have resulted in death.'

'You say that death was almost instantaneous, and you suggest that it could have occurred in less than twenty seconds. How can you be so sure?'

'You will see on the general photograph the bruising that occurred at the pressure point. Bruising can only occur when a body is still alive. Bearing in mind the internal damage done, the bruising is very concentrated, and there is no bruising of any internal features.'

'Dr Keating, you have been responsible for forensic investigations for a number of police forces. How many of those involved murder?'

'I don't remember exactly, but it would be over sixty.'

'Have you ever seen a murder carried out in this manner before?'

'No.'

'Do you think that this is a case of murder?'

'I'm not qualified to comment.'

'Thank you, Dr Keating.'

Maclean had seen the drift of Palmer's questions and stood up to re-examine his witness.

'Dr Keating. Just one more question. In your opinion

could the pressure applied to this place on the deceased have been applied by any other means than by human agency?'

'I don't see how it could have been applied in any other way.'

'Thank you.'

Palmer was uncertain about what order he should play his cards with the character witnesses. If he put the Chief Constable in to bat first it would dilute the value of the others, but if he put him in last it might look as if he was just using him to sweep up at the end. He decided to put him on first.

The Chief Constable spent far less time in court than most of his men, and he didn't much like the dilemma he had been placed in by Palmer. Of course Connors wanted to back up his officers, but a Chief Constable appearing as a character witness for a man accused of murder. It wasn't quite the done thing, somehow.

Connors sat at the back of the court waiting to be called. But Lord Justice Hacker had words to say first.

'The court sits a little later than I had forecast because I had a short meeting in my room with my learned friends, counsel for the Crown and for the defence.

'My learned friend the "amicus curiae" had claimed the right to bring witnesses to the character of the accused. The general rule is that evidence of character is excluded except in certain well-defined circumstances. One of these circumstances is that the accused himself may wish to do so. Even then, certain conditions apply. But in this case, with the accused standing mute, no such request has been or can be made. However, my learned friend as "amicus curiae" has made such an application himself. There is normally a possible risk for the defendant inasmuch as by seeking to prove his own good character he opens the door for the prosecution to prove otherwise. In the circumstances I have decided to allow the evidence of character to be put forward because of the unusual aspects of this case. I want all concerned to see that the accused was not put at a disadvantage in this court because of his silence.' He nodded to Palmer. 'Call your witnesses, Mr Palmer.'

Connors was sworn in and he stood looking at Palmer as he rose to his feet. Even stationary on the witness stand he had almost a swagger about him, his alert cockerel's head ready for trouble.

'You are Algernon Marvin Connors, Chief Constable of the Kent County Constabulary and Rear-Admiral, retired?'

'That's right.'

'The accused, James Harmer, is one of your senior police officers?'

'He is...was...is.' Connors bridled a little at being made to sound indecisive. He had merely been trying to work out what Harmer's technical position was.

'He is now in his eleventh year of service with your force?'

'Correct.'

'During that time has the accused been subject to any disciplinary action?'

'No.'

'Has he been charged with any crime or criminal offence in that time?'

'No.'

'Not even a driving or parking offence?'

'No.'

'Have there been any complaints from the public regarding the performance of his police duties?'

'No.'

'Would you tell the court in your own words your opinion of the accused.'

Connors had been told that this would happen by the police solicitor and he had rehearsed his little party piece a dozen times to ensure that it was neither too strong nor too weak. And now he couldn't remember the opening sentence. He'd have to make it up as he went along.

'I have found this officer to be hard-working and conscientious. He is respected for his experience and skill by his colleagues at all levels. And I find all this business very regrettable.'

'Thank you, Chief Constable.'

Maclean bobbed towards the bench. 'No questions, Milord.'

Palmer was amused and delighted by Connors' last sentence. It would impress the jury even though it would irritate His Lordship.

Phillips was sworn in, looking every inch a policeman in his dark blue serge suit and his Royal Artillery tie.

'You are Frank Phillips, Detective Inspector with the Kent County Constabulary?'

'I am.' Phillips' voice was very soft.

'How long have you known the accused, Inspector?'

'Ten years.'

'What is your relationship with the accused?'

'He's my gov'nor.'

'Inspector Phillips, have you ever seen or had knowledge of the accused showing disrespect for the law?'

'Never. Just the reverse. He's a stickler for the book.'

Palmer saw that Hacker was looking across the court at Harmer.

'Have you ever seen the accused strike anyone?'

'No.'

'Would you consider the accused capable of violence to another person?'

'We're all *capable* of violence, sir. But him no more than me . . . or you.'

'Thank you, Inspector.'

Archibald Truman was sworn in and he stood like a farm-horse in its stall. Stolid and uneasy, his two massive hands on the shelf of the stand.

'You are Archibald Truman, you work as a farm-worker at Lye's Farm, Marden?'

'Yes.'

'And in your own time you work as gardener and handyman for the defendant?'

'I do.' There was a touch of defiance in the old man's voice.

'How long have you worked for the defendant?'

'Ten years.'

'How did you come to work for him?'

'He stopped some hop-pickers from beating me up.'

'What happened?'

'I was acting as foreman for my boss. Paying them out. They disagreed about their pay. I was knocked on the ground and they was booting me. He arrested all three of them.'

'He overpowered them?'

'No. He just walked up, told 'em to stop and they did. He's a very commanding man. Then he arrested 'em.'

'Has he been a good employer?'

'The best.'

Hacker's testy voice interrupted. 'We don't need any more, Mr Palmer. I'm sure the defendant is kind to old ladies and dumb animals.'

'As you wish, Milord.'

251

Eighteen

Palmer stood waiting for Lord Justice Hacker to stop writing. He didn't, but he did say, 'Carry on, Mr Palmer.'

'Your Lordship. I should like to make a submission that there is no case to answer.'

Hacker leaned back in the green leather chair, pushing his glasses back up his nose. Then he leaned forward in his habitual crouch over his notepad. He turned to look at the jury.

'Ladies and gentlemen of the jury. I am going to ask you to retire for a short time, while I hear counsel on this matter. I shall ask the bailiff to tell you when you are needed. We shall not keep you long, I suspect.'

The jury shuffled out under the watchful eyes of the bailiff, and the court settled down again.

'Right, Mr Palmer.'

Hacker settled back. He had expected the submission of no case to answer, but he couldn't really see how Palmer could establish the submission. The prosecution's case was a real dog's breakfast. Even the circumstantial material had a false ring, like a paper model stuck together with glue that wouldn't set. But the jury would be sure that the defendant was guilty because he stood mute. All the little homilies from the bench on the right not to speak never made any difference in the long run. It may be the law, and it was sound law, but unless some obvious good reason was given they took a defendant's silence as a sign of guilt. And more often than not they were right.

'Your Lordship, there have been several points in this trial where I felt that perhaps I should make this submission, but because of the sequence in which the Crown put foward its evidence, I waited. However, in my opinion, your Lordship, I waited in vain. Bearing in mind the difficulties of both prosecution *and* defence when a defendant stands mute, I feel that the Crown has merely gathered together a rag-bag of bits and pieces and thrown them at the court...'

'Is it only on the point of insubstantial evidence that you make your submission, Mr Palmer?'

'Yes, Milord.'

'In that case I am of a mind to reject your submission. I take your point, but you can make it to the jury in your closing speech. And I will also cover it in my summing up. The matter of insubstantiality of evidence is for the jury to decide.' Hacker nodded at the bailiff. 'Ask the jury to come back.'

The jury settled in their places looking slightly mystified, like children who had been sent outside at a party and were now to be told to find the parcel. What was it that the public could hear that they could not?

Maclean was already standing, sure now of the outcome, and aware of the relief that he would now get from the pressures that had been put on him from several quarters to ensure a conviction. He still had the feeling that there was more behind this case than he knew. The Home Secretary had been very insistent on the grounds that Police were his responsibility. But Maclean had moved in government circles too long not to sense other influences. It *was* a rag-bag of evidence, and he had played his cards in an unorthodox way, but he felt now that there would be a finding in his favour. And it was too late now for second or third thoughts. He took a sip of water, put down the glass, and turned to face the jury. Solemn-faced and earnest.

'Members of the jury. In presenting the prosecution's evidence to you I have been concerned to establish three things. That a murder was committed. That the defendant had the opportunity of place and time to commit this murder. And that it was not only possible that he committed this crime, but probable that he did. You will note that I have not attempted to establish a motive for the murder. It is not necessary in law for the prosecution to do this. It is irrelevant *why* the murder was committed, this trial concerns only one thing. Did the defendant, James Harmer, murder Montague Carter. That is the central issue. The "why", and even the "how", are secondary issues.

'This brings me to another point. The evidence itself. The evidence is what is called circumstantial evidence, and there is sometimes an implication in lay minds that circumstantial evidence is not enough. As if it were in some way inferior evidence. This is not the case. In a court of law circumstantial evidence is as valid, as conclusive, as any other evidence. Convictions based solely on circumstantial evidence are both normal and common.

'Now to the evidence itself. In the first place . . . '

It took Maclean to the lunch-time adjournment to make his closing speech. Palmer had the feeling that Maclean was less sure of himself than when he had started the case. He had made a good job of presenting the evidence he had, but Palmer had wondered from the start why Maclean himself should take the case. Like some of the evidence, there was a faint touch of bluff about it. The DDPP himself presenting a case that had no element of national security or politics was

254

unusual enough. For him to handle personally such a ram-shackle case could only mean that the Crown was waving flags. Signalling to somebody the importance that they attached to this particular case.

They wouldn't have deceived Hacker for a moment. He was a lawyer's judge. Blind to flag-waving, no respecter of persons, impervious to public or political pressures, he was only concerned with the facts and the law.

He drank the last of his coffee and headed for the toilet. Uneasy bladders and bowels could distract a man.

When Palmer stood up he looked across to the jury, waiting in silence until he had their attention.

'Ladies and gentlemen of the jury. When this trial started His Lordship instructed us on the subject of the defendant's silence. He told us that such silence should not be interpreted as guilt. I want to remind you of that. It is the defendant's *right* not to answer questions. It is as much his right as any other right granted by the law. And when His Lordship warned you that no guilt should be attached to that silence he meant *no* guilt. Not even the smallest prejudice. As we are all human beings we may speculate on why a particular defendant chooses to exercise this right. So let me enlarge on this point.

'If one evening you are walking to your home and you are stopped by a police officer who asks you to go with him to the police station, a reasonable citizen may choose to go. If, at the police station, you are not charged with any offence but a police officer starts asking you questions that seem to concern some crime of which you know nothing, it would perhaps alarm you. You have the right to say to that police officer that you will answer no questions unless you are charged with an offence. Would you feel that by so doing you are in some way establishing your guilt? I think not. The defendant is exercising such a right in remaining silent in this court. Exercising that right makes him neither innocent nor guilty. It leaves him a neutral status.

'My learned friend representing the Crown told you that the Crown does not need to establish motive and that is perfectly true. However, the absence of evidence on motive is significant. There are only two reasons why such evidence is not put forward. The first is, that although the motive is known, or suspected, or patently obvious, it cannot be proved. The second reason can be that there *is* no motive on the part of the defendant for the simple reason that he or she did not commit the crime. I won't dwell on this, but I don't want you to be misled by my learned friend's comments on motive. If the Crown *could* have put forward a motive I have no doubt that they would have done so.

'I come now to the evidence which the Crown has put before you. It strikes me as being like one of those boxes of chocolates called "Selections". Try this strawberry cream; if you don't like that, try the marshmallow and if you don't fancy that then there's always the one with the nut. There was something for everybody, and nothing much for anybody. And I draw your attention to the fact that we were several days into the trial before the Crown even decided to establish with you that the deceased man was actually dead. And when it came to establishing that a murder had been committed we heard the evidence of an eminent forensic scientist. But in my opinion they merely established the cause of death. I suggest to you, ladies and gentlemen of the jury, that the Crown did not establish that murder was committed. And when we listen to the parade of those who the Crown suggest would have the necessary strength and knowledge to commit such a murder we are indeed in strange company. Wrestlers, surgeons, veterinary surgeons – I won't go on. But you will notice that Detective Chief Superintendents were not on the list.

'As I listened to the prosecution's witnesses I had the impression that I was seeing them through a mist, always out of focus. It was evidence of course. But evidence of what? People *thought* they saw something. Things *might* be connected with other things. Never did I . . . '

Palmer had trudged on, taking each piece of evidence and displaying its worn fabric. Hacker sat impassive with head bent as his pen scrawled on his foolscap pad. It was 4.25 when the court adjourned.

The court was adjourned until 10 a.m. but on the morning the jury had been notified of a later start at 10.30. Lord Justice Hacker was passing sentence from an earlier trial in another court. He was now back in Number One Court.

As he turned towards the jury Hacker took off his glasses and placed them at the side of his note-pad. He preferred the blurred anonymity of their faces when he was summing up.

'It is my duty, ladies and gentlemen of the jury, to sum up after my learned friends for the prosecution and the defendant have made their closing speeches.

'You may have found this a strange trial, with the defendant silent, and the "amicus curiae" limited to rebutting what evidence the Crown put forward. But such cases occur from time to time. I have had to hear several in my time as a judge, and we take them in our legal stride. And I have to remind you again that the defendant's silence is a right given by law and not to be seen in any other light.

'Learned counsel for the defence made much of the Crown not bringing evidence of motive. It is a point, but again, motive does not have to be proved. When murder is committed in the course of robbery or passion then of course motive is part and parcel of the indictment.

'The essence of what the Crown has established, or attempted to establish, is that the defendant and the deceased were together on the defendant's boat on the day when the murder is presumed to have taken place. That the defendant was the only person to be with the deceased that day after the deceased's mistress had left for London. That evidence, you may feel, establishes opportunity.

'The medical evidence put forward by the Crown seems to establish the cause of death whilst leaving the manner of the killing less certain.

'I come then to the character of the defendant. You have heard his superiors, his colleagues and his juniors testify that he is an excellent police officer, doing his job with impartiality and skill, with respect for the public and the law. We have no reason to doubt this body of opinion given by men whose duties require them to assess and make judgments on many classes of people. However, I must point out to you that we are not considering here whether Detective Chief Superintendents of police are *capable* of committing murder, but whether this *particular* man, the defendant, has committed murder on the evidence put before you.

'There are no difficult points of law for me to explain to you. This is not what is sometimes called a judge's case, bristling with intricate points of law. It is very much a jury case where your own common sense will be most important. You will be taken by the bailiff to your jury room and your foreman will notify the bailiff when you are ready to give your verdict.'

His Lordship stood up, gave the traditional short bow to the court and left.

Maclean and Palmer left their papers on the long front table and walked out together to the restaurant.

Maclean smiled as he stirred his coffee.

'What do you feel?'

'I'm damned if I know. It was a messy trial.'

'That couldn't be helped.'

'So why did you bring it to trial?'

'My masters wanted it. Mine but to do and die.'

'How long do you think they'll be out?'

'If it's over a couple of hours they'll find him guilty. Have you picked up any tittle-tattle as to why he wouldn't talk?'

'Not a thing. He hasn't said a word to me.'

'That must have been pretty frustrating.'

Palmer shrugged. 'Not really. It's just another case as far as I'm concerned.'

'You'll be able to get back to the model railway.'

'No such luck. I'm sorting out a rape case at the moment. Starts next week in Number Four.'

'I'm going to the Listings Office, can you send for me when they're coming back?'

'Sure.'

In his chambers Lord Justice Hacker was eating a smoked salmon sandwich and reading the letters page of *The Times*. His mind was far away from the case he was hearing. He was thinking of his children. His son who was a doctor in Sydney, Australia, and his daughter in Boston, Mass., who was in the middle of divorcing her husband. He missed his children now that he was alone. Hearing murder cases could be as grindingly boring in its routine as assembling Ford cars at Dagenham. Noting down the obscenities shouted by some man before he was struck down by a spade in a moment's anger. Murder seemed to have become a commonplace. There were three murder trials going on at the Old Bailey at that very moment. He wondered how things would have been for him if his wife were still alive. She had often come in at the lunch adjournment to have a snack with him in his rooms. She used to do a quite perceptive impersonation of him at parties. But there were no parties anymore. They reminded him of her, and he had never liked them all that much.

He looked at his watch. The jury had been out for two hours and that meant they were disagreeing. And that would surely mean a 'guilty' verdict. He sniffed in self-admonishment. Only fools speculated on jury verdicts.

He stood up, wondering what to do. He wouldn't have minded a breath of fresh air but it wasn't really on. Get knocked down by a bus and somebody would have to go through the whole rigmarole all over again. He wasn't a man for crossword puzzles. They were for men with shifty minds. He walked over to the window and looked out. It was quite sunny. The men looked drab and weary but the wind was catching the girls' skirts, pasting them to their bodies and revealing long nylon-clad thighs. He wondered how men like the deceased, a merchant banker, fixed themselves up with young girls. Where did they meet them? How did they find out that they were willing? And what did they say to them when they were suggesting it? She was a very pretty little thing. And that rather childlike voice must be . . . He turned impatiently to the darkness of the room. That sort of thinking could get you into the *News of the World*.

No sooner had he sat down than the bailiff came in with a message from the jury foreman. They would like to ask him a question.

He nodded. 'Get everybody back in court.'

Half an hour later he was back in chambers. The foreman of the jury had asked if the defendant had been examined by a psychologist. He explained the legal position to them and read a piece from Blackburn. It wasn't going to help them, but at least the question showed that they were putting their minds to the verdict rather than their emotions.

At five o'clock Hacker had sent a message to the jury that hotel arrangements had been made for them and messages would be delivered to their nearest and dearest. They would restart their considerations the following day at ten.

The following morning the jury came back into court just after eleven o'clock. Maclean and Palmer were sitting side by side at the front table, and Maclean whispered, 'I'd say old Hacker will give him seven years, not more.'

Harmer was standing, his face impassive between the two policemen.

The foreman of the jury was standing, and in the sudden silence the clerk's voice seemed to echo round the court-room.

'Mr Foreman of the jury, do you find the defendant guilty or not guilty?'

'Not guilty.'

There was a clamour of voices and Hacker rapped angrily with his gavel and the court usher shouted, 'Silence in court.'

The clerk continued, 'Is that the verdict of you all?'

'It is.'

Palmer turned to look at Harmer but his face showed no emotion as one of the court policemen led him to the open door.

As they gathered up their books and papers Maclean said, 'And what do you make of that?'

Palmer smiled. 'I can only quote Lord Camden. "Trial by jury is indeed the foundation of our free constitution; take that away and the whole fabric will soon moulder into dust." '

Maclean smiled. 'Are you going to Wentworth tomorrow?'

'No. I'm too busy.'

'See you.'

Nineteen

Jane Frazer had read every word in every national newspaper reporting the trial. She had been tempted to go to London and sit in the public gallery. Perhaps it would cheer him to see her there. To know that he and she were the only people in that court, or maybe in the world, who knew why he had done it. And maybe he would look up to find her face in the gallery and be sad that she wasn't there, and think that she didn't care.

It was her father who told her the verdict. He had made arrangements with a friend at *The Scotsman* to phone him as soon as it came through.

When her parents went to bed that night her hand had reached out a dozen times for the telephone, to dial that Marden number. What would he do? How would he cope? The trial had probably served as some kind of catharsis. She felt like the survivor from some terrible natural disaster, like an earthquake or a flood. It was as if some fundamental lesson had been learned. As if someone had drawn a line under that terrible account from the past and said that the credits now balanced the debits.

She was almost sure that she could sleep with him now. Maybe not with enthusiasm as first, but at least with acceptance, and with mental pleasure instead of with physical pleasure.

It was nearly two o'clock when her father came down in his dressing-gown.

'Have a whisky with me, Janie. It'll help us both get to sleep.'

'I don't like whisky, Father, you know that.'

'Doesn't matter. Have one with me, just to celebrate.'

She smiled. 'You're a cunning man, you know.'

'That's wisdom,' he said. 'Not cunning.' And he handed her her glass as he sat down opposite on the old settee. He looked at her as he swirled the whisky in his glass.

'What's worrying you, girl?'

'I've been tempted to phone him. He must feel terribly lonely and deserted.'

'I think you're probably right.'

'You mean I should phone him?'

'No. I mean that he will be lonely and feel deserted. But not deserted by you. Much as I love you, I'm sure that by now you're only a postscript in his life.'

'I don't understand.'

'He always was lonely. He was a lonely boy, he had a lonely childhood without warmth and affection. He was a lonely young man. And then came the war and he did a job that absolutely fitted him. People wouldn't have described him then as lonely. There was a more romantic word. He was a loner. And it was loners who survived in that sort of work. He met you. And I suspect that you were the only person in all his life that he ever felt love for. And then he was betrayed. You all were. Some of you came back. Some of you survived better than others. Some just existed, like the man you told me about in the asylum.

'Somebody high-up decided that a handful of people should be thrown to the wolves. Nobody will ever know if it was justified. One man, your Jimmy, would *never* see it as justified. His kind of people don't do things like that for any reason. To find that his kind of people *did*, and thought nothing of it would be almost worse than the things you all suffered in the camps. To him, what he did, if he did it, will have been for more than just squaring the account. To him, they totally abused his weakness, his loneliness. They used his loneliness, his courage and then threw him away. And the rest of you with him. It takes a different kind of courage to face up to that. He hasn't got that kind of courage. That kind of courage comes from having self-confidence, friends and a background. He never had that.'

'There will be people who know what was done, and they will know why he did it.'

'He knows that, too.'

'But they could have exposed him. Proved that he did it out of revenge.'

'And admit what they did? I think not. They will have prayed that he didn't expose *them*.'

'Why didn't he just expose them, then?'

He sighed deeply. 'How does he prove it? The records have been destroyed. If he had named names he'd have had libel writs on his desk the next day. They wouldn't have to prove a thing. *He* would. He couldn't, and he knew it.'

'So how did he know for certain what happened?'

Her father looked at her and spoke very softly. 'I don't have to tell you, do I?'

'I guess not. So what do I do?'

'For him, or for you?'

'For him.'

'Leave him alone. That's what he chose when he first set out to confront Carter. He knew what he was doing. And he'll know what he's going to do now. He's that kind of man.'

'And for me?'

'I suggest you close down your flat and come back here, where you're loved and cherished. Keep on your translations, and read Victorian novels.'

She frowned. 'Why Victorian novels?'

'Because in those days women found it possible to love just one man in a lifetime. If he didn't come back from the wars they went on loving him. And no other.'

'I wish Jimmy was being loved and cherished.'

'It's too late for that, my love. That has to start when you're a child.'

She sighed. 'You're a wise old bird, and I'm glad I've got you and mother.'

'I'm not all that wise. I'm much the same as your Jimmy. I'm a black and white man. I don't believe in the grey bits. It's not popular these days, but it means I know where I am.'

'Pour me another whisky and then I'll go to bed. Maybe there's something I could do.' She looked at his face. 'Can I talk about it with you again?'

'Of course.'

Harmer brushed aside the outheld hands and ignored the pleasantries. He shaded his eyes from the sunlight as he walked out of the Old Bailey and waved down a taxi, ignoring the reporters and photographers who crowded round him on the pavement.

He changed trains at Tonbridge and took a connection to Marden. He walked from Marden station the two miles to his cottage. It seemed to be smaller than he remembered, but the garden was still trim and tidy. He packed a small canvas case, and after locking up he walked to the lean-to garage. The car started easily enough and he drove through the evening sunshine down to Dymchurch. He booked a room in a small guest-house.

All night he sat in the old armchair, fully dressed, dozing and waking in the darkness. Early next morning he drove to Lydd, to the British Car Ferries airport. The first plane was at ten o'clock and he walked outside the small airport building to sit on the grass, his knees drawn up, encircled by his arms. A man-sized foetus staring into space.

Nobody seemed to notice the name in his passport, either at Lydd or Le Touquet. He bought a train ticket for Paris.

In Paris he called at a pharmacy by the station, and then took a taxi to the Rue Roger. The restaurant had been renamed but it looked much the same from the outside, and he felt faint as he walked across the cobbled street.

They no longer let rooms on short lets so he paid in advance for three months after checking that the two rooms he wanted were available.

The patron looked at him as he took the money and said in broken English, 'You feel yourself OK?'

He smiled when Harmer reassured him in fluent French.

Harmer walked through the bead curtains and turned instinctively to walk up the narrow stairs. Half-way up he had to stop and lean against the wall. Then slowly he mounted the stairs to the small landing. His eyes were closed as his hand turned the brass knob on the door, and he shivered as he walked into the room. He closed the door, dropped his bag, and walked over to the window. He didn't remember the view, in those days they had always been watching the street. But now he could see across the tiled roofs to where the domes and pinnacles of Paris were washed with the rose-coloured light of the setting sun. The sky was a pale blue, streaked with red and orange. It was going to be a fine day tomorrow.

Slowly he unknotted his tie and the top two buttons of his shirt. Bending over, he opened the canvas bag and his hand closed round the small cardboard box. The capsules were bright yellow, and he reached for the glass and the bottle of Vichy water. He took the capsules two at a time and when they were all gone he lay back on the pillows and closed his eyes. He breathed gently and evenly, and behind his closed eyes he could still see the sky. The sky that was everywhere, over Natzweiler, Buchenwald, Edinburgh and Paris. The patient sky.

In the south-east corner of the small church at Beaulieu there are two graves under a rowan tree. The headstones are identical, except for the words carved in the lichen-covered stone.

> In loving memory of
> Capt. James Harmer
> Born 1 December 1919
> Died 23 June 1958
>
> In loving memory of
> our daughter
> Jane Menzies Frazer
> Born 24 October 1920
> Died 9 August 1979